Knot So Perfect *Omega*

MAYA NICOLE

AUTHOR'S NOTE

Omega Match is an omegaverse reverse harem romance series of standalones. That means each of the main characters will have a happily ever after with three or more men. Recommended for readers 18+ for adult content and language.

Contemporary omegaverse has non-shifting alphas, betas, and omegas. Alphas have knots and omegas go through heats, but they do not turn into wolves.

CHAPTER ONE

Kayla

I propped my combat boots on the railing, looking out over the Alphaball field as the Killer Gnomes started their third and final round against the Monster Chickens. How could anyone take a game seriously when every other announcement was about chickens or gnomes?

I certainly couldn't.

"And the Gnomes take down a Chicken in the first ten seconds with a tackle by Abbott! Perez tosses his ten to Thomas and... Perez takes the thirty! The Gnomes are headed to their hole with four balls! Can the Chickens stop them or are they going to let them get away with a quadruple homicide?!"

The crowd roared as the Killer Gnomes worked their

way across the field toward their hole, all three of their weighted balls still in play, plus the one they'd stolen. They were obliterating the Monster Chickens, and this round was just for show since there was no way the Chickens could come back from the point deficit they had.

Alphaball was like if cornhole, football, and dodgeball had a baby. A very competitive and sexy baby. I never watched the sport, but maybe I needed to start.

It was set up in a tournament format, which had four teams to start, playing two separate games with three rounds or periods each game. The winners advanced to face off for first and second place, while the losers played a game for third and fourth. It was much like how the Olympics was set up with gameplay.

My twin sister, Kara, sat down next to me and scrunched her nose in disapproval as I lifted my elote to my mouth and took a bite out of the cob, dropping a glob of cheesy mayonnaise goodness on my light blue sweater.

I held out the Mexican street corn to her in offering, and she leaned away from it like it was the most disgusting thing she'd ever seen. "At least try it. You don't know what you're missing, sis."

"It's so messy." She grabbed a napkin that was shoved in my cupholder and wiped at my sweater, making the situation worse. "We're meeting the Killer Gnomes after their game. Don't you want to be at your best?"

I took another bite and snatched the napkin from her, wiping the mess from my face. "Why would I want that? If alphas aren't going to accept me with corn stuck in my teeth and a little mayo on my sweater, then I don't want them. Besides, they named themselves Killer Gnomes, didn't they? Major red flag."

"You have to start taking this seriously. We're only a few days away from matching, and I'm worried for you. You don't want to end up at one of the omega compounds, do you?" She leaned forward in her seat, her attention now on the game that was unfolding below. "We have the open house tomorrow on campus that will bring out a lot of packs to meet us."

With a sigh, I continued eating. I knew what was coming up, and it was making me full of unease. On one hand, I couldn't care less if a pack selected me as an omega, but it was in my nature to want a pack. My prospects were slim to none, while my twin was going to have enough packs vying for her to supply the entire class of omegas.

Over the past several months, the omegas in their final year at Elite Omega Academy had met with countless packs. We were supposedly the cream of the crop when it came to omegas, although I often felt out of place. I was definitely an omega, but the only reason I even attended EOA was because my sister had been accepted and our parents refused to send her unless we stayed together.

Kara was the perfect omega in every way; beautiful, intelligent, and proper. Any pack would be lucky to have her as theirs, and she had the added bonus of being the academy's *Omega of the Year* for all four years we'd been in attendance.

It was unheard of.

Also unheard of was omega identical twins. But that mattered little when one was the black sheep. I was combat boots, while she was stilettos. She liked to use a knife and fork, while I preferred to eat off a stick or with my hands.

I'd spent my entire life being compared to her, and now that we were on the verge of graduating, I was glad the comparisons would stop. There were only so many times a woman could hear about how great her sister was before she wanted to sew her ears shut.

None of my shortcomings were her fault, though. She couldn't help that she was omega to her very core, and I wasn't.

The crowd roared and I put my feet down, leaning forward as the captain of the Killer Gnomes closed in on the goal, which was a hole just big enough to fit the weighted ball in a slanted metal surface.

My mouth hung open as Nazario 'Rio' Perez whizzed past the captain, Beckett Thomas, taking the thirty-pound ball worth three points and throwing it at the hole in a tremendous display of strength and agility. The ball went in, and the crowd went wild as they won the game thirty-four to fourteen.

Jerseys were ripped off and chests were bumped in a show that had the omegas around the suite whimpering and the other alphas on the field growling. Despite their ridiculous team name, the pack that made up the Killer Gnomes was the strongest in the league, and they were on their way to winning the championship if they kept playing like they did today.

At least, that was what the announcers kept saying.

One of our escorts clapped her hands to get our attention. "Ladies! The team will be up in about ten minutes, so if you need to prepare yourselves, now is the time!"

"Come on, Kayla. Let's go freshen up." Kara grabbed the hand that wasn't holding my finished corn cob and led me to the bathrooms off of the suite.

I chucked my trash in the garbage as we entered the bathroom that was already nauseatingly scented with a mixture of omega perfumes. None of us perfumed enough to send alphas into a frenzy since we were on a cocktail of medicine that dampened our pheromones.

Perfume blockers, heat suppressants, and birth control implants made our scents almost nonexistent, but in large groups, with all the omegas perfuming just the tiniest amount, alphas could smell us from a mile away.

I lifted my arm and sniffed, scrunching my nose when I caught a faint whiff of my sweet scent. My sister caught me doing it and smacked my arm with the back of her hand, rolling her eyes as she opened her purse and pulled out a compact.

"I wouldn't be surprised if they smell like corn." She took the small round sponge and rubbed it on the powder. "Your T-zone is a bit shiny."

She blotted my face with her make-up before doing her own. It was a waste of time putting it on me when I could feel the corn juice residue. Before she could stop me, I stepped up to an empty sink and splashed cold water on my face, scrubbing off the make-up and the mess from my delicious snack.

I wasn't a barbarian by any means, but it was hard to pass up the culinary offerings at the Alphaball stadium. If they didn't want us to eat it, they shouldn't have put it in our suite. The academy didn't let us eat junk food, so if the opportunity was there, I was taking it.

A squeal came from the entrance, and the ten of us that were crammed around the five sinks all turned our heads like lemurs toward it. "They're here!"

Water dripping from my face, I grabbed paper towels from my sister and quickly dried myself and blotted the mayonnaise spot on my sweater. Now it was an even larger, darker spot, but I didn't care. I just wanted to get this whole thing over with so I'd be able to sit in the corner and play on my phone while the other omegas fawned over the alphas.

"There's no time to fix your hair." Kara smoothed my hair across my scalp and sighed. "Flyaways everywhere.

♡ 6 ♡

That's what happens when you don't take care of your curls."

"Just because you spend half your life on your hair doesn't mean I want to." I batted her hand away and tightened my ponytail.

Both of us had wavy hair, and while Kara embraced it, doing everything in her power to make it curly as hell, I chose to throw mine back in a ponytail or a bun. On rare occasions when I felt like it, I'd run a straightener over it. Today wasn't one of those days.

Taking my hand, Kara led me out of the bathroom, the four alphas that made up the Killer Gnomes already mingling amongst the other omegas in attendance. I refused to breathe through my nose, while my sister took in a deep inhale.

"They smell divine. Too bad they won't be able to smell any of us with all of the omega scents." I didn't see why Kara was worried about that; her perfume was a very neutral, melted chocolate scent that would please almost all alphas.

Mine was similar to hers but had a distinct note of hazelnuts to it. Unfortunately, that also limited my pack prospects because of nut allergies. Not that my scent itself would set off an allergic reaction, but in one of our courses, we learned our slick might. After that lesson, I'd had a nightmare where an alpha who was eating my pussy died with his tongue inside me.

How traumatic.

The alphas' backs were to us, and I appreciated their

tight team shirts pulling across their broad muscles. But that meant absolutely nothing because I didn't want alphas lording over me. I had plans for my future, and it didn't include rolling onto my back and catering to a pack, even if the idea of a knot filling me during my heat made me a little weak in the knees.

Kara and I were raised in a pack and had witnessed the love between our parents, but we also saw the heartbreak when one of our dads passed away from a heart attack when we were only nine. It hadn't only devastated my mom but had weakened the bond between our other five fathers. Things were only going to get worse the older they got, and since my mom was six years younger than them, she'd most likely die before her time of a broken heart.

I shook my head of my morbid thoughts and squeezed my sister's hand, my heart needing something solid to connect to. Omegas weren't usually that close to each other, but my sister and I were an exception, and it pained me to think about us parting ways soon. She could end up clear across the country from where I was.

"Be on your best behavior and try to smile," Kara whispered out of the side of her mouth as if I needed the reminder.

Okay. Maybe I did.

"I think I have corn stuck in my teeth." I brought my nail to my mouth just as Kane Martin turned and watched as I slid it between my lips.

Oops.

Nothing like a sinfully sexy alpha watching me dig a wayward kernel from my chompers.

He was just shy of six feet tall, with warm brown skin, black buzz cut hair, and facial hair groomed close to his face. I'd seen photos of him with his shirt off, and the man had enough abs to feed an army of omegas. The whole pack did.

"Hello, ladies. I'm Kane." He held out his hand to my sister first, his brown eyes twinkling from the overhead lights and possibly because he was enamored by the mere presence of her. "What's your name, beautiful?"

My sister let go of my hand, slipping it smoothly into his, her cheeks turning pink from the compliment. "I'm Kara Sterling. You played a fantastic game out there. I'm a really big fan."

Do not roll your eyes, Kayla.

I wiped my hands on my jeans and then shoved them in my pockets as he released my sister and held out his hand to me. I didn't take it because who knew where it had been? I'd read somewhere that over half of men did not wash after using the bathroom. I'd rather not risk it, especially because I'd probably forget I'd touched him and then stick a finger in my mouth.

I nodded my chin in greeting instead. "I'm Kayla Sterling." I wasn't going to kiss this guy's ass just because he was a rich as fuck alpha with a banging body.

Kara nudged me, and I sighed, my eyes roaming to the seats outside the open sliding doors where we'd watched the game from. I yearned to escape this pony show. This pack was not only one of the best Alphaball teams in the country, but they were also a top pack in our society, running several profitable businesses.

"Twin omegas? Well, isn't this something." Rylan Abbott, another member of the Alphaball team, clapped Kane on the shoulder as he came to join his pack mate in greeting us. "I hope you ladies are enjoying yourselves."

Rylan was a few inches taller than Kane and was just as striking in appearance. He looked younger and had a clean-shaven face, showing off his smooth porcelain skin, messy brown hair, and was sporting a grin that promised a good time.

"We are. We really appreciate your pack inviting us to the game and taking the time to meet us." Kara was always so gracious and proper. *Barf.*

The two of them moved on, clearly not interested in talking to us further. But then again, there were over twenty omegas to meet, and I vaguely remembered our chaperones saying they only had ten minutes. Although ten minutes didn't seem like a lot of time, the pack would receive profiles and scent cards on each of us after this.

"I'm going to get some air," I whispered in my sister's ear as she was drooling over the alphas we'd just met.

"Kayla." The disapproval in her voice left a bitter taste in my mouth. I just wasn't in a social kind of mood. But was I ever?

I slipped away out the sliding doors of the suite,

finding a spot I'd seen earlier where a column hid a cluster of seats from the view of the rest of the area. I pulled my phone out of my crossbody purse and opened the game I was playing. There was something mind-numbing and calming about solving puzzles and then building an estate.

I passed a few levels when my reprieve was inter-rupted. "We told you we didn't want an omega," a male voice said, his voice lowered so only whoever he was with could hear.

I peeked around the corner of the column to see the head of the pack, Beckett Thomas, with a man in a suit. Both looked tense, but it was clear to me from how they were standing that Beckett was the alpha and the man in the suit was either a low-ranking alpha or a beta.

"Having an omega will only make the pack stronger so you can keep winning! All of the top teams have omegas except yours. This is how you take yourselves to the next level: champions." The two men walked to the railing, their backs to me.

I slid back in my seat so I was hidden again just in case they turned around. With all the smells in the stadium and the ones coming from the suite, they were none the wiser to my presence hidden in the shadows.

"An omega will make us weaker, especially right now. What if her heat is in the middle of playoffs or during the championship? You don't think these things through, Brian. It's almost like you want us to be thrown off our game and lose."

"That would be ideal for the omega to be in heat during the championship. You'll be more aggressive. If you get the best of the best, then it will only help you. Elite Omega Academy has that. They are well educated in how to take care of a pack both domestically and sexually. It will strengthen your pack bond as well."

I wanted to gag. Sure, part of being an omega was taking care of the home and our alphas' needs, but we were more than just a maid and a hole to fill.

"We already have betas to fulfill all of those needs," he growled, the frustration in his voice making my spine tingle with awareness.

"You met Kara Sterling, right? She won *Omega of the Year* for four years." Brian sounded like he was pleading now. "An opportunity to get an omega of her caliber won't happen again. I suggest we put her at the top of the match list. I know it was hard to smell her perfume, but none of the omegas in that room smell bad, I can guarantee it. As your manager and coach, I insist that you consider it. If it doesn't work out, we can ship her back to the academy and they can deal with the fallout."

My stomach dropped at that. I'd never heard of a pack rejecting an omega after matching with them and taking them in, even though it was in the contract. It would be a major blow to an omega to be sent to an omega compound.

It was quiet for a minute before there was another growl from Beckett. "Fine, but when this blows up in our faces, it's on you." He punctuated his words, and I could practically visualize him poking Brian in the chest as he said each one.

I didn't know where my sister stood on ranking the packs, but I couldn't let her put them on her list when they would so easily cast her aside.

CHAPTER TWO

Beck

Fucking Brian.

I knew he had our best interests at heart when it came to completing our pack by adding an omega, but the thing was, I felt like we were already complete without one. We'd been doing just fine for almost a decade without an omega, so why change things now?

Entering back into the room with all of the omegas just made my insides twist with an overwhelming need to protect. The last thing I needed to be thinking about was whether an omega was safe or if they needed me.

And that was exactly what omegas did. They sucked the life right out of an alpha and a pack. They made our instincts rule over us instead of us running the show.

Brian elbowed me and then nodded his chin toward Kara. "Try to be nice."

I hated taking direction from him, but when it came to our Alphaball career, he was the best one for the job. We'd been fortunate to snag him about a year ago when his old team retired from the game.

Kara's eyes lit up as I approached, and I smiled, despite wanting to head straight for the door. She was a beautiful woman with the most striking blue eyes I'd ever seen, curly brown hair that fell over the front of her shoulders and brushed her breasts, and she had a body any alpha would be happy to sink into.

But there was something missing as I took her hand in mine and gave it a solid shake. *I should feel something, shouldn't I?*

Although there were a lot of scents in the room, I could pick up a hint of chocolate as she brushed her hair back. I could only imagine what her full-on perfume smelled like.

Brian was right next to me and cleared his throat to get Kara's attention. "Beckett is the head of the pack, and we were just discussing our intent to put you at the top of our match list."

Her lips parted the tiniest amount as she took a sharp inhale of air. "Wow. I don't know what to say. I will take that into consideration when listing my matches."

Brian winked at her and then turned to me. "We need to get going. Our plane is waiting."

Kara's shoulders dropped, and she bit her lip. "It was really nice to meet you, Beckett. We all appreciate you-"

"What's up, sis?" The almost identical replica of Kara came up beside her, throwing an arm around her shoulder.

They would have been identical if she had her hair curled and had any semblance of manners. She narrowed her eyes at me and Brian and looked us up and down in disgust.

Kara said her sister's name under her breath in warning, but I didn't catch it over the noise in the room. Her smile was tight as she pried her sister's arm off her shoulders. "Forgive her. She was rooting for the other team."

"Oh, really?" I couldn't stop from smirking because the sister was practically foaming at the mouth. "Sounds like someone likes their alphas weak."

"No, I just don't like my alphas with shrimp-sized dicks," she spat with a venom that made me think this was more than just an Alphaball thing.

Kara gasped. "Kayla!"

Something about this chick was riling me up, and I stepped forward, ready to stare her down and make her whimper.

Brian grabbed the sleeve of my shirt to stop me. "It's time to go."

"It was nice to meet you, Kara. I can see why you've been selected as *Omega of the Year*." I stepped back and then looked at Kayla with a sneer. "But there can only be one *Omega of the Year,* am I right?"

Anger and hurt flashed in Kayla's eyes before she stood up straighter. "You're an asshole."

I threw my head back and laughed, drawing the attention of quite a few omegas around us. I'd never had an omega call me a name before. This chick had balls.

If we did end up matching with her sister, holidays were bound to be a shit show.

AFTER THE MEET and greet that left me more than a little irritable, we headed to the airport to go home. We were no strangers to the attention of others, but something about being in a room packed with omegas made me antsy. It was like my alpha instincts had kicked into overdrive, despite not being hit full-on with any perfume.

Thank fuck for the invention of perfume blockers.

We boarded our private plane and took our seats around the small conference table. Just because we were professional Alphaball players, didn't mean we could neglect our other businesses that brought in ten times the amount our athletic prowess earned us.

Brian gave us a nod as he walked past us with his cellphone to his ear and sat in the back of the plane. He wasn't an official member of our pack—there was no

MAYA NICOLE

way in hell I'd bite him in, no matter how good of a beta he was—but he ran the Alphaball side of things for us.

Apparently, now he was handling all things omega, including going through the profiles, filling out our Omega Match paperwork, and showing us where to sign.

A few decades ago, Omega Match was created to prevent the major issues that were happening when it came to alpha packs finding and bonding with omegas. Now, instead of a free-for-all that often led to omegas being hurt and packs ripping each other apart, it was streamlined across the country.

When omegas emerge around the age of sixteen, they immediately go to a boarding school to finish out their high school years. From there, they either go to an academy, which is essentially college with courses geared toward omegas, or they enter the matching system.

Alphas can decide whenever they wish to utilize the matching system, as long as they've declared themselves as a pack or a solo alpha. Usually, meet and greets are arranged, and then profiles and scent samples are used to decide who would be a good fit.

The computer then makes matches based on how each participant ranks each other. It might seem like a flawed system, but most of the matches work out, with both the packs and omegas happy with the pairing.

As soon as we were in the air, I pulled out my laptop and powered it on, glad I wasn't dealing with the paperwork involved with Omega Match. "Our spring campaign starts next Monday, and we have an in-person interview and mini-fashion show scheduled with *Good Morning Pack* on Tuesday, plus a launch party that evening. We'll be staying in New York Monday and Tuesday night and flying back to L.A. on Wednesday for a game and then dinner with the CEO of United Alpha Sports to talk about our brand being the official gear for Alphaball."

Rio looked up from his phone with a frown. "If we match with that omega who Brian was going on about, I think she'll be coming on Monday evening. Shouldn't we be there to greet her and get her settled in?"

"Where will her nest be? We have that guest room, but I don't think it's a good room for that." Rylan turned and glanced back at Brian and then lowered his voice. "Don't you think it's odd he's pushing this omega thing when we're well on our way to the playoffs? Why now? Why not during the fall?"

Kane snorted and ran a hand over his face before putting his head back against his seat and shutting his eyes. "Brian does whatever the fuck he wants. Are you really surprised?"

"She won't need a nest right away. Unmatched omegas are on blockers, and it takes time for them to wear off if they stop them. She'll probably talk to us first before she goes off them." Rio put his phone on the table in front of us with a webpage pulled up. "I think we should order a nest starter kit and have it there for her to set up since we don't have anything already."

A growl bubbled in my throat, and all three of my packmates looked at me. "She's supposedly the best of the best and went to this academy for what? Four years? I'm sure she doesn't need us to help her. She seemed to have her shit together, unlike her twin. Besides, those kits cost thousands, and if this chick doesn't work out, we're already going to be out money."

Kane let out a low whistle without opening his eyes. "We have the money regardless, asshole. I think we should be there when she arrives."

How many times was I going to get called an asshole in one day?

"I'll take care of it all." We'd been so focused talking about the omega, none of us noticed Brian had moved to stand by our seats. "I sent the paperwork to you all to sign. Need I remind you that if this doesn't work out, the restitution to the omega is one hundred thousand."

My fists clenched, and I resisted the urge to throw my laptop at his head. "If this doesn't work out, you're paying half."

"I'll gladly do that, but I know this is going to make your pack the strongest it's ever been. You met the girl. She's perfect. This is going to give the pack more networking opportunities as well. She can charm the investors and their omegas." He grinned as if he was the best beta on the planet.

"You're forgetting that we have to match with the girl

first." Rio picked up his phone again, probably to order that damn kit. If that was how he wanted to spend his money, then fine.

"Don't you worry about that. It will happen." Brian turned and headed back to his seat before I could ask him what he meant by that.

"He's right, you know." Kane opened his eyes, meeting mine. "At the very least, it should help mellow your ass out. You're getting more and more aggressive and irritable. The last thing we need is for you to lose your shit and for us to be put on watch by the World Pack Health Organization."

"It takes a lot for the WPHO to get involved with a pack." I leaned back in my seat, crossing my arms. "And I am not irritable."

The fuckers laughed, amusement thrown at me through our pack bond. I growled, glaring at each of them before turning back to my laptop.

What was making me irritable wasn't not having an omega, it was the idea of having one come in and fuck up everything I'd built from nothing.

CHAPTER THREE

Kayla

Omega Match Results.

We'd been clicking refresh on Kara's phone for the last fifteen minutes in the hopes the results of Omega Match went up early. I hadn't bothered opening my email, instead I enjoyed my sister's excitement of four years of hard work paying off.

Not all omegas had the privilege we did to attend the best academy in the nation. Hell, some omegas never even went to an omega academy and went straight into searching for their packs after the mandated two years in an omega boarding high school.

Things would have been easier for me had I gone that route. Instead, I'd spent four years awaiting the day I could select the checkbox that stated I wasn't interested in any packs at this time.

My parents were going to be disappointed, and so was the academy, but it was my life, my choice. And currently, my choice was to focus on myself and start my own quilting company specifically geared toward omegas and their nests.

I'd first fallen in love with quilt making after taking an introductory course a few years ago and had taken every course on it since. In my free time, I watched countless videos on how to make certain patterns. I'd gotten so good that most of the omegas at the academy had some creation of mine.

There was something about an omega getting a handmade quilt that just filled them with the warm fuzzies and brought them comfort. My goal was to open a shop where omegas or their alphas could come in and select the materials they wanted and mark them with their scents if they wished. I'd probably have to forever be on scent blockers and wear some kind of special protective gear so my own scent wouldn't get on them, but I could figure that all out later.

"I think I'm going to puke." Kara put her phone down without opening the email and took a long, shaky breath. "You open it for me."

Snatching her phone, I clicked on the email, my breath catching in my throat as I read the words no omega wants to read: *No match.*

That was impossible.

I clicked out of the email and opened it back up

before hitting refresh a few times, but nothing changed. Kara didn't get a match.

I'd been with her when she filled out her list, and she had listed twenty, which was the most an omega and a pack were allowed to put. The system then used the information to pair omegas with packs. Luckily, I'd convinced her not to put Beckett and his pack after relaying the conversation I overheard.

But maybe I should have let her. Even that fate was better than her not matching. It wasn't the end of the world to not match, but for Kara, I had a feeling it would be.

"Which pack did I get?" The hope in her voice made my chest ache, and I set the phone on the desk in front of her.

I was so glad I'd talked her into staying in her room to read the email because, had we been around the other omegas, it would have been ten times worse. Especially because I could hear the squealing out in the hall as others began sharing their match successes.

Kara looked down at the phone and took it with a shaking hand. "What... I don't understand..." She whined, letting the phone drop from her hands and fall to the floor.

I bit back my own whine, hating to hear my sister's pain. I wrapped my arms around her, trying to give her comfort as she broke down in tears. I'd expected her to get her top pick, but no match at all?

A lot of packs should have put her at the top of their

lists, but if they hadn't, then it was possible a match wouldn't have happened. It was modeled after how doctors matched into residency programs, and even the best of the best sometimes weren't the best fit at that moment in time.

"There's always the match in the fall. This is just fate's way of telling you your pack wasn't in this batch." I didn't know if that was helpful or not, but she had to know it would all work out eventually.

She shook her head. "The best packs match in the spring."

"Maybe this was a mistake and you did match."

With a shaky sigh, she scooped her phone up and wiped her cheeks. "You're right. Let's go see the dean. It's probably just a glitch. Maybe I matched with several in a tie and need to pick."

Matching didn't work like that, but I'd go along with it for now. "Definitely a glitch. Technology these days; you can't trust it."

She stopped at the door, nearly causing me to run into her. "Wait, which pack did you match with?"

I bit my lip and looked at my shoes. "I opted out."

I could feel her eyes boring into me as she silently stood there. "Mom is going to be upset."

"Well, that sounds like a her problem and not a me problem." I shrugged even though my sister's comment made me want to scream.

I loved my mom and valued her opinions, but we always seemed to walk on eggshells around her in order to not upset her. It had gotten worse since we emerged as omegas. Our designations made us much more vulnerable, and she wanted us protected at all costs.

I felt like an asshole for my thoughts and inwardly smacked myself. It might have been over a decade since my father passed away, but my family's grief was still fresh. A pack bond is something that doesn't quite fully recover from a death; like a crumpled-up piece of paper that's still wrinkled, even when you attempt to smooth it out.

With her head down, Kara grabbed her sweater, opened the door, and walked into the hall where we could hear the celebrations down in the common room. I looped my arm through hers, and we walked as quickly as possible down the stairs and past the common room that had comfortable seating, a large fireplace, and a television.

There were four dorm buildings at our academy, each housing a year. We stayed in the same building all four years, and next year, an incoming class would take our place. It had been my home away from home, and I hated to admit it, but the comfort of leaving it made me anxious.

I was sure those that were going to packs weren't anxious, though, judging from the excitement in the air as we slipped by unnoticed. Once we were outside, we both let out a collective sigh of relief; Kara because it was obvious from her tear-stained face that Omega

Match hadn't gone her way, and me because I didn't want to hear about the heat plans of my friends.

We walked across the courtyard and past the other dorms to the administration building. It was a bit chilly, and I shoved my hands in my hooded sweatshirt pocket. It might have been May, but it was cold in the mornings.

The administration building loomed ahead, three stories tall with red brick and windows reflecting the gray sky. A security guard opened the door for us, sympathy on his face as he nodded to me, assuming we were there for me. There was only one reason you'd come to the administrative building on match day; if you didn't match.

"What if this isn't a mistake?" Kara whispered as we took the elevator to the third floor.

I took her hand in mine. "Like I said, maybe there was a reason you didn't match."

"I should have put down Beckett Thomas's pack." She sniffled and froze in place when the door dinged and slid open. "I don't know if I can handle this."

"I'm here for you Care Bear." I squeezed her hand and led her out of the elevator into the reception area.

There was a lot of activity with phones ringing and people rushing around, no doubt fielding phone calls from students, parents, and packs. The academy had nothing to do with the match results, but they were responsible for arranging moving to our new pack houses. Those who didn't match would stay a few more weeks before moving to an omega compound of their choice.

"Ah, the Sterling twins. What can I help you with?" The secretary was simultaneously writing something on a sticky note, typing something on her computer, and looking at us with a smile as we approached the reception desk.

"Can we please speak to the dean? I know she's probably swamped right now, but we really need to speak to her about Kara's match results." Kara was shaking, and I held her hand tighter. "We'll wait if we have to."

"Let me check here..." She finished her two tasks and then picked up her phone. "Kara Sterling would like to speak to you if you're available... perfect! Go right on back, ladies."

My phone buzzed in my back pocket as we walked down the long hallway to the dean's office, and I pulled it out. My mom was calling, no doubt to see what packs we had matched to.

"She's probably freaking out because I didn't call her right when the match results were sent. I left my phone in my room." Kara knocked on the partially opened office door before entering. "Ms. Monroe, thank you so much for seeing me on such short notice."

The dean smiled at us, although the smiles she gave never quite reached her eyes. Ella Monroe was the youngest dean in the history of the academy system, being thirty years of age. None of us really knew her story, but judging by the sadness in her eyes, it wasn't good.

"Not a problem at all." She folded her hands on her desk, giving my sister a knowing look. "I'm sorry the match didn't work out for you this time around. There's always the fall or waiting until next spring. Sometimes the timing is just not right. It doesn't mean you're any less of a wonderful person and a perfect omega for a pack." She spoke with sincerity, as if she wasn't just saying the words to pacify my sister.

"But..." My sister cleared her throat and wiped at a wayward tear. "It has to be a mistake."

"I looked over all the match results before they went out. While I was a little surprised, you have to remember that it's not just our academy vying for the packs, but all omegas who are looking for a pack. Meeting the packs isn't required, so a given pack might have over a hundred omegas with that pack in their top spot and if they put even one of them before you, they'd match."

Basically, the system calculated scores based on where you ranked a pack. So, if Kara put a pack third and they put her fourth, that would be a score of seven. If another omega put that same pack second and they put her fifth, that would also be a seven and then the highest omega score would match to the pack.

"What about the Thomas pack? They said they were going to list me at the top of their selections and I... I must have forgotten to put them." Kara sat up taller, scooting to the edge of her chair. She reminded me of a golden retriever begging for a treat.

We both knew she didn't put them at all because I talked her out of it. There was a slight twinge of guilt in my stomach, but I shook it off. She deserved a pack that *wanted* an omega, not just one that was doing it for a gain or to tick off a box for their manager.

The dean looked over at me with a frown, and I squirmed in my seat under her stare. "I'm afraid that's impossible. They matched with Kayla."

"What?!" Kara and I both screeched at the same time.

I jumped to my feet, my heart thudding so hard that I wondered if I was about to have a heart attack. Looking back and forth between Kara and Ms. Monroe, I tried to find my words, but they were stuck in a lump in my throat.

Kara found her words, though. "You lied to me! You told me they were assholes, and I trusted you!"

"Kara, I swear to you, I opted out!" I tried to reach for her as she stood and headed for the door.

"You're dead to me." The door slammed shut behind her, my heart shattering at her words.

What the fuck had just happened?

I STARED up at my ceiling through a small gap in my blankets so I could breathe, my phone lying on my chest. There were twenty missed calls from my mom and dads, and texts asking me to call them. They'd undoubtedly heard about what had happened and wanted to rip me a new asshole for deceiving my sister.

Only I hadn't deceived her.

I didn't know what I was going to do. I was set to leave in two days, my sister hated me, and there was no backing out of going since I'd supposedly signed a contract when I submitted my online form.

There had to be a mistake because I was certain I checked the opt-out button and didn't even pull up the pack names to select any.

Pushing the blankets off me, I jumped to my feet and grabbed a tote bag that was hanging on the back of my door. I shoved my hidden stash of emergency chocolates and tiny bottles of liquor into it. I was of legal drinking age, but alcohol was banned on campus. No one wanted to deal with a bunch of drunk omegas making bad decisions.

It was nearly midnight, which was our curfew to be in our rooms, but luckily, Kara's room was right across the hall from mine. I knocked softly before using a copy of her key to go in.

The room was dark besides the faint glow of a night-light she had plugged in under her bed. I could see her in her bed, a million blankets and pillows piled around her and on top of her.

"Care Bear, I brought chocolate and rum," I whispered, not sure if she was asleep.

"Go away," she said through a whimper.

Setting the bag on her nightstand, I pulled back the blankets and slid into bed next to her. She scooted over, making more room for me, but turned to give me her back.

"I swear to you, I didn't put them or any pack. You have to believe me." My voice caught in my throat, and I cleared it. "I'm certain I opted out, and even if I hadn't, I didn't even open the search to select any packs. I don't know how this could have happened."

I turned toward her and put my hand on her arm, hoping she wouldn't lash out at me more than she already had. It could have been a lot worse; she could have smacked me or gone to my room and trashed it. Not that Kara had a bone in her body that would allow her to be violent or vindictive.

But maybe I'd changed that and set off a spiral.

A whimper escaped and tears sprung to my eyes. I rarely let that side of being an omega come out, but I couldn't help the pain it was causing me to see my sister hurting because she thought I wronged her.

"They picked you." I could hardly hear her because her face was buried in a pillow she was hugging. "They picked you and you picked them."

"I didn't. I swear on everything." I moved closer to her and nuzzled my face into her back. She didn't shrug me off, which was a win. "Ms. Monroe called the Omega Match office and they told her that there wasn't an error, but there has to be."

She turned over, and even though I couldn't see her

face, I knew it was red and puffy from crying. "Call them or message them on social media."

"I don't have their numbers. I did message them, but the last time I checked, they hadn't seen them. They probably get thousands of messages."

"Did you try their manager or whoever that guy was? Maybe he can get the message to them." She pushed the blankets off of our heads and leaned over me to grab the bag I'd put on her nightstand. "But even if it was a mistake, it's not like it changes the fact I didn't match."

I turned on the small bedside lamp and we both squinted as our eyes adjusted to the soft light. "They probably just got our names mixed up... but that doesn't explain how I got a match." I took a small bottle of coconut rum from her and opened it. "Are you still mad at me?"

She moved a few pillows against the headboard and sat against them, bringing her tiny bottle of alcohol to her lips and drinking it in one gulp. "No. I believe you."

Relief flooded my system, and I scooted next to her, putting my head on her shoulder. "The fine for backing out of a match is too much for me to not go... I can't stick our parents with that burden."

Kara dug in the bag and pulled out a package of peanut butter cups. "And if you start to throw around accusations about the matching system being broken or wrong, the government is going to rain hell."

"Fuck, Kara. I can't join a pack. I feel like this is being

forced on me. Do you think it's karma for saying they had shrimp dicks?"

One of the many reasons the alphas that ran our government didn't take lightly to omegas and packs backing out of matches was because then it might create a domino effect. If a pack matched with an omega who refused to go after already matching with them, that pack might become possessive anyway. It had happened in the early days of the matching system, so now there were financial penalties great enough to prevent it from happening.

We both were lost in our thoughts as we had our fill of chocolate and booze. I eventually pulled out my phone and pulled up one of Brian's active social media accounts. He mostly posted pictures of the team during games and some behind-the-scenes pictures during practices and interviews.

Me: *Hi. This is Kayla Sterling, and I was trying to contact one of the guys, but they don't seem to check their messages. Can you have them check?*

The message was read almost immediately. Did this guy not sleep?

Brian: *What is this regarding?*

"Seriously?" I showed my sister, and she rolled her eyes.

Me: *I matched with them, and I thought they were going to put my sister. Neither of us put them on ours.*

Brian: *Are you rejecting the match? Have you notified the Omega Match offices?*

Me: *They said there wasn't an error, but there has to be because I didn't list them or any pack, for that matter.*

Brian: *What are you suggesting?*

"Careful," Kara warned. "We don't know this guy and he's being pretty cagey."

Me: *I need to confirm the match with them because if there's been a glitch of some kind, it needs to be remedied.*

Brian: *It wasn't a glitch. I'll see you on Monday.*

Me: *Can you please have one of them contact me? The match email doesn't have their phone numbers because they're 'celebrities.'*

The message stayed unread for a solid minute before I threw my phone on the bed in frustration. "This is bullshit. I'm just supposed to get on a plane on Monday with no contact information for them?"

"Maybe you should give it a shot." Kara got off the bed and went to her dresser to pull out pajamas. "Are you staying here tonight?"

I nodded. "What do you mean, *give it a shot?*"

"Well, think about it. You go there, be your charming self, they send you back, and boom! You're a hundred thousand dollars richer. You can start your business." Kara threw a tank and pajama shorts at me. "Or you can fall madly in love with them, and I can live vicariously through you."

"Did that alcohol go straight to your brain?" I got up, feeling slightly buzzed myself. "I can't do that!"

"Why not? It's the perfect opportunity for you to get your start-up costs and show just how fucked Omega

Match is." Kara rarely cussed, and I gasped. "My guess is they put the wrong name down, and when there wasn't a match, they paid to have it happen."

"Then you should go. Say you're me." I crawled back into bed, leaving my clothes in a heap on the floor. Kara immediately picked them up and folded them to put on her desk chair.

"We're twenty-two years old, Kayla." She sat on the edge of the bed and grabbed a scrunchie from her nightstand to tie her hair back. "They would know immediately, and who knows what the fines would be? Do you think our parents are going to want that?"

I sighed because she was right. "You aren't mad?"

She lay down and flicked off the light, dousing us in darkness. "I was, but if no packs want me, then maybe I'm doing something wrong."

"You aren't." I checked my phone one last time for a message from Brian. "I bet you anything, I get to their house, and they'll realize they put the wrong name. We'll be back to drinking contraband liquor and chocolate together in no time."

"I'm sorry I told you that you were dead to me." She whimpered and leaned in to hug me. "Maybe you're onto something about not caring about this whole omega role business. It consumed me, and now look at what happened. It almost ripped us apart."

"I'm sorry too. If you would have put them, maybe it would have been a match and-"

"It's not your fault." She pulled out of our hug and

pulled the covers around us. "This is an opportunity for you."

"Yeah." I grabbed one of her Squishmallow pillows from the foot of the bed and hugged it. "I'll be the *best* damn omega they've ever seen."

CHAPTER FOUR

Kayla

A freaking private jet.

I didn't even know what to think when my driver had taken me and two other omegas to a side entrance at the airport where small aircrafts departed from. There was minimal security and a waiting room that was straight out of a magazine.

The free donuts and coffee helped calm my nerves slightly, but I was still all twisted up inside about leaving the security of the academy and my sister to go into the unknown. This pack could be my worst nightmare.

I could have raised a much bigger stink about the whole thing, but Kara did have a good idea about letting it play out until they sent me back.

"I can't believe this is happening so quickly! It's exciting, don't you think?" One of the other omegas, Charlotte, was sitting next to me on the plush loveseat facing the giant windows looking out onto the tarmac. "I couldn't believe I matched with my dream pack. I'm glad they came to our open house a few months ago."

I looked over at her as I took a bite of donut, sprinkles dropping down my shirt. "What if they're complete assholes though?"

Mackenzie, the third omega in our little group of luxury fliers, laughed. "Why are you always so cynical? You do realize you matched into one of the most sought-after packs? Not only are they rich, but they're also sexy as fuck and smart. You have to be to run the empire they do."

"Makes you wonder why they picked me," I muttered with a mouthful of donut.

"You must have made an impression on them. What did you think of their scents?" Charlotte brought her own donut to her mouth and nibbled on it.

While I wasn't close to the other omegas, most of us considered each other friends. It was hard to build strong relationships when we were all vying for the same packs, and our instincts often left us grumbly around each other.

"I didn't smell them. One of the only classes I aced at the academy was Olfactory Management." It was hard to not use your nose, but I was a master of it.

They both gave me a funny look. I knew it sounded psycho to them that I'd pick a pack not based on how I reacted to their pheromones, but it wasn't like I'd actually picked them. I wasn't about to tell them that, though.

"That's going to really suck if you find their scents repulsive." Mackenzie laughed uncomfortably. "Do you plan on going off your blockers?"

I scrunched my nose. "Heck, no." The last thing I needed was to go into heat when I wanted them to send me packing, but they didn't know that. "I mean, I'll wait a bit so we can get to know each other. The first heat after being on blockers for as long as we have can be crazy, and I don't want it to be awkward."

Charlotte was staring at me without speaking for an awfully long time. "Kara didn't match. I find that interesting. I swear I overheard that pack saying they were going to put her first when we were at that meet and greet at their game."

"Maybe they didn't find her scent appealing." I wanted to get away from these two before the discussion spiraled out of control, but there wasn't anywhere else to go besides the alpha and beta waiting area, and that wasn't going to happen.

Instead of running away, I pulled out my phone, hoping they took the hint that I didn't want to talk anymore. They were nice enough, but I didn't need anyone ruining my now solid plan.

Luckily, Charlotte and Mackenzie were both called for their flights within minutes of each other, and I was left with my thoughts. Maybe the pack *had* smelled my scent card and gone nuts over it. I did smell like a jar of Nutella when my full perfume hit.

Damn it. I should have at least smelled their scents and really examined their profiles. I'd been so caught up in making things right with Kara and my impending move, I hadn't taken the time to prepare. But that was the story of my life; unprepared and scatterbrained.

Except when it came to quilting.

"Kayla Sterling? Your plane is ready to board."

Here goes nothing.

I grabbed the one suitcase I'd brought to get me by until the rest of my belongings arrived in a week. I would have preferred not having them shipped at all, but that would have raised suspicion about my plan to be the worst omega ever.

The plane was a ten-seater from a private jet rental company that catered to the rich and influential. I was the only one on board and sat at a table with four over-sized leather seats around it. I braved a subtle sniff but couldn't smell anything.

"Welcome aboard, Ms. Sterling. We'll be arriving in Los Angeles in about three hours. Once we're in the air, you'll be able to connect your devices to our Wi-Fi and enjoy the snacks and beverages we have aboard." The flight attendant was a tall, blonde woman who had an award-winning smile as she went through safety information.

She left me as the plane began driving to the takeoff point, and I relaxed into the soft leather seat. I'd be lying if I said the butterflies were from being on the plane, but really, they were because I didn't know what I was getting myself into.

WAS I a little disappointed it was Brian who picked me up from the airport? Absolutely.

What kind of pack picks an omega and then sends their lackey instead of welcoming me themselves? A pack of rich assholes, that's who.

We were currently stuck in rush hour traffic and had gone about a mile in ten minutes when we still had about fourteen miles to the pack's house in the Hollywood Hills, according to the GPS.

Brian hadn't said much to me yet, and I was beginning to wonder if he was avoiding the elephant in the car.

"So... where's the pack?" I was sitting in the backseat of the SUV, so all I could see were his eyes in the rearview mirror and part of his face.

"They had some business in New York and then have an Alphaball game and a dinner they have to attend."

"And I can't attend the game and dinner?" Wasn't that one of my purposes? "Also, you never messaged me their phone numbers."

"They've been busy. Why bother them when you're completely capable of settling in on your own? You'll just distract them from their jobs." Wow, he was a complete asshole. "They'll be back Wednesday night."

"And what? You're keeping me company until then?" I crossed my arms, already feeling my hopes and dreams being flushed down the toilet.

If they weren't going to be around, how were they going to see that I was the last omega they should have put on their list? I wanted to ask Brian about why they'd chosen me, but I didn't trust him at all.

"No. Unfortunately, I have business to attend to. I'll get you settled in at the house and then you can do whatever you need to do to make yourself comfortable." He met my stare in the rearview mirror as we came to a stop in traffic again. "You're a very fortunate omega to be matched with such a prominent pack."

Don't roll your eyes.

"I'm very fortunate their beta is at their beck and call to take care of their omega." I knew it was going to rub him the wrong way, and I smirked when he stiffened.

"I'm not part of the pack, and I will not be taking care of you besides setting you up in their house and giving you a pack credit card." His hands were tight around the steering wheel as the traffic started to move at a decent pace. And by decent, I meant twenty-five miles per hour.

"Seems a little idiotic to give an omega free use of a credit card," I muttered, turning my attention out the window.

We were just about to the Hollywood Hills, and I

couldn't help but wonder what their house looked like. They all made good salaries as Alphaball players and had endorsements and other business ventures. Hell, they'd sent a private jet to retrieve me.

"They'll spare no expense to make you happy. From the looks of your clothes, shoes, and suitcase, you are not the caliber they need to present to the world. There will be dinners and events you need to attend eventually. Plus, your everyday attire isn't up to par."

I looked down at my ripped skinny jeans, N'Pact band T-shirt, and combat boots. "What's wrong with what I'm wearing? You're telling me they walk around in suits all the time?"

He pulled off the highway without answering me, and we spent the rest of the drive in silence. I wished Kara was with me to see all the humongous houses we were passing as we started into the Hollywood Hills area. She spent a lot of time on real estate websites, looking at properties. I couldn't have cared less as long as it had a cozy place for me to set up a nest.

I might not have enjoyed all the things that came with being an omega, but creating a comfortable nest where I could hide out and calm my nerves was vital to my well-being and mental health.

We stopped outside a solid black gate, and Brian pulled an opener out of the center console. The gate swung inward, and I gasped as we pulled up into the driveway of a two or three-story ultra-modern-looking house that looked like it was made out of white marble.

I couldn't quite tell how many stories it was because most of the houses in the area were built into hillsides. The two black, double garage doors were on the driveway level, and then back behind it up higher looked like two stories. There was a retaining wall at least ten feet high made of white marble with a subtle gray veining and a wide set of black marble stairs leading up to the front.

What happened when it rained? Were people just expected to slip and slide down the smooth surfaces?

A black stone ball sculpture sat on the corner edge of the retaining wall, serving no purpose other than to contrast dramatically with the sharp angles and light coloring of the house. It wasn't inviting at all, and as much as I didn't want to admit it to myself, I was disappointed.

"Are they compensating for something with that ball?" I chuckled to myself, trying to ease the small bubble of anxiety that was pooling in my gut. I could only fight my instincts so much, and this house screamed bachelor party pad.

"This house is an architectural masterpiece, and that's an Alphaball art piece commissioned by Rio by his favorite sculptor." He opened one of the garages with another click of a button but didn't pull inside because there were vehicles parked there. "Eight bedrooms, ten bathrooms, ocean and city views, a gym with a sauna, cryotherapy chamber, and state-of-the-art equipment."

"Jesus. What the hell does someone need ten fucking

bathrooms for?" I grabbed my backpack and got out. The weather was very mild and sunny; I already loved it.

"Watch your language. Most of the rooms have one. The main level and entertainment and gym levels each have one."

I had to bite my tongue from saying something else and followed him into the garage. "Hey, wait. My bag is in the back of the car."

"I'll let you in and then grab it for you." He put a code in the door leading into the house and it opened into a space that had two large sectionals, a bar area, a giant television, and an all-glass wall looking out onto a lap pool and greenery. "I'll give you a code to get in and out, and that sets the alarm and disarms it."

"Is this the ocean and city views?" I gestured to the pool and outside area.

The room was cozier than the outside but was still mostly shiny stone and dark colors. At least the couches looked comfortable.

"This is the ground floor. Why don't you explore while I grab your bag?" He went back out into the garage, leaving me standing there in awe of the space.

Down a short hallway to the left was the gym, which was practically the size of the one back at the academy. There were four treadmills and bikes, all the weight equipment four athletes could possibly imagine, and a glass sauna that looked out over it all.

I took my phone out and snapped a picture, sending

it to Kara. She'd wanted pictures of their house, and I certainly was going to give them to her.

It was no wonder Brian and Beckett's conversation had been so flippant about sending an omega back if they didn't work out. A hundred grand was a drop in the bucket to these guys, and the tiny part of me that felt guilty for what I was doing decreased to just a tendril.

On the other side of the gym was another hallway that led to the opposite side of the entertainment space. The place was gigantic, and I could only imagine how many square feet it was if there were still two more stories.

Down another hallway, there was a movie viewing room with tiered recliners and loveseats in front of a massive screen and a guest suite. Brian still wasn't back inside yet, so I went to the wide staircase leading up to the main level and had to pick my jaw up off the floor as I took in the view out the floor-to-ceiling windows.

The main living space was large, with a sitting area, an electric fireplace spanning a wall between the living room and the dining room, and a kitchen barely visible through the dining area.

But the dark colors and geometric elements of the space weren't what I was focused on. The view was of the Los Angeles skyline, which was turning a faint pink as the sun began to lower in the sky.

I went to the large windows which were telescopic sliding doors that opened across the width of the entire wall. My first thought was of how many bugs and birds must fly in through it when it was open.

The outside wasn't exactly a yard, more of a giant patio with an infinity pool reaching to the edge, where it looked like it dropped right off the side of the hill we were on. It was amazing, and I found myself walking to one of the lounge chairs outside to sit and enjoy the view.

"It's quite the view, isn't it?" I jumped as Brian came to stand beside the lounger. "This is your home now too. They want you to make it your own."

I glanced up at him, annoyed he had ruined my moment of peace and even more suspicious because he seemed to have changed his tune. Why did he sound nice all of a sudden?

"It's a party house." I looked back out at the skyline. "I'd hardly call this an ocean view, by the way."

He shoved his hands in his pockets and stood there for a minute that lasted what felt like ten. "I left pass-codes, cell phone numbers, and the pack credit card on the kitchen counter. If you need anything, call me first before you call or text the pack. They are pretty busy these next few days and don't need to worry about how you're settling in. Buy what you need to build a nest. Anywhere would be suitable."

"Wait, that's it? You're just leaving me here in this giant house with a credit card? What if I need to go somewhere?" I stood, a sudden panic welling up inside me out of nowhere.

"There's a list of omega services on the counter. The credit card has a large credit line, so don't worry about cost. They will spare no expense when it comes to making you comfortable and happy." He started walking toward the house, and I grabbed his sleeve, a whimper threatening to embarrass the hell out of me in front of him.

"Are you sure this wasn't a mistake? You were standing right there when Beckett and I got into it." I watched his face carefully, but the guy didn't let any hint of his feelings peek through.

He stepped back from my hold, his eyes not leaving mine. "It surprised me just as much as it probably surprised you. I really need to go. You'll be fine. You're an Elite Omega Academy graduate. You should be able to handle setting yourself up."

And with those departing words, he left me in a giant house that made me feel more alone than I'd ever felt.

CHAPTER FIVE

Rio

There was so much excitement in our car as our driver zoomed along the highway, the traffic light since it was nearly midnight. Not only had we won our Alphaball game and sealed our position in the playoffs, but we'd just landed a deal with United Alpha Sports, making our athleticwear line the official gear with an initial payment of a quarter of a billion dollars.

How was this our lives?

Things hadn't always been so good for our pack. We'd all really been into sports and easily bonded with each other through our college years. It had taken a lot of hard work to work our way into the professional league, and we'd only really come out as a top contender in the last few years.

And now everything was about to change with the addition of an omega. The timing was all wrong, but sometimes good things came when we least expected or wanted them. We'd been so focused on our careers and building a solid pack foundation, for the longest time we hadn't even entertained the idea of adding an omega.

But we needed one.

I glanced over at Beck, who had been over the moon when we'd first gotten in our ride, but now he was staring quietly out the window, his cheek on his fist.

We all worried about him. As the leader of the pack, our successes were his, but so were our failures. He liked to be in control of every situation, and over the last year, he'd slowly started to become more and more agitated with the little things.

It was a sign that we desperately needed an omega to calm the instincts that raged inside of us. Biology waited for no one, and our time of putting off finding and bonding with an omega was up.

He was stubborn, though, and would never admit to any of us that he needed an omega. An omega would change everything, and Beckett did not do well with change.

"You all right over there?" I was nervous he was going to be a complete asshole as soon as we got home. I at least wanted him to try to accept Kara.

"I'm fine." He glanced over at me and ran a hand down his face. "Just tired as hell and ready to sleep."

I turned and propped my leg on the seat. "It's normal

to be nervous for a new chapter in our lives to be open-ing. I know we've been super busy and kind of just went with who Brian thought would be best, but she is perfect for us. It's going to be great, and maybe you'll find that the weight you constantly have on your shoulders and chest is lessened."

"We don't even know her." He turned back to the window, his shoulder practically up to his ears.

Rylan leaned forward from the rear row of seats to join our conversation. "We'll get to know her. That's the fun part."

"What if she-" Rylan stopped Beck from spiraling by putting his hand on his shoulder. "I just don't want her to ruin everything."

"She's not going to ruin everything, man. This has been a long time coming. All of the other packs at our level have omegas. Our bond will be stronger, and then we'll be unstoppable." Rylan sat back and elbowed Kane, who was on his phone. "Right?"

"Right." Kane turned his phone so we could all see. "Did any of you go on a shopping spree, or is this all Kara?"

I took the phone from him and scrolled down the list of charges from the last few days. "Jesus." Even I was shocked at all the charges from various online stores. "Brian said he was taking care of everything, but I didn't think he meant he was giving her free rein of the pack card."

Beckett grumbled and took the phone, scrolling

through the charges. "She spent five hundred dollars at a craft store."

Rylan laughed from behind us. "Maybe she's planning on bedazzling your nuts."

"She's doing something to my nuts, and it's not that." Beck handed the phone back to Kane. "Maybe that's why Brian ran off right after our game. He knew he fucked up by giving her the credit card."

"After this season is over, we need to have a serious conversation about whether we want to get a new coach and manager. I know things are easier in a way with him around, but I question some of his decisions when it comes to our team." Kane put his phone away and crossed his arms. "Like this omega thing. He didn't even ask us, just scheduled the meet and greet and expected us to jump on board."

There were small things Brian did that drove the alpha sides of us nuts. He had been great for us in terms of Alphaball, but now he was overstepping his boundaries. We did not claim him as our beta, yet he acted like he thought he was part of our pack and our leader.

While we all fell into contemplative silence, the driver turned off the freeway toward the hills. I hated that we hadn't been there for Kara when she arrived, but hopefully she had settled in without us breathing down her neck.

Omega Match was a necessary evil, but I still wondered what it would be like to meet an omega the old-fashioned way. When my fathers met my mother, it had been back when alphas and omegas mingled on a more regular basis without the restrictions the government placed on us. No perfume blockers. No heat suppressants. No applications and hoping for the best.

But as the populations of alphas continued to flourish, so did the problems. It had been a daily occurrence in every city where there were fights over omegas and kidnappings. The worst was alphas bonding to omegas without their consent. Alphas had turned into absolute animals.

Beck opened an app on his phone as we approached our house and opened the gate for the driver to pull inside. The outside lights were on, and it made it look like a display in a museum. My favorite part was the lights that ran the lengths of the stairs, making it look like the steps alternated black and white.

It was a dream home for us, with plenty of space for the four of us and an omega. Although I never vocalized it when we were house searching over a year ago, in the back of my mind, I'd wondered how an omega might like the space.

After the driver helped unload our suitcases and pulled out of the driveway, we went in through the garage, the alarm disengaging as we opened the door.

What none of us expected was to be greeted with a mound of empty boxes and a sweet chocolate and nutty scent lingering in the air. I inhaled sharply, shutting my eyes and savoring the perfume of our omega.

"Fuck me," Kane practically growled. "She smells like hazelnut spread."

Even with her probably on scent blockers still, when an omega was alone in a closed-up space, their scent lingered. I could only imagine what she smelled like without them.

"Look at this mess." Beck kicked the pile of boxes that were stacked haphazardly and sent them scattering across the floor. "She didn't even break them down."

I smacked him on the back of the head. "Don't be a dick." If I needed to, I'd show my more dominant side.

Rylan put down the retractable handle on his suitcase and grabbed the strap, heading for the stairs. He hadn't said a word, but judging by the pace he was walking, he was excited and anxious to meet Kara.

So was I.

We followed him upstairs, where the faint sound of the television greeted us. My eyes zeroed in first on the woman sleeping on the couch, blankets and pillows from our room piled around her. Then I noticed the mess.

I cringed and looked over my shoulder at Beck as he crested the top of the stairs and stopped dead in his tracks. He set his suitcase down and then put his hands on his hips, walking forward with a scowl.

"Beck," I warned under my breath.

He went to the couch, staring down at our sleeping beauty, who had a bowl of popcorn clutched in her hand with half of it scattered next to her on the couch and blankets. On the coffee table sat two Twisted Knot wine bottles, one empty and the other only about a quarter gone. There were candy wrappers, a pizza box, and half-full cups of water, orange juice, and soda on the end tables and coffee table.

She looked as if she'd had a grand time the past few days, and I couldn't help but smile thinking of her enjoying her freedom for the first time in years.

"Wake up." Beck's bark popped the bubble of happiness I had started to feel, and I felt the tension through our pack bond. He was so angry he was letting his emotions bubble over.

Kane grabbed the back of Beck's shirt and tugged him away toward the stairs leading up to our rooms. Thankfully, he went without being an asshole.

Kara didn't wake up, so I turned off the television and lowered the lights so the room had a subtle orange glow but wasn't completely dark.

Rylan and I went upstairs, venturing to Beck's room, where we could hear Kane laying into him.

"You don't get to treat her like shit because you're put out by her presence. You agreed to doing the match thing, and we aren't just going to send her back because you don't like that she spilled some popcorn and drank a bottle of wine you were saving."

"She's changing everything!" Beck was kicking off his shoes as we entered the master suite, where the smell of Kara was strong. "She slept in my bed! How am I supposed to sleep?"

He sat down on the bench at the end and put his face in his hands. It had been a long time since he'd had an anxiety attack or a freak out about something.

I sat next to him, putting a comforting hand on his back. "Breathe, Beck. It's going to be fine. You can sleep in my bed."

He shook his head. "This was a stupid idea. I'm not ready. What if this is only the beginning and she makes a mess of everything? What if she breaks our bond?"

"Our bond is strong." Rylan went to the bed and picked up a pillow, bringing it to his nose and inhaling. "Damn. You're one lucky fucker to have her scent all over your bed. You should be celebrating that an omega felt comfortable enough to sleep in your space, not upset she spilled some popcorn and left boxes everywhere."

Beck's shoulders sagged a bit, and he sighed. "I'm sorry. You're right. I'm being ridiculous."

"Don't apologize. We get it." Kane was leaning in the doorway, his eyes half closed from exhaustion. "She's not here to hurt us or take away everything we've worked for."

"Get some sleep. We'll all sit down tomorrow and get to know her." I slapped his back and stood. "The offer stands about sleeping in my room. Or there's the guest room since she seems to have picked your room as her own."

Beck stood and went into his bathroom, closing the door. We all gave each other concerned looks before Kane shrugged and headed for his room.

"He'd better not mess this up." Rylan threw the pillow back on the bed, even though he looked tempted to take it. "Because with this perfume, there's no way I'm letting her go."

"He'll come around." I shut the bedroom door behind us. "There just haven't been any big changes in our lives in a while, especially not any that encroach on his space and belongings."

"He hasn't been homeless for ten years now. I don't understand how an omega would trigger him." Rylan brushed past me as we entered the hallway leading to our rooms.

"It's all about control of the situation. That's why I let him be the head of our pack. He has some semblance of control over everything, but with this new addition, he doesn't know what to expect."

Rylan stopped at his door and looked over at me. "I hope for all of our sakes you're right."

CHAPTER SIX

Kayla

I woke up, my mouth feeling like a cotton ball was inside it. The television was off and the lights were dim as I sat up, rubbing my eyes from the blurriness that had overtaken them. Definitely had too much wine.

Scooting off the chaise, popcorn crunched underneath me as I moved, and I grimaced. I hadn't meant to drink the whole bottle of wine and pass out, but the longer I had sat waiting for the pack to come home, the more I drank.

As much as I'd tried to fight it, my instincts had taken over and I'd gone a little bit bonkers for their scents. I wasn't sure what scent belonged to who, but each one made me feel safe and a certain kind of way I hadn't felt before.

So much for acing Olfactory Management.

I took one of the blankets that smelled like a hot toddy with me as I went to the kitchen to get a drink of water. Part of me was really fucking glad they hadn't come home because I'd left dishes in the sink, empty and partially eaten takeout containers on the counters, and the dining room table was covered in quilting materials.

Brian had been useless when it came to helping me get settled in. His number went straight to voice mail every time I tried to call. I couldn't tell if he'd read my texts or not, but something told me he had and was choosing not to respond.

I could have called the other numbers he left me for the pack, but he'd told me not to and I knew that they were busy men. Honestly, the first day of independence had been great.

Until it wasn't.

I threw the blanket on a clean part of the counter and went to the sink, frowning at my mess. I'd never been an overly tidy person, but now I was going to be staying here for a few weeks or maybe even months, I needed to at least attempt to not appear like a slob.

Wait.

That was part of the plan; annoy them enough for them to send me back. I bit my lip as I had an internal battle of whether to put the dishes in the dishwasher. Now that I'd smelled their scents, it was like a light switch had been flipped, and I had the urge to do things to please them. That's what had made me so tired the past few days because leaving my shit everywhere was wearing me out.

Shaking my head, I filled up a glass with water from the refrigerator and went to stand by the floor-to-ceiling windows. It was just after two in the morning, and the city lights had dimmed a bit. The view really was breathtaking, and I had found myself drawn to it several times a day.

My eyes closed as I tipped the glass back and gulped down the ice-cold water. I'd need at least two glasses to quench my thirst. My body wasn't used to drinking bottles of wine and gorging on junk food.

"What are you doing?"

I jumped at the gruff voice right behind me, the glass slipping from my hand and shattering at my feet. My wide eyes met Beck's over my shoulder as I turned and winced as my foot came down on some glass.

"Fuck. Don't move." He jogged out of the kitchen, leaving me standing there with my heart nearly beating out of my chest and a pain in my foot that I was trying to keep pressure off.

A minute later, he came back, flip-flops on his feet, and scooped me up like I was his bride. My skin heated at his touch, and I looked away. "You scared the shit out of me."

He set me on the counter near the sink and paused, looking inside it. "We have a dishwasher, you know."

I narrowed my eyes as he flicked on the light over the sink and grabbed my ankle, bringing my foot up to examine it. His fingers sent tingles across my body as he made a disapproving noise.

He was shirtless and only wearing a pair of basketball shorts. His skin was lightly covered in freckles, and I found myself wanting to touch them. I hadn't paid much attention to him at the meet and greet, but up close and personal like this, he was a stunning man. His green eyes assessed the damage, and I couldn't look away.

Damn it. This wasn't how this was supposed to go.

"It doesn't hurt that bad." I wiggled my toes, and he released my ankle. "You aren't going to kiss it and make it better?"

He braced his hands on the counter on either side of me, his lightly stubbled jaw ticking. "I need to go get the first aid kit. Don't get off the counter." He pushed off and walked out of the kitchen; his scent hit me like a freight train. I inhaled deeply.

I'd been sleeping in his bed and using his blanket.

"Damn it, Kayla." I brought my foot up across my knee and glanced at the bottom. There was a small piece of glass in there, blood getting ready to drip onto the floor.

Beckett came back with a first aid kit, his frown still firmly in place. "You have to eat and drink at the table or counter. These floors make glass shatter."

I bit my tongue, stopping myself from snapping at him like I wanted to. "Usually, I don't drop glasses, but someone decided to scare me." I stared at the pair of tweezers he pulled out of the kit, not liking the idea of him digging around in my foot. "Do you know what you're doing?"

He poured some rubbing alcohol on them and moved in close to me, his bare abdomen brushing against my leg and making my body tingle. "I've taken out splinters before. Just hold still and don't look."

His touch on my ankle was light, and the way he was leaning in blocked my view. The temptation to run my fingers through his short, dark red hair was nearly killing me.

I sucked in a sharp breath as pain radiated from the bottom of my foot. Beck leaned in closer, more of our bodies contacted, and a light purr came from him, immediately making me forget about the pain in my foot.

Before I knew it, he was moving away from me, the bottom of my foot covered with a thick bandage. "All done."

"Thank you." I lowered my foot as he wiped up a small spot of blood on the floor.

"You should get to bed. It's late." He closed the first aid kit and then finally looked up at me. "You've been sleeping in my bed."

My face felt like it was on fire under his gaze. I couldn't tell exactly how he felt about my taking over his bed. I'd tried to stay in the guest room on the first level, but it was so far removed from where they slept and where their scents were concentrated. His scent had called to me the most with him being the pack leader, so I'd chosen his room.

It just so happened that I knew it might piss him off too if our first encounter was anything to go by. "The guest room isn't ideal." He was going to flip his lid when he discovered where I'd set up my nest.

He chose to ignore my comment, and after washing his hands, he stood in front of me and grabbed my ankle again. "Just checking to make sure it's not bleeding through the bandage."

The smart thing to do would have been to pull my leg away from him and get off the counter. But I sat still, my heart thudding much harder than it needed to since I was just sitting there.

His thumb ran along the arch of my foot, and I bit my lip in an attempt to not moan or whimper. Why was he torturing me by touching me? Had he turned over a new leaf since I'd heard him balk at the idea of an omega?

"What are you doing?" I whispered as he bent down and brushed his lips across my ankle.

Goosebumps erupted across my skin, and a pleased shiver raced down my spine. My head fell back against the kitchen cabinet with a soft thud.

"Are you still on perfume blockers?" He put my leg down, but instead of backing away, he pushed between my thighs so he could get closer, and buried his face in my neck. "Fuck, you smell good."

"I'm still taking them." My nipples pushed against my

tank top, and I tilted my head to the side so he had better access to my neck.

"If you smell like this while still on them..." He inhaled, his stubble brushing across my sensitive skin as he moved his nose along the column of my neck. "Stop taking them."

I was starting to get turned on by how he was touching and speaking to me. Instead of pushing him away, though, I wrapped my legs around him and finally buried my fingers in his hair. It would be okay just for a minute.

Who was I kidding? My body had been starved of the affection of an alpha, and now I was getting it, I didn't know why I'd ever been so against having a pack.

He groaned, his arms going around me, our chests pressed against each other. "Do you have any idea how difficult it was trying to fall asleep with your perfume in my bed and you not in it with me?"

I did know because, as soon as I smelled their scents, I knew it was going to take everything in me to not give in to my needs. Their scents called to me, which was probably why, even with perfume blockers, I was releasing more than usual.

My body wanted them.

"I didn't want to want this," he mumbled against my neck, his lips brushing against my skin, sending a throbbing pulse to my clit. "But now you're here..."

His lips ghosted up my neck and across my jaw until they were centimeters from touching me. I'd never been kissed or *anything* before. There had never been any opportunities to explore sex while locked away at the academy besides with ourselves.

The tiniest of whimpers escaped my slightly parted lips as I thought about how different a real alpha cock would feel compared to a silicone one. "Please-"

I didn't get to finish because his lips took mine in a hungry kiss that both excited me and scared the crap out of me. It was as if I was feeling desire for the first time in my life. Sure, I'd masturbated during my subdued heats, but it had never felt so right and so good. And all he'd done was kiss me.

My fingers tugged at his hair and his tongue probed at my lips, seeking entry. I opened for him, not sure if what I was doing was correct, but it felt right. The wetness of my slick between my legs made me tingle and ache, and the need to move against him was too strong to resist.

I barely knew this man, yet there I was, ready to hump him on the counter. If he was causing this strong of a reaction now, I could only imagine what my heats would be like, especially if I went off my heat suppressant.

Beckett's hands moved under my shirt, starting at my lower back, and then traveling up along my spine. I arched into him, our kiss becoming even more frantic. He groaned, his lips moving back down to my neck, right under my ear.

"Stop me now." His voice was lower and filled with

lust. "Stop me now or there's no turning back."

His hands moved to wrap around my sides, his thumbs brushing under my breasts and making me feel dizzy. Did I want this? Did I want to give in to this over-whelming physical pull I had to this man?

I was naive to think I'd be able to resist alphas once I was in the thick of them. There was part of me that didn't want the all-consuming need and love. I had goals and plans, and what if this pack didn't let me see them through?

Beckett pulled back, gripping my chin gently after I didn't respond quickly enough. "I need to hear you say it, Kara."

Kara.

Whatever I'd been feeling quickly shattered, just like the glass I'd dropped. I shoved him away, embarrass-ment and anger making my eyes burn. I hissed as my feet hit the ground, my cut stinging.

Of course they'd wanted my sister. I didn't know or care how the mix-up had happened, but it had, and now the sliver of feeling I'd let myself have was dashed away.

It was painful, and I could only imagine how much more painful it would be to bond with a pack and then have something tragic happen.

"What's wrong? Did I move too fast?" Beckett gently touched my arm as I pushed past him.

How did I even begin to tell him I wasn't Kara?

So, I did the only thing I could.

I ran.

CHAPTER SEVEN

Kane

Groaning, I rolled over and touched my cell phone to see what time it was. It was nearly three in the morning, and the anxiety coming through the pack bond from Beck was nauseating.

Most days, our emotions didn't seep into the bond, but they had several times in the past few days. We could usually control and block things from getting through, but when it came to this whole omega situation, emotions were strong.

I got up and shuffled to my door, my feet practically dragging from the half-asleep daze I was still in. It was doubtful the onslaught of emotion woke up Rio and Rylan, who both slept like fucking logs.

Why did Beck's room have to be so far?

I grumbled as I went down the hall in the wing

my room was in with Rio's and Rylan's and walked across a small sitting area none of us used at the top of the stairs. Beck's room was the primary suite, and he had the largest bed since sometimes we all slept together as a pack. We hadn't in a while, but maybe we needed to if Beck was starting in a downward spiral.

The door to his room was open, and I peered inside, finding the bed a mess but no Beck. I moved back down the hallway and stood at the top of the stairs, straining to hear if he was downstairs.

With a sigh, I slogged down the steps. I was glad we had the day off to recover from our game before we kicked it into high gear for the playoffs and hopefully the championship. We'd made it into the playoffs the year before, but were knocked out of contention when Rylan dove to stop a thirty-pound ball from the opposing team from going into the hole and broke his arm.

I could still hear the bone snapping.

There was a light on in the kitchen, but with a quick glance in that direction, I found it empty. The couch was abandoned too. "Beck?"

"Come on, Kara. Open the door." I barely picked up on his voice and turned toward the hallway where we had an office and a gamer room.

Beck was sitting on the floor next to the gamer room door, his head back against the wall. What had the asshole done now?

"What are you doing?" I stood in front of him, my hands on my hips.

"I don't know." He peered up at me and scrubbed his hands over his face. "We were making out in the kitchen, and I told her if she wanted me to stop, she needed to tell me, and then she ran off. She locked herself in here."

"Did you try the door through the bathroom?" There was a bathroom connecting the office we used for meetings and the gamer room where we had computers and gaming systems. "There's the key thing that will unlock the door."

I reached for the small, metal key that unlocked all the interior doors that sat on top of the doorframe. Kind of pointless to have locks that could so easily be unlocked if you asked me.

"Of course I checked the bathroom door. It's locked." He pushed up off the floor and snatched the key away from me, putting it back. "We aren't going to just barge in there."

I put my ear against the door and heard a muffled whimper. "What the fuck did you do to her, man?"

"Nothing! We were both into it. At least, I thought she was." He looked dejected as fuck, which surprising considering his feelings on welcoming an omega in the first place.

I put my hand on his arm. "I heard that the omegas that end up at academies are all virgins and inexperienced unless they were sexually active before emerging.

Think about it, dude... since they were sixteen, they've lived away from everyone else in their little bubbles."

One of the things I hated most about our society was how omegas were treated like fragile little porcelain dolls that had to be locked away so the big bad alphas didn't destroy their innocence. It should have been the opposite. Alphas should be the ones to take scent blockers and rut suppressants to curb the need to take an omega and bond with them.

"I was in the moment and just... fuck!" He put his forehead against the door and banged it a few times with a growl. "Please, Kara. Open the door so we can talk."

"Why don't you go get some sleep? She's clearly not going to come out of there right now." I grabbed his shoulder and he let me lead him down the hall to the living room.

"My room is filled with her perfume. Those suppressants don't work for shit," he grumbled and shrugged off my hand. "I need to clean up the glass on the kitchen floor."

I followed him and pinched the bridge of my nose. "Maybe that's what scared her into hiding."

"No. She got a sliver of it in her foot after she dropped it and I took it out." He went to the pantry and grabbed a broom and dustpan. "It's not like I came down here and expected to be swept away by her."

"Pun intended?" I gestured to the broom and then began cleaning up the first aid kit next to the sink. "I wasn't accusing you of anything, by the way. I'm just a little surprised you're all worked up over her."

"You and me both."

AFTER A FEW MORE HOURS OF restless sleep, I finally got out of bed to start my day, hoping whatever had upset Kara was now forgotten. I'd managed to convince Beck to sleep in the guest room and wondered if he actually had or if he'd gone back to his post outside the locked door.

An upset omega was the last thing we needed when we were about to start heavy training for the playoffs. What we needed was a sit down to get to know each other and lay out our expectations of one another. In a way, this was like an arranged marriage, and it wasn't like the love was going to be immediate.

I showered and dressed in my favorite pair of dark wash jeans that fit my muscular thighs and ass perfectly. I paired them with a solid white Alpha Fit T-shirt. Looking in my bathroom mirror at the Alpha Fit words across my chest, I still couldn't believe we'd landed a deal with United Alpha Sports.

Not bothering with shoes, I headed downstairs to find Rylan eating a breakfast sandwich and drinking coffee at the kitchen island. Out of the four of us, he was the youngest, and also the earliest riser. It didn't matter what day of the week it was or how late he was up the night before, he was up at six every day.

"No Kara yet?" I went directly to the coffee maker and poured myself a cup.

"She wasn't on the couch when I got up." Rylan popped the last bite of his sandwich in his mouth and jumped up. "I have a gaming date with my sis."

"That's where she's locked herself. Something happened between her and Beck last night." I sipped my coffee as I walked out of the kitchen area and toward the room in question, Rylan right behind me. "It sucks because the more I've thought about having an omega, the more I want it. We don't want to end up like one of those older packs that start to go a bit feral because they don't have an omega to keep them grounded."

"True, but a lot of those packs are in the government or high up in society. But I agree, we are long overdue to have an omega. We should have done this back when we graduated." Rylan passed me in the wide hallway and got to the door first. "Kara? Open up." He tried the door and then knocked before putting his ear against it.

I rolled my eyes and grabbed the key from the door-frame. "We're going to unlock the door. Beck isn't with us."

We needed to at least make sure she was okay. It had to be a lot going from an academy where all the students were other omegas and most of the staff were female. She didn't know us at all besides the brief meeting we had, which wasn't nearly long enough, and now she was just thrown in the middle of a pack of alphas.

There was something seriously fucked up about Omega Match.

Rylan unlocked the door and opened it slowly, light spilling into the pitch-black room. There was a loveseat and four gaming chairs that reclined enough to sleep comfortably, but it wasn't an ideal place to sleep. It was dark, though, with black-out curtains, and was the farthest room away from any rooms that had noise.

The four desks that held our computers were all shoved into a corner, the height adjusted as high as possible, and there were dark sheets hanging to make what I guessed was a makeshift nest. It made sense she'd pick this room, but I wished we'd been there to get it set up properly.

Rylan pulled his phone from his pocket. "Fuck, my sister is calling. I was supposed to be on ten minutes ago."

"Go talk to her. I don't think you'll be gaming today unless you plan on moving your shit somewhere else." I stepped into the room, listening for any signs of omega duress but was met with silence. "Kara? It's morning. Do you want to come out and get some breakfast?"

I put my coffee on the entertainment center that held more gaming shit. We worked hard, but during our downtime, we liked to play hard too, and for us, that was playing hours of video games.

She wasn't answering or making any noise, but I

could smell her perfume that had accumulated in the closed off room. It made me feel a certain way, and I had to remind myself that now was not the time to get turned on.

But it was definitely hard.

Shaking my head at my train of thought, I knelt next to the enclosed nest and lifted the sheet. She was in there but seemed to have every spare blanket and pillow in the house inside with her, including one from my bed.

One of her feet was sticking out, and I tried to stop myself, but since she wasn't responding, I needed to make sure she was still breathing. It was a better alternative than diving into the blankets with her when we'd only met for a few minutes.

I ran a finger up the arch of her foot, careful not to touch the bandage. She inhaled a sharp breath, pulling her foot to safety. At least she was alive and hadn't suffocated under all the shit she was buried under.

"You can't stay in there forever. What's wrong?" I crawled under the desks, sitting on the edge of one of the mattresses she must have ordered and had delivered. It was a special nesting one that was waterproof.

"Leave me alone." The blankets moved like she was rolling over and away from me. "As soon as the Omega Match offices open, I'll be leaving."

Leaving? What the fuck had Beck done?

"I don't understand." I had been respectful, but now she said she was going to leave, I crawled across the mound of blankets until I got to where her head was and pulled the blankets away. "You can't just decide after less than twenty-four hours to reject us."

"I can. And it has been longer than that. You weren't even here when I arrived." Her back was to me and her hair was a mess in the bun it was in. I wanted to run my fingers through it and comfort her.

Wait.

"I thought you had curly hair." We'd met a lot of omegas that day, but I could have sworn Kara had curls and her sister didn't.

"That's Kara." Her voice cracked, and she blindly reached for the blankets, but I was quicker and pulled them away so she couldn't hide under them again. "I tried to tell everyone it was a mistake, but they wouldn't listen. Even your beta said you'd put me down."

"Our beta? Brian is not our beta." I was starting to get annoyed that people always referred to him as ours just because he was always around and made decisions when it came to Alphaball. He was our manager and coach, not a part of our pack.

"I opted out of matching, but the results came back and I matched to your pack." She had her face buried in a pillow she was hugging, so it was hard to figure out what she was saying and make sense of it. "And I just thought... might as well give it a shot if they want me, but you wanted Kara."

I wasn't equipped this early in the morning to deal

with something of this magnitude, and my coffee was on the other side of the room. "So, you're..."

"Kayla."

It honestly didn't matter to me what her name was. She smelled like fucking heaven, and it wasn't like we knew Kara. The only reason we'd let Brian submit our interest in Kara was because he said so.

"You told Brian you were Kayla? What did he say?"

"I messaged him and said there must have been a glitch because neither of us put your pack, and he said there wasn't one. I just assumed you guys decided to pick me and then paid someone off at Omega Match to make it happen." Her accusation shocked me a bit, and I was left speechless for a minute.

My silence must have pissed her off because she sat up suddenly, her face puffy from crying. I reached out to touch her cheek, and she flinched away from me. That hurt more than I expected it to.

"Let me fix you something to eat and then we can figure out everything." I scooted out of the nest and, surprisingly, she followed.

I didn't know what the hell was going on, but there was one person who could tell us.

CHAPTER EIGHT

Kayla

A girl had to eat, and as much as I wanted to stay in my makeshift nest I'd thrown together, I knew I needed to clear things up. It was stupid to even think for a second they'd put me down on their match list.

When Beckett had said my sister's name, something in me had broken a little, and my instinct was to run and hide from it all. I hadn't given a lot of thought to the fact that maybe they had put Kara, and there'd been a mix-up. Although, now I knew, it still didn't change that the whole thing had happened in the first place.

Someone had fucked up, and for once, it wasn't me.

As I followed Kane, I couldn't stop myself from checking him out during the trek to the kitchen. He had a muscular back I could catch outlines of through his shirt and an ass that was rock solid under his jeans. Added to his entire appeal was that he was barefoot and sipping coffee.

I looked down at my pajama shorts and tank top. "I should go get changed."

"Your stuff is in Beck's room, isn't it?" Kane looked over his shoulder at me, his eyes immediately falling to my breasts before he looked forward again. "I'll give you my shirt."

I wasn't nipping out that hard, was I?

Kane set his coffee on the island once we were in the kitchen and reached behind his neck to pull off his shirt. He was trying to kill me, wasn't he?

A knowing smirk graced his plump lips as he handed me his T-shirt, his chest and abs on display. I was blatantly checking him out because there was no use in hiding it after he'd not so subtly looked at my nipples showing through my tank top.

"Shut up." I snatched the shirt from him and pulled it over my head, his campfire scent making my toes curl into the cold stone floor.

"I didn't say anything." He laughed and went to the refrigerator. "You look good in my shirt, Kayla."

Was he flirting with me even after finding out I wasn't who he expected? I guess I had expected more anger and not him giving me his shirt so everyone wouldn't be greeted by my nipples.

I sat at the island as he pulled eggs and cream out. "Do you like French toast?"

"I love French toast." I should have been the one cooking for him, but I needed to remember my goal was to be myself so they'd ship me back. But they'd be doing that anyway, and I probably wouldn't get any money because it was an error.

"Your thoughts are loud." He got a griddle out and a dish to mix the eggs.

"Yeah, well, things aren't exactly going to plan." I slid off the barstool and went to the coffee maker that had a carafe half full to pour myself a cup.

"And what plan is that?" Kane finished mixing up the egg and cream mixture and turned on the stove. "Do you want cream for your coffee?"

"Yes." I grabbed the pint from him and poured it in. "I opted out of Omega Match but instead got a nice surprise."

"Why would you opt out when your biology pushes you toward having a pack?" He put butter on the griddle, and it sizzled. "Even with the heat suppressants you guys are on, it has to be uncomfortable."

"It's manageable." I didn't want to get into specifics with him about my dildo collection that satisfied my needs just fine. Was it ideal? No, but the alternative of having a pack and being expected to go through a full-on heat made me sick to my stomach.

When omegas first emerge, there is no suppressing the first heat because it would inhibit our bodies from adjusting to being an omega. It's beyond painful, and it made me feel so vulnerable and needy that even with reassurances from my mom that it was great when there were alphas involved, I didn't want to experience it again.

Plus, it could be several weeks long, and with me wanting to run a business, dealing with raging horniness and out-of-control slick and perfume was out of the question. I couldn't be scent marking other omegas' nesting quilts.

"You didn't answer my question." I'd hoped with Kane focused on putting the egg-covered slices of bread on the griddle, he'd forgotten he'd asked me why I didn't want a pack.

"There are things I want to accomplish for myself before being tied down to a pack where I might not be able to explore those things. Being expected to be at a pack's beck and call, spread my legs multiple times a day for whoever wants their turn, and dealing with a heat that might last weeks at a time every few months isn't my cup of tea." I'd never expressed myself so clearly before, and it made me sit up a little taller. Something about Kane made me want to spill my soul to him. "I want to start my own business."

He put the last piece of toast on and went to the sink to wash his hands. I'd expected an immediate response telling me all the reasons why omegas and alphas were meant to be together, but instead, he was silent as he lathered his hands and rinsed them.

"Is that the type of environment you grew up in? A pack that didn't support their omega?" He grabbed a spatula out of a drawer and turned to look at me. "I know a lot of packs are like that, but this one isn't."

"You say that now... And no, I grew up in a pack that was supportive, but there was no time for my mom to explore her interests beyond being an omega. She got pregnant with me and Kara pretty early on, and we have six dads." I sighed and rested my cheek on my fist. "I don't even know if I want children. It doesn't seem fair to match into a pack that definitely wants offspring when all I want is to make quilts and freely eat chocolate."

"I think it's hard to imagine children running around when you're so goal-focused. There's no law saying packs have to have offspring, and ultimately, it's the woman's choice." He turned back to the stove to flip the toast, and I tried to calm the beating of my heart.

If the pack felt that way, maybe they weren't so bad after all.

"But what are you doing quilting? Isn't that for... you know..." He turned back to me, his plump bottom lip between his teeth as if he were biting back what he wanted to say. I knew a lot of younger people didn't talk about quilting, but that didn't mean we didn't do it.

"Say it, Kane." A smile broke free as he shifted from one foot to another. "Just know that I know where you lay your head at night."

"Are you threatening me, sweet cheeks?" He grinned, his entire face lighting up.

"Me? Threaten you? Never." I nodded to the griddle. "Don't burn my breakfast."

"Shit." He turned back to the stove and turned it off. "They didn't burn, thankfully."

"Good morning." I stiffened at the greeting coming from Beckett as he walked into the kitchen. "Kara-"

"I'm not Kara," I blurted, deciding to rip the Band-Aid off in one fell swoop. "I'm Kayla."

It was like my body could sense his sudden shift in mood as he stopped abruptly and did a pivot to stare at me from across the island. "What do you mean you're not Kara?" His tone was a partial growl, and my heart nearly stopped.

I'd been on the receiving end of many angry alpha growls in my younger years, and I hated it. I preferred Beck's *I'm going to fuck you senseless on this counter* growl.

"I told you, I'm Kayla. By some horrible twist of fate, we matched." I was starting to feel the same sass I had at the Alphaball meet and greet coming out. "I knew calling you a shrimp dick would turn you on."

His nostrils flared and his eyes narrowed as he put his palms on the counter to lean toward me aggressively. I sat taller because he didn't scare me. I'd braced myself for his wrath to be the strongest given our first interaction.

I just hadn't expected to shove my tongue down his throat the night before.

"You will not speak to me that way when you so clearly are involved in some kind of deception with your sister. I almost fucked you last night thinking you were her!" His voice was starting to rise, and I bit inside my cheek to stop from whimpering. "Pack your bags. You're going right back to where you came from."

I didn't move or take my eyes off him. He couldn't just boss me around like he owned me. "Is your poor alpha ego bruised? I'm so sorry, but I barely passed Submission 101."

His hands fisted on the counter. "That's an actual fucking class?"

Kane made a disgruntled noise in his throat and slid a plate of delicious French toast across the counter, along with some syrup.

"Don't act so surprised. The academy's whole purpose is to prepare omegas to roll over on their backs for their alphas." That wasn't necessarily true, but it did feel like most of my peers would do just that if that meant they could live a life of luxury.

"If that's the case, then how the hell did you make it past the first semester?"

I shrugged because I honestly didn't know. "Fake it 'til you make it."

"Is that what you were hoping to do here? Fake being your sister until we bonded with you?" My mouth opened in shock at his accusation. I'd tried to tell everyone it was impossible for me to match with this pack.

"Beckett," Kane growled in warning. "You don't have

to be an asshole. It honestly seems like a mistake on Omega Match's end."

"That's enough," Rio barked from the entry of the kitchen. I hadn't even realized he'd been watching the whole exchange. "Let's go call Brian and discuss this as a pack in private. Tossing accusations around isn't helping anyone."

Beckett pushed away from the counter and left the kitchen without another word. But he didn't need to say anything for me to know he was thinking about wringing my neck.

"Eat your breakfast. This shouldn't take long. I'm sorry he's the way he is." Kane tapped the counter as if that was going to comfort me any and followed Rio and Beckett.

I heard them yell for Rylan, and a minute later heard him ask what was going on. The French toast was calling to me, but the need to know what was happening was strong, so I jumped up and quickly went toward their voices coming from downstairs.

From the kitchen, I wouldn't have been able to hear them, but I was able to sit about halfway down the staircase without them seeing me from where they were.

"Brian isn't answering his fucking phone," Beckett said. "What does the paperwork we signed say?"

"You don't list your matches on it. That's just to agree to all of the government's rules about using Omega Match... which we broke by letting Brian take care of it all for us." Rio sighed. "Let me call them and see if it was a mix-up."

"Even if it was, we aren't sending her back," Kane grumbled. "Just because Beck has his panties in a knot doesn't mean we all have to suffer."

"We could send her back, but then what? We'd have to wait a whole year to match again. I don't know her well enough yet to say what we should do, but shouldn't we give her a chance?" Rylan said.

"Look at the mess she's already made and imagine this next week during playoffs or the championship." Beckett seemed to only care about his precious Alphaball, and I clenched my fists in my lap.

"Omega Match, this is Brandie. How can I help you?" I was so grateful for speakerphone.

"Hello, Brandie. This is Nazario Perez, part of Beckett Thomas's pack. I wanted to check to see who we put on our match list."

"Let me see... I see here you matched with Kayla Sterling, and she was marked as moved into your pack house. Was there an issue I could help you with?" Brandie sounded confused, and I couldn't blame her.

"Was she the only one we put on our match list?"

"Yes, and it looks like your pack is the only one she put on hers. That's fantastic that you liked each other enough to only put each other. Romantic, really. Is there a problem?"

"No, not at all. Just some confusion is all. Kayla tells us she opted out of matching but somehow still matched with us." Rio was doing a good job of not bringing up Brian, but maybe he should have.

"That's impossible. Hold on just a moment while I look at her file." There was silence, and it seemed to stretch on forever. "Her signature is on the forms as accepting the match as final along with your pack being the only one listed."

Impossible.

"Thank you so much, Brandie. We really appreciate you answering our questions." I heard the tone of the call ending and held my breath.

"She lied about opting out." Beckett sounded smug as hell, and if I'd been downstairs, I would have smacked it out of him. "I know it's going to cost us, but let's start the paperwork now to send her back. We don't have the time to deal with this."

"Now, wait just a fucking second. You don't just get to decide this." Rio's voice was louder now and coming closer to the stairs.

I moved like my ass was on fire and ran back to the kitchen, nearly falling over my own feet as I got on the barstool and started shoveling French toast into my mouth.

This was exactly what I wanted. So, why did it make my chest hurt to hear it?

CHAPTER NINE

Rylan

I was about to punch Beck in the jaw if Rio didn't beat me to it. We all loved each other like blood brothers, and we didn't always see eye to eye, but when it came to Kayla, Beck was out of line.

There were a lot of questions surrounding her, but did they matter? We could at least all agree that her scent was highly appealing to us, which meant we were biologically compatible. Personality compatibility was easily workable, but the natural urge to love and protect either existed or it didn't.

And the fact I wanted to punch Beck in the jaw said enough.

I stood from the couch and glared down at Beck, who had his arms crossed and looked like a petulant child. "You're supposed to lead this pack, not cause a rift because you can't let your past go. With all of our investments, Alphaball, the brand, we're about to be billionaires, yet you're concerned that an omega is going to take all of that away? We get that change and unpredictability makes you nervous, but there is nothing she can do to bring our empire down."

Well, unless she has some twisted plan to kill us.

"You're the one that agreed to do this in the first place. It was never a question of if we were ever going to have an omega but when. And I can't speak for Rio and Ry, but I've been ready since I first emerged." Kane grabbed the television remote from the coffee table.

"I wouldn't say I've been ready, but for an omega like Kayla? We aren't going to match to someone like her again, and if we did, it wouldn't be fair because I'm pretty sure she is it." I felt that with every ounce of my soul.

If Kayla ended up not bonding with us, it was going to be hard, if not impossible to forget her scent. I hadn't even spent time with her yet and I just knew it to be true. While that feeling excited me, it probably terrified the crap out of Beck.

"Regardless of how she ended up with us, we haven't even given her a chance. The shit storm of sending her back because you aren't even willing to open yourself up to the possibility of her isn't fair to us. You were willing to when you thought she was her sister, and while wanting someone perfect is great and all, come on, man. Do you really think you'd be happy with an omega that won *Omega of the Year* four years in a row?" Rio was standing at the bottom of the stairs and looked up them, his frown deepening. "She was listening. I can smell her."

"Great, so she eavesdrops too." Beck got to his feet and headed for the garage. "I'm going out for a bit."

"When you come back, make sure the stick that's up your ass is removed," Kane said as he turned on the television.

The door slammed, and I rolled my eyes at the tantrum. "What are we going to do about that?"

"Nothing. He'll come around. Hopefully we'll get some answers from Brian soon about what the hell happened so Beck will stop thinking Kayla is lying." Rio started up the stairs. "I'm going to check on her, and then I'll be back to watch the game footage, Kane."

"I'll go check on her." I moved up the stairs past Rio, who had paused. I could smell the lingering scent of Kayla where there hadn't been any when we'd come down. "The sooner you two get done picking apart every one of our plays, the sooner we can relax."

I hated watching replays of the games and ripping apart our every move. When we'd first started playing Alphaball more seriously, it had been fun to move up the ranks, but now we were at the top of our game, the fun had been sucked out of the sport for me.

After I'd broken my arm, I had a lot of time to think about just how much time and energy we put into the sport. While it did give us the launching point for our sportswear brand and our nutritional brand that was being developed, it also took a lot out of us mentally and physically.

I walked to the kitchen and found Kayla finishing her breakfast. She hadn't noticed I'd walked into the room yet, and I cleared my throat, causing her to jump.

"You're awfully jumpy. Are you scared of us or something?" I went to the refrigerator and grabbed a coffee drink. I hated brewed coffee but loved the sugary coffee drinks. Not the best choice, but I hadn't had the chance to go get one.

"Not used to men sneaking up on me." She put her fork down and closed the lid to the syrup. "So, what's my fate?"

I took a drink of my coffee and leaned against the counter, crossing my legs. "We know you were listening. Your perfume was in the stairwell."

She cringed. "Can you blame me?"

"No. I would have wanted to know what was being said about me too." I pushed off the counter and grabbed her plate to put in the sink. "I am curious as to why you didn't make a bigger stink out of the whole thing though."

She looked down at her hands for a moment before her blue eyes lifted to meet mine. "What good would that have done? Even if I had gotten into contact with you guys or Omega Match would have even listened, didn't you guys have Brian do all the paperwork and submitting?"

"Yes. We trusted him to take care of everything.

Clearly, we had a lapse in judgment." I hated that we were the ones that had caused this whole debacle because we were too busy and lazy to take care of it ourselves. It wouldn't have taken us more than thirty minutes. "But what's done is done, and honestly? Now that I think more about it, I don't think your sister would have been a good fit for us."

"I overheard them talking." I gave her a confused look. "Brian and Beck. At the meet and greet they stepped outside, and basically, Brian said with the perfect omega, it will only help you guys, and if not then you can just ship her back because you can afford the fine. I told my sister not to put your pack."

I ran my hand down my face and shook my head at the nerve of Brian and Beck. "Their ideas of a perfect omega aren't mine. There is no such thing as perfect. Some award isn't going to make you perfect for every pack."

"I won't change who I am and what I want out of life for a pack. Especially one that doesn't seem to know what the hell they want." She stood and adjusted Kane's T-shirt she was wearing.

A bit of jealousy crept in. I wanted her in my shirt and marked with my scent too.

I rounded the island and took her in my arms. She stiffened the slightest bit, and I started to doubt my move, but then she melted into me. "I never want you to change who you are."

"You don't even know me." Her hands were braced

against my chest, but instead of pushing me away as I nuzzled into her neck, she gripped my shirt. "I'm messy, opinionated, and just a bit stubborn."

"Don't let our clean house fool you. We have people that come to clean. They should actually be coming today." *In fact, they're supposed to be cleaning right now.*

She pushed away from me, and I grumbled my dislike of our separation. "I don't want them touching my things."

"They seem to be no shows, which is weird because they usually text if something comes up." I pulled out my phone and sent a text to them.

"Brian probably told them not to come." She crossed her arms over her chest. "He wasn't very nice to me."

"He can be a little blunt." I read the text message I got back. "They were told not to come today since we didn't know your feelings on having people you haven't met clean your space."

Brian should have been telling us these things instead of taking it upon himself. His job was to manage our team, not our damn pack.

"There's no way I'm cleaning this house, but I'd like to meet them before they're all up in my business." She walked over to the windows, looking out at the pool and skyline.

"We can arrange that. What are your plans for today?" My plan had been to play video games all day, but now I was in her presence, I didn't see myself leaving her side.

"No clue. I've just been online shopping, reading, and watching reality TV." She turned, and a smile lit up her face. "Since you're here now, you could take me shopping. There's this huge fabric shop I found, but I didn't want to leave the property without alpha protection."

"We can do that. Rio and Kane will be a while watching footage from our games yesterday, and Beck… he went out for a bit." Her face fell at the mention of Beck, or maybe it was because Rio and Kane wouldn't join us. "I can ask them if they want to come too."

"No. If you guys have stuff you need to do, you don't have to cart me around anywhere." She shrugged and started walking out of the kitchen. "I should go shower and probably move my stuff to the guest room."

"Go shower and then we'll go. Leave your stuff in Beck's room. He can just move his growly ass to the guest room. I'll even help you move it all." It would piss him off further, but I had no fucks to give.

I'D NEVER SEEN someone light up as much as Kayla did when we stepped foot in the fabric store. It was like we had taken a trip to a magical theme park instead of a giant warehouse filled with bolts and bolts of fabric in every color, texture, and pattern.

I didn't mind pushing the cart as we went down row after row and then had to wait for someone to cut all of them. She had a pretty good idea for making custom quilts, but there were a lot of things she needed to consider... like her own perfume getting on the material.

Now wasn't the time to talk about all the considerations she would need to have if she was going to go forward with her plan. Especially now that she lived with four alphas.

"Let's go swimming, and then we can work on getting your room set up and all talk about your nest." I dropped her bags of material in the dining room where she had a quilting area set up. We hardly ate at the big dining room table, so I didn't see an issue with her using it.

"I don't know if I want to encroach on your space if I might not even be staying." She pulled a stack of folded fabric from one of the bags. They were in all shades of blue and green.

"Why would you not stay?" I didn't want her to feel like she was going to be sent away just because of a mistake on Brian or Omega Match's part.

My morning had been one of the best I'd had in a long time. We hadn't even done anything special besides shop and talk about the academy, Alphaball, and the reality TV show about selling houses we were both addicted to.

"I'm not going to stay where I'm not wanted by a pack. The *whole* pack. I'd be gone already if I could afford the fine." She bit her lip and looked away from me. "That came out wrong."

I squeezed the back of one of the dining room chairs. "If you don't want to be here, we aren't going to force you to stay. I will personally pay the fine for you if you decide we aren't what you want, but give us a chance. Beck will take longer to come around, but that's normal for him."

"Being an asshole is normal?" She put her hands on her hips, fire in her eyes. "He talked about me like I'm dirt beneath his cleat."

"Pack leaders are under a lot more stress than everyone else. That's not an excuse for him, but he already struggles with change." It wasn't my place to talk in-depth about Beck's issues.

"Let's just… enjoy today and worry about everything tomorrow. Ready to go swim? We should see if Rio and Kane want to join us." The excitement was back in her eyes. "We can play chicken. Me and you against them."

Having Kayla wrap her legs around my neck as she sat on my shoulders? Hell, yes.

My cock twitched in my pants at the idea of her so close to me. This was either going to be the best idea in the world or leave me with an epic case of blue balls.

CHAPTER TEN

Kayla

I didn't know what I was thinking when I suggested we play chicken. Oh, that's right, I wasn't. I played all the time at the academy, but playing with three alphas who all looked at me like they were about to eat me like a chicken dinner was completely different.

The first few rounds, Kane had let me win despite him being stronger than me. I protested the special treatment, and he and Rio did not hold back. I'd hit the water more times than I cared to count.

"I'm starting to feel like a drowned cat," I whined, coming up from going under for the hundredth time. "I call for halftime."

"You look like a drowned cat too." Kane splashed water at me, and I spluttered before charging at him. "The poor pussy doesn't like to get wet."

I jumped on him, attempting to dunk him under, but he barely budged and instead wrapped his arms around me. "You don't fight fair."

He grabbed the back of my legs and urged me to wrap my legs around him. I didn't hesitate, but as soon as I did, I knew it was a mistake. His erection was pressed right up against my wet pussy. Not that he could tell through my swimsuit and the water.

"Stop wiggling." His hands moved up to rest on the small of my back, and I wrapped my hands around the back of his neck.

"I'm not wiggling." Okay, maybe I was just a little. I shouldn't have wanted any of their dicks anywhere near me, but there I was, unable to make myself swim away.

"Bro, it's the middle of the day." Rylan swam up behind me, sandwiching me between the two of them. "We probably shouldn't move too fast."

"No! I mean..." My cheeks heated more than they already were, and I wanted to swim under the water and hide. "I'm not a fragile little virgin. If I didn't like it, you'd know."

A growl came from Rylan. "Who took it?"

"Took what?" I put my palm to my forehead. "No one took it. I just meant, I might be a virgin, but that doesn't mean I haven't explored things... with myself."

I swear I could feel Kane's cock pulse between us. I leaned back against Rylan's chest and looked over my shoulder to see Rio getting out of the pool.

"I'm going to go try to call Brian again and make us

some snacks and drinks. Any requests? Kayla, do you have any food allergies or dislikes?" Rio stood at the edge of the pool, and I forgot how to speak.

The only thing that would have made the whole situation worse was if I could smell them over the chlorine because I was sure they were sending out pheromones. Campfire, fresh-cut wood, and the scent right before it rains was a heady combo.

Water dripped down Rio's tan skin, and my eyes were drawn to the trail of dark hair that dipped into his swim shorts. There was a bulge behind the swirling design on them, and I looked back up to find him smirking.

"Busted." Kane chuckled, which made him rub against me in just the right spot.

"Kayla? Are you going to answer my question?" Rio ran his hands over his arms and chest, getting some of the water off his skin.

"What? Oh! No, I like everything. Kara sometimes calls me a kitchen sink."

Man, I missed her. She had been quiet on calls and not said much in text. I knew she just needed some time to process everything, and I was careful with what I said so it didn't upset her more.

Rio went inside the house, leaving the three of us in the pool, the warm sun beating down on us. The weather in Los Angeles really was perfect, and I was glad they didn't live somewhere too hot.

"Your hair is curly. Why do you wear it straight?"

Rylan ran his fingers through my ponytail, drawing my attention back to the sandwich I was in.

"It's not super curly, so it takes longer to make them look good than just running a brush through it and throwing it into a ponytail or bun. Kara does all kinds of shit to her hair to get the curl perfect, and I'd rather be doing anything but that." It was nice to be able to bring up my sister with them, but I did worry it would remind them about how I ended up there.

I'd started thinking this would be an easy way to earn some cash when they decided I was too much of a pain, but now I wasn't so sure. Part of me wanted to get them to send me away as fast as possible, and the other part of me liked the attention and affection I was getting.

I needed to be careful because I was one knot away from becoming a whimpering mess of omega goo.

"We need to talk about some things before we get carried away." I didn't want to have the sex talk with them, but they both had their hands and dicks against me.

"Anything you want." Kane touched my cheek and ran his thumb across my bottom lip. "We can wait if that's what you want."

"Well, it makes me nervous that we'll do things we regret when you send me-"

"Not happening unless you want it to." Rylan's voice had lowered and was on the verge of a growl. "You talk like you want it to."

"I don't know what I want." I turned my head, letting Kane's hand fall away from my face, and my eye caught on movement up on the balcony off of the main bedroom.

Beck was leaning on the glass partition, sunglasses covering his eyes and an unreadable expression on his face. He was wearing just shorts, and I wondered how long he'd been standing there watching us.

"Ignore him," Kane said loud enough for him to hear. "If he wants your attention, he can come down here instead of creeping."

I snorted a laugh and unhooked one of my legs so I could turn my back to Beck and see Rylan. "So, we were about to talk about sex. No knots. No biting. I'm staying on my heat suppressants and perfume blockers, although just being around you guys makes me perfume some."

"We can do that. What about anal?" Rylan's fingers tightened where his hand landed on my waist.

"I'm down for anything. I've messed around with a butt plug a time or two. I'm not opposed to anal sex, but a knot better not come near my ass. Heat or no heat." Just the thought of it had my ass cheeks clenching. "I know your knots don't get as big or last as long during non-heat sex, but that's a level of intimacy I don't think I'm ready for."

"Well, your first time with a real dick isn't going to be in the pool." Kane kissed my cheek then moved his lips across my jaw.

"Then let's get out of the pool." I tried to wiggle away from them, but they both had a hold of me.

It was amazing and scary how comfortable I was with these men already. I'd always thought it was ridiculous hearing how omegas just quickly fell into place with packs they'd never even met before, but now I understood because I was experiencing it.

"I think we should get a little appetite going before Rio comes back with food." Rylan grabbed the leg that Kane had released so I could turn sideways between them and pulled it around him.

I was spread open for them under the water, and a throb pulsed between my legs. The water made the ache worse; it felt both right and wrong at the same time, and I was conflicted about whether I should stop them.

"But he could be back any minute." I turned my head to look back at the house but was stopped by Kane's lips pressing against mine.

The apprehension I'd been feeling melted away. I wanted this, even if I didn't know what the hell I was going to do in the long run.

Rylan peppered kisses across the back of my neck and one of his hands moved underneath my breasts, resting there as if waiting for permission.

I broke my kiss with Kane and turned to Rylan. "Touch me." I kissed him, his groan against my lips making my stomach swirl with butterflies.

These men wanted me just as much as I wanted them, and I was going to seize the moment and let them bring me the kind of pleasure I'd only ever dreamed about. Pleasure by another's hand.

Kane slid between my legs, cupping my sex. "This is ours," he growled. "We'll be the first and last to touch it."

A shudder overtook my body, and my nipples pebbled with an ache. I didn't want to like his possessiveness, but it made heat rush between my legs, preparing my cunt for them.

"Look at how responsive she is." Rylan ran his fingers across a nipple and then tweaked it between his fingers. "Is she slick for us?"

I could handle the touching and kissing, but hearing them talk to each other was going to be the end of me. I was going to come before they even did anything.

Kane pulled my bikini to the side and ran a finger through my folds, a light purr vibrating against me. He liked what he was feeling. "She's slick, even in the water."

"I want to taste her." Rylan pulled the string behind my neck, and my top fell down with a plop on the water. "First each nipple, then we'll put her on the side and have a snack."

"Please." I was starting to pant from my need to be touched.

"What, baby girl? Do you want us to eat your delicious cunt?" Kane lazily ran his finger up and down, never reaching my opening or my clit. It was driving me crazy. "Or do you want my fingers buried inside you?"

"Both." My voice was shaking, and I whimpered as

Rylan leaned down and sucked a nipple into his mouth. "Yes, please, just…"

I lost my train of thought when Kane lowered his mouth to my other nipple, still stroking me between my legs. It was an odd sensation being wet with my own slick and the water.

As if communicating through some kind of mental link, they both bit down at the same time and Kane slid a finger in. I cried out, my head falling back, and if they didn't have a hold of me, I would have sunk to the bottom of the pool and drowned in pure heaven.

"Fuck, feel how hot and tight she is." Kane pumped his finger slowly. "Baby, do you want to feel both of our fingers in you?"

My body was overwhelmed, and all I could do was offer a weak nod. I gasped when Rylan's finger joined Kane's. In all my fantasies, I'd never imagined something so perfect.

Before I knew what was happening, we were at the side of the pool and I was lifted onto the edge, my breasts bared to the world and the cool air making my skin erupt in goosebumps.

Kane grabbed the top of my bottoms and pulled them down. I was barely able to lift my ass for him to slide them off since they'd already turned my bones into jelly.

"Scoot so your ass is right at the edge." Rylan's hand was under the water, and I could barely make out his dick as he stroked it. "And spread your legs wide."

"What if someone sees?" I looked around the backyard as I scooted forward, but we were on the edge of a hill without any houses visible. The only ones that might see were Rio or Beck, which I didn't care about.

"Then let them see how alphas take care of their omega." Kane's patience seemed to have left him, and he pried my legs open and buried his tongue where his fingers had been only moments ago.

"Oh my God!" My hands grabbed his head, not to push him away but to push him deeper. "Kane! Yes, more. I need more."

"Lie back." My attention had been solely on the head between my legs, and I hadn't noticed that Rylan had climbed out of the pool and was now standing naked right next to me.

My mouth opened on a gasp from both what Kane was doing with his tongue and fingers and from the sight standing before me. I'd seen plenty of alpha dicks before on the internet, but never one up close and never one so absolutely perfect.

It wasn't too gigantic that it was going to rip me in half, but it was going to pack a punch when we did have sex. At the base, his knot was slightly swollen, and down the length were five barbells. Sweet baby omega, I wanted that inside me.

"Don't inflate his ego by staring too long." Rio's smooth voice was a shock to my system, and I glanced behind me to find him sitting at the outdoor dining table, a beer in hand. "Do as he says, sweetheart."

He was just going to sit there and watch? I didn't know why, but that turned me on even more.

I laid back, the smooth cement around the pool warm from the sun. Kane pushed my legs so my feet were flat on the edge, and Rylan lowered next to me and straddled me so his ass was in my face.

"You don't need to do anything if you don't want to." Rylan lowered down, his dick hanging right over me as he kissed down my lower belly, over my mound, and circled his tongue around my clit. We were in a sixty-nine position, and the thought of both Kane and him with their mouths on me at the same time made heat flood to my core.

I was scared to take him in my mouth in fear that I might bite it, so I wrapped my hand around it and began stroking at the same pace Kane's tongue moved in and out of my pussy.

Rio knelt next to my head, his cock out of his shorts. "Do what I do, you'll have him coming all over your chest in no time."

My entire body was on fire and my eyes threatened to shut from the pleasure of the mouths on me and taking direction from Rio.

I did exactly what Rio did: even, firm strokes, my thumb swiping over the head at the end of each. He used his other hand to gently roll his balls.

Rylan turned his head to the side and cursed, biting into my inner thigh. "Don't fucking stop."

The pressure of a finger against my ass refocused my

attention on what they were doing, and I tried to relax. It pressed slowly into me, using my slick as lube.

"You're doing amazing. He can barely even eat your pussy with how good you're stroking his cock." Rio's praise caused me to clench around Kane's tongue. "Now let go of his balls and wrap your hand around his knot. Yes, just like that."

Rylan's legs were shaking, and he groaned as he sucked my clit into his mouth, sending me over the edge right along with him. He exploded, his cum covering my chest as his knot grew slightly against the grip I had on it.

"Fuck, yes." I couldn't see Rio, but the sounds he was making let me know he came.

Kane removed his tongue and finger, and I shivered at the loss. He pulled my legs down so they dangled in the pool and kissed my inner thigh.

Rylan chuckled and flopped over onto his side next to me after I let go. "Well, that was hot as fuck."

It was something dreams were made of; really hot, sexy dreams.

Kane grunted and then he disappeared under the water, bubbles rising to the surface. I was sad I didn't get to hear him come like I had with Rylan and Rio.

Rio grabbed a towel from a lounge chair and wiped off his hand and dick before kneeling next to me and wiping my chest. His eyes were hooded, his breaths still causing his chest to rise and fall more than usual.

"You were so beautiful jacking him off." He bent

down and kissed my forehead. "I imagined you doing that to me the whole time."

Rylan yawned. "I need a nap after we eat some real food."

It would be a perfect end to a perfect afternoon. My three favorite things back-to-back: orgasm, food, and sleep.

CHAPTER ELEVEN

Kayla

Taking a nap was a mistake, and now I couldn't sleep. It wasn't just because I napped too long with Rylan, but because Beck had moved all of my things to the guest room downstairs and Rio still couldn't get in contact with Brian.

He was obviously avoiding dealing with his mistake, but it just didn't make sense that I was able to match when I was one hundred percent sure I'd opted out and not put any packs. It had even asked if I was sure before submitting.

I should have taken a screenshot.

Brian would have to answer eventually and then we'd have to decide what to do. Although, it seemed Rio, Rylan, and Kane had already made up their minds to keep me.

I didn't know what the hell I wanted.

The room I was in was two floors away from the pack and while normally I'd be happy to have my privacy, being in a new place made me want the comfort of protection nearby. I would have been content sleeping on the couch upstairs or in the little nest I'd made.

The guys had offered to let me sleep in their beds—with or without them—but I figured I needed the space to get my head straight.

Because I was losing it.

All I could think about was them, and while that wouldn't be a problem to any other omega, I was struggling with it. For years, I'd pushed back against the biological urges that come with being an omega, but put me in a room with four delicious alphas?

I hated it and I didn't know what the hell I was going to do. The tables had turned, and now I was actually giving thought to this whole match.

I checked my phone to see it was past midnight, and I'd been attempting to sleep for over an hour. There was no point in continuing to toss and turn when my brain wouldn't shut off. I got out of bed, hoping a snack would help.

Learning my lesson from the night before, I slid on a pair of slippers. There was a tiny cut on the bottom of my foot that stung a little when I stepped a certain way, but it wasn't inflamed.

The hallway was dark, and I flicked on the light. It

wasn't a horrible room by any means, none of the rooms were, but I'd found comfort in being in Beck's. It completely sucked that it had to be his.

The lights in the stairway up to the main floor were on, and I headed across the large space but stopped when I heard the faint sound of instrumental music coming from the direction of the gym. It was far too late to be working out, but maybe someone had left it on.

Changing course, I went down the hallway to the gym and opened the door. Some of the lights were on, giving it a warm glow inside. I didn't see anyone at first, but then my eyes landed on the pile of clothes right outside the sauna across the room.

It was dark inside, but I could see condensation on the window and a person moving around inside. What the hell were they doing?

I walked in and was hit in the face with Beck's scent. It felt like a warm hug, as much as I hated admitting that to myself.

The closer I got to the sauna, the more my cheeks heated. He was stretching naked inside, and I stopped behind some workout contraption with pully things to keep myself partially hidden as I watched him lunge forward with one foot and lift his arms. Was he doing naked hot yoga?

I shouldn't have been watching him, but there was something about seeing him completely unaware and comfortable in his own skin. And dare I say, relaxed?

His shoulders were down, and he moved his body

like it was as light as a feather. I'd never realized just how tense he always was until seeing him like that. The last thing I wanted was for him to catch me and have him tense up again.

With a final look, I went back toward the door, my mind back on my snack. There was a bag of chocolate candies with my name on it.

"*Stop*," Beck suddenly barked.

Shit on a stick.

I was left with no other choice but to heed his alpha command. I could have tried to fight it, but I was tired, and it was time we had it out so we could move on.

"Yes, master alpha?" I turned around and batted my eyelashes at him because I knew it would goad him into not holding back what was eating him inside.

"What are you doing in here?" He strode toward me, his dick slapping against his thigh. I couldn't help but look at it as he stopped a few feet in front of me.

"I couldn't sleep, and I wanted a snack." I looked up, bit my inner cheek, and hoped that my perfume didn't surge from looking at his cock. I wondered if they had made it a requirement to have perfect dicks to be in their pack.

But it wasn't really about what their dicks looked like, it was what they did with said dicks. Not that I wanted Beck's to come anywhere near me.

Maybe. The jury was still out on if I wanted to let myself entertain the idea. He'd been a complete asshole to me.

He lifted an eyebrow. "You want a snack?" His eyes held a challenge and my body immediately felt flushed at the glint in them. "Then get on your knees."

Was he fucking joking? The expression on his face and his eyes told me he wasn't. Seeing him all sweaty and red from his explicit sauna yoga made me want to do whatever he asked but also punch him in the balls.

I stared blankly at him, and he shook his head, taking a few steps away from me. But then my traitorous body moved forward, dropped to my knees, and reached and grabbed the back of his thigh so he couldn't escape.

He said my name with some kind of growl and purr combo that really spurred me on. With my other hand, I grabbed his dick and popped it right in my mouth. He sucked in a sharp breath, and his cock twitched as it came to life right in the palm of my hand.

"Fuck. I was joking." He grabbed onto my ponytail, wrapping it in his fist. "Don't fucking stop."

I sucked the tip and squeezed where his knot was, drawing a groan from him. It didn't take long for him to grow rock-hard, and I couldn't help but smile around him knowing that, even though he hated me, he certainly didn't hate my mouth.

His hips rolled toward me, his cock hitting the back of my throat and making me gag. I didn't like that at all and dug my fingernails into the back of his thigh. He was lucky I didn't have his balls in my hand.

"Swallow your snack like a good little omega." His

words pissed me off, and instead of swallowing, I pulled back, my teeth dragging lightly as I got to the tip. "Jesus."

His head tipped back, baring his Adam's apple to me, and his hand speared through my hair under my pony-tail holder. He'd liked that.

I swirled my tongue around the head of his cock and took him all the way to the back of my throat again, my eyes watering with the urge to gag and cough. I didn't know what he meant by swallow, but fuck if I was going to try it.

I pulled back off, dragging my teeth again. His legs trembled slightly, and I lapped at the bead of pre-cum on his tip. His fingers were moving against my scalp, making me feel almost sleepy, and his strong cinnamon and clove musky scent made me wet.

"Stand up." His alpha bark was unforgiving, and I released him and stood, wondering if I'd done something wrong. "Do you have any idea how difficult it was to hear you come earlier today and not throw myself over the balcony?"

I cringed and started to step back, but he grabbed my face between his hands with a growl. My eyes widened, not understanding if this was a good thing or a bad thing. "I'm sorry my pleasure makes you want to crack your skull open."

One of his hands moved down to my neck, circling it like he might choke me. I gasped right before his lips connected with mine.

I should have shoved him away, but instead, I moved

KNOT SO PERFECT OMEGA

so our bodies were pressed together, his erection pressed against my lower belly.

He replaced his hand with his mouth, sucking the skin hard enough to leave a mark. My hands explored his back and then moved to his ass, my nails digging into the muscular globes.

I was already past the point of no return. I didn't care if he was a complete asshole and sent me away. All that mattered was how he was making my body feel.

"Tonight, you're going to cry out for me. I want every last whimper, moan, and scream." He grabbed my chin, his darkened green eyes filled with thunder.

I clenched my thighs together, the ache and wetness between them overwhelming. "I want your knot."

What the hell was I saying?

A low growl came from his chest, and he backed me up and then spun me around in front of the mirrored wall. He lifted my tank top off and then pushed down my sleep shorts and panties. I was left completely naked in front of the mirror with him standing behind me.

"I want to watch your face as I ruin you for any other alpha." He wasn't gentle as he pushed me so my hands were on the rack of weights under the mirror.

"Do it." I pushed my ass back, presenting it to him for the taking. "Make me scream."

His hand came down against my sensitive skin, and I whimpered, wiggling my ass in a display of neediness that I didn't know I was capable of. We might have hated

MAYA NICOLE

each other's guts, but I could feel his desire for me in the way his eyes darkened.

He kicked apart my legs, and I gasped as he dropped to his knees behind me and buried his face between them. My back arched, and my hands gripped onto the dumbbells my arms were resting on.

"Beck!" I was panting like an omega in heat and widened my legs further. "Oh, God!"

I thought what had happened in the pool was intense, but Beck's face buried in my cunt, eating me like a starved wolf, was a whole other level.

Just when I was barreling toward an orgasm, he stopped and stood. "You want my knot, little omega?"

I shuddered, the thought of him burying it inside me making my pussy even more slick in preparation. "Yes."

"Then beg for it." His hand smoothed across my ass cheek, and then he smacked it again. "Tell me how bad you want it."

"I won't beg you for it." If I could have growled, I would have. It was bad enough he was calling me *little omega*, but now he wanted me to beg him for his knot?

He slid his hand between my legs, his finger pushing the tiniest bit inside my pussy. "Then this is all you get."

I lowered my forehead to rest on my forearm, my entire body trembling as he moved the tip of his finger in and out. It wasn't nearly enough, and I pushed back, his finger sliding all the way in.

"Naughty girl." His hand came down again on my ass,

♡ 116 ♡

and I clenched around his finger. "You like to be spanked."

"Shut up and fuck me before I just go use a dildo." I didn't want to get off from a hunk of silicone, but I would if he was going to torture me.

His finger left me, and I sighed in frustration and started to stand up. His large hand splayed across my upper back, pushing me back down with a growl, and then his cock filled me in one smooth thrust that had me crying out.

I was so ready for him that it didn't hurt like I'd expected it to, but then again, my dildos weren't men that got me so slick it felt like I was dripping.

"Fuck, your cunt was made for me." He pulled almost all the way out and slammed back into me. "Watch in the mirror as I fuck you."

My cheeks burned brighter than a freshly bloomed rose, but I did what he asked, the fight leaving my body as he began a torturous snap of his hips. His eyes met mine in the mirror, and I didn't look away, even though the intensity in them made me nervous.

This was no hate fuck. This was a claiming.

His fingers dug into my hips, holding me steady. Even if I wanted to, I couldn't look away from the intense look of concentration on his face. His mouth was slightly open, his chest heaving, and his muscles flexing.

My breasts swayed and my entire body was flushed

with a light sheen of sweat. I could get addicted to this. To him.

He released one of my hips and adjusted his stance so he could reach my clit. My orgasm was building somewhere deep inside me and I hated the needy mewls I was making.

"Beg for it," he growled between gritted teeth. "Beg for my knot."

I wanted it so bad it hurt. "Please, Alpha! Oh, God!"

My orgasm ripped through me before I could say more, and he buried himself in me as far as possible and circled his hips, working his knot in. It stung for a second but only served to amplify my orgasm as my pussy clenched around him.

"Fuuuuuck!" Beck spilled inside me, his hips making small thrusts and rotations as he milked every last drop out of his cock.

I was struggling to hold myself up as my orgasm continued to make my body twitch, my pussy convulsing around him like it was starving to drink him up.

He removed his hand from my clit, his arm wrapping around my waist. "Do you trust me?"

My chest was heaving, and I must have lost my damn mind letting him knot me. I knew it wasn't going to last as long as a knot would during a heat or a rut, but being stuck with him for any amount of time when he was so hot and cold wasn't ideal.

"You have your knot stuck inside me, so I guess for as long as it lasts, I'm going to have to."

"Close your legs together and keep them that way. I'm going to spin you around so you can wrap your legs around me." He had to be kidding, but I did because I was curious how he was going to manage to spin me on his dick. "Relax. It won't hurt if you stay still and let me do all the work. Try to stay bent, though."

I nodded, hoping like hell he didn't drop me and rip his knot from me. The last thing I needed was a bruised pussy.

He lifted me slightly and grunted as he maneuvered me around like I weighed nothing. My abs strained to hold my torso up, and as soon as my legs were straight up in the air, I wrapped them around him. It hadn't hurt at all, but it felt like he'd spun his dick around inside me.

The only problem was, now I was facing him.

With his hands resting under my thighs, he walked toward the gym door. "Your room or mine?"

Instead of looking at him, I rested my head on his shoulder, my face in his neck. I was completely ravished, and as much as I hated the answer I was about to give him, I needed to be somewhere I could sleep comfortably. "Yours."

By the time he got there, his knot would probably be ready to slide out, but now that I was clinging to him like a spider monkey, I didn't care.

This had been a horrible idea.

CHAPTER TWELVE

Beck

Something in me had snapped like a violin string pulled too tight. One second, I'd been ready to lay into her for sneaking around the house in the middle of the night, spying on me. The next, I'd wanted nothing more than to claim her.

And I definitely claimed her, if the way she was wrapped around me with her head buried in the crook of my neck was any indication.

It had taken all of my fucking willpower not to claim her as my knot had filled her, which made no sense considering our relationship so far. But it wasn't like I could control an alpha's biological need to claim an omega.

By the time I got to my room, I could already feel my

knot deflating. I was torn between wanting to send her back to her room and sleeping still buried inside her. There was something seriously fucked up with my brain.

I felt like I was being pulled in two different directions. My heart and body wanted one thing, while my brain was pushing back. I had my issues and while I dealt with them fairly well most of the time, this was exactly why, as leader of the pack, I'd never entertained the idea of us having an omega.

An omega meant our world changed. It meant the potential to lose everything, not just what we'd built, but our minds and hearts. I'd already lost enough to last me a lifetime.

I lay down carefully on the bed with her on top of me and then rolled so we were on our sides, our legs tangled so we were both comfortable being stuck together.

I shouldn't have knotted her.

She sighed and snuggled in closer to me, nuzzling my neck. I wasn't usually into cuddling after sex, but the need to protect her and take care of her was overwhelming.

Everything was overwhelming.

My fingers danced along her back before going to her hair and working the ponytail holder out of it, letting her wavy hair fall free. I couldn't believe I hadn't noticed her hair was different at first, but then again, women liked to style their hair many ways day to day. I ran my fingers through it, gently working out the tangles.

"Beck?" She yawned, her hands resting on my chest between us.

"Hm?" I was purring lightly, hoping it kept her from pulling away from me in the next few minutes. An alpha's purr was the ultimate comfort to an omega, and she was the first person I'd ever been compelled to purr for.

Not that I'd been with any other omegas—that was nearly impossible anyway without breaking laws—but there had been plenty of betas. The thought of them made my stomach turn over, like I had cheated on Kayla or something, which was ridiculous.

"Why do you hate me?"

"I don't." I kissed her shoulder and then moved up to nuzzle into her neck. "It's complicated."

"How so? You just have a stick up your ass?" And just like that, the honeymoon was over. "Because I've done nothing wrong, yet you treat me like I'm trash."

I pulled back so I could see her face. "That wasn't my intention. I just... I'd been expecting one thing and then to have the rug pulled out from under me after I'd already wrapped my head around the whole thing was too much for me. That's no excuse for me being a dickwad, and I don't deserve you or your forgiveness."

"If it's going to cause you emotional duress to have me here, then you need to send me back." She looked past my shoulder. "I never wanted this, just like you never wanted an omega."

"Yet here we are, stuck together." I cupped her cheek, and her glossy eyes met mine. From the dim light coming through the sliding glass door, they were dark like stormy waters. "Do you want us to send you back?"

She bit her lip. "I don't know," she whispered. "I thought I'd come here, you'd all hate how I wasn't the perfect omega you wanted, and then you'd send me back with a nice check. I tried to tell the academy and Brian there was a mix-up, but even if they believed me, it's not like the government would care."

Extreme possessiveness welled up inside of me. "Don't say his name when my dick is inside you."

A small smile spread across her face, and my anger at Brian fell away as quickly as it had appeared. I had practice tomorrow to be angry with him, if he even showed up. We'd put too much trust in him since he was one of the best coaches and managers there was. Yet another reason for me to be apprehensive about Kayla too.

No one could be trusted except ourselves.

"You sound jealous, snookums." She patted my cheek, and I turned my head and kissed her palm. "You're kind of sweet when you want to be."

I'd done it without thinking. Kind of like how we'd come to be in this very position in the first place. "Don't get used to it, and don't call me snookums."

"Then don't call me little omega. It's condescending coming from you, and I'm not into the daddy kink."

"Neither am I." My knot was completely deflated, and I slowly pulled out with a heavy sigh. I would have stayed buried in her all night, but we were both a mess. "Let's take a shower and then go to sleep."

I rolled off the bed and held my hand out to her. She stared at it for a few heartbeats, and I was just about to shrug it off and go take a shower by myself when she grabbed it.

"You want me to sleep in here? You moved my stuff as far away from you as possible." She stood and pulled her hand away from me.

"I just thought... you don't have to, Kayla. I just thought it would be the polite thing to do seeing as we just had sex and I knotted you." I shrugged as if the thought of her sleeping elsewhere didn't bug the shit out of me.

"I think... maybe I should go back to my room." She looked around as if searching for her clothes but then grabbed some tissues from my nightstand. "Thanks for ummm... the fun." She patted my chest, and I captured her hand before she could pull away.

"Stay." I grabbed the tissues from her. "I want you to stay."

"You're giving me whiplash." She crossed her legs. "Can I shower first?"

I was thinking we'd shower together, but on second thought, that was a pretty intimate thing to do. "Sure, just don't use all the hot water."

She rolled her eyes and pulled her hand away,

leaving me staring after her and wondering what the hell I was thinking.

My brain wasn't completely sold on having Kayla become our omega, but my heart and body were quickly overpowering it.

And that scared the shit out of me.

I EXITED the locker room at our training facility, and my eyes immediately landed on Kayla.

Somehow, she'd convinced all four of us that coming to our practice was a good idea, but now that we were there, I regretted agreeing to it.

She was a distraction, and we needed to give the next two practices before playoffs our complete attention. How was I going to focus when I was going to worry about the other alphas in the facility trying to worm their way into her pants?

Because that was exactly what was going to happen. She was unbonded, and even though she had a mark on her neck I'd left the night before, she didn't have the silvery claim scars of our bites.

"Thank fuck Brian is here. I was about ready to go to his condo and kick in his door." Rio came out of the locker room behind me and threw his arm around my shoulders. "Perk up, Alpha. We've got our girl to impress."

"That's the problem," I muttered as we strode toward

Brian, who was setting up an agility course for us to warm up on.

I clenched my fists at my sides, my anger at the beta coming back tenfold. I didn't like to fight, but if I needed to, I'd punch him in the face.

"Brian. Where have you been? We've been calling and texting you." Rio squeezed my shoulder in warning —or maybe comfort—before moving away from me. "We have some things we need to talk about before practice."

"Oh, hey." He threw a cone down and turned around to face us. "Sorry, my phone service has been shoddy."

I narrowed my eyes, not believing that bullshit for one second. "Why did you put down Kayla on Omega Match?"

He looked between both of us, confusion on his face before he looked over at Kayla on a bench in front of Rylan and Kane, who were on the ground stretching.

I moved my body in his line of sight and growled. "Don't look at her."

"Woah, okay, sorry." He held up his hands in apology. "And what do you mean, why did I put Kayla down on Omega Match? That's how it works. You submit the omegas you are interested in."

"We'd discussed Kara, not Kayla." I crossed my arms over my chest. "Kayla didn't even put our pack down, yet somehow we matched with her."

"Kayla was the one we discussed. Curly hair, *Omega of the Year* at the academy four years in a row..." His brows furrowed and I couldn't tell if he was being honest or was completely full of shit. "Right?"

"No, you fucking idiot. That's Kara. Didn't you double-check the profile before submitting our shit?" Rio was next to me again, probably to stop me if I got the urge to lunge forward and wring Brian's neck.

"No, I'm pretty sure it was Kayla." Brian pulled his phone out of his pocket and started scrolling through it. "No. Fuck. No, no, no."

I squeezed my temples between my fingers. "You fucked up. She tried to tell you and you didn't listen."

"I... fuck. This is so unlike me." He frowned at his phone. "Their names are just so similar and... fuck!"

Rio and I exchanged looks, both of us not sure what to think. Why would he purposely mix up the women?

I sighed. "Look, everyone makes mistakes, but this is a fucking huge one. Not to mention she says she didn't list any packs. So, how did we match?"

Brian slid his phone into his pocket, his face a mask I couldn't get a reading on. "She must have put the pack down. Omega Match isn't a perfect system, but it wouldn't just override her decision. Does she want you to send her back?"

"She doesn't know what she wants and neither do we..." I looked over my shoulder as Kayla threw her head back and laughed at something.

"What we need to focus on right now is the playoffs and, hopefully, the championship. We shouldn't have had you take care of something so important. We won't make the same mistake twice." Rio went to join the others, leaving me to deal with Brian.

"I honestly didn't do it on purpose. Their parents are idiots for naming them such similar names." Brian shook his head, and I wanted to smack him for speaking badly about Kayla's parents. "Go get your pack. We need to start practice."

I stepped into his personal space, causing him to freeze in place. "If I find out you're lying, I'll end you."

"Are you threatening to kill me?" he scoffed, backing up a step. "I'm on your side. Why would I do anything to hurt the pack?"

I glared at him for a few moments, a growl bubbling in my throat. "Remember your place, Brian."

He'd fucked up royally, but I was also partially to blame for giving him the chance to. That mistake wouldn't ever happen again.

Kayla watched me as I walked over to them, the smile falling from her face. Fuck, that was the worst feeling in the world.

Internally kicking myself for letting her get under my skin, I looked at my three packmates instead of at her. "Time to practice. Kayla, don't move from this bench."

"Yes, daddy." The sticky sweet sarcasm dripping off her words made me growl and before I could stop myself, I was leaning down toward her ear.

"Be a good little omega and I'll reward you later." I

nipped at her neck and then walked away before I did something stupid like kiss her.

Rylan ran to catch up with me. "Dude, what the hell was that?"

"What was what?" I avoided his stare as we started to jog around the practice field.

"Be a good little omega and I'll reward you later," he mimicked in a growly voice that sounded nothing like me. "Did something happen? You smell like each other. Then there's that hickey on her neck she didn't have last night before she went to bed."

I hadn't told them anything about the night before and hadn't planned to. "She was probably just rolling around in my dirty laundry or something."

"But then why do you smell like her?" His questioning was irritating me. "And the hickey? How'd she get that?"

"I don't know. Maybe she smells like me because she's staying with us, and maybe she burned her neck with her hair gadget." I sped up, leaving him in the dust.

"Liar!" he shouted after me, laughing like he was going to have a lot of fun teasing the fuck out of me.

It was going to be a long practice.

CHAPTER THIRTEEN

Kayla

Sometimes I was a little impulsive, which led me to my current situation sitting on the sidelines watching the Killer Gnomes run through drills and plays. I didn't even like to watch sports, yet there I was.

I'd woken up wrapped in Beck's arms and still couldn't lie to myself that it didn't put me in a good mood. A good enough mood to ask if I could watch their practice.

What had I been thinking?

But now that I was there, I was already growing bored and didn't like sitting out in the open. I hated that I felt things just because of what I was. There was no control over it, and that was what frustrated me the most about being an omega.

None of the other alphas had said anything to me yet, but a few eyes had looked at me appraisingly as they passed by. I could see the guys watching out of the corners of their eyes, and something about that made me happy.

The facility was several Alphaball fields set up to practice on and a giant weight room through two doors. There were locker rooms and a small area for people to watch practice.

The bench I was on was on the sidelines where the coaches stood when play was in action, but neither of the coaches was anywhere close to where I was.

I grimaced as Rio was tackled by another team they were practicing with. I didn't understand what was so appealing about Alphaball. Who in their right mind would want a weighted ball to hit them in the ribs or someone to mow them down to the ground?

I pulled out my phone and saw Kara had finally texted me back. I was starting to worry about her, and had she not responded to that morning's text, I would have called our parents.

Me: *Good morning! I am up before the sun and going to watch men hopefully take their shirts off.*

Kara: *Are they forcing you to go at gunpoint?*

Me: *Haha! No, I was tired of being cooped up in the house. Plus, I plan to get them to take me to the mall when they're done.*

Kara: *It sounds like things are going well...*

Me: *I wouldn't go that far. I'm still not sure what I want.*

Kara: *I think you should give it a chance. You might not get another.*

Me: *Have you gotten any answers from Omega Match?*

Kara: *No. They just said I need to be patient when it comes to finding a pack. Like, what does that mean? Don't they care that something might be wrong with their program?*

Me: *They don't even follow their own damn policy. Look at what's happened with me. It makes them look bad that the best omega there is didn't get a match.*

Kara: *I'm not so sure being the best is all it's cracked up to be.*

Me: *It's going to be fine.*

Kara: *Sleeping all day and eating a pint of ice cream every night for dinner isn't fine.*

Me: *Maybe you should see about going to visit our parents... our heats aren't even close to starting.*

She didn't respond, and I hovered my finger over the call button. Would that just make things worse? I didn't want her to hear any of the pack and get even more depressed.

Our whole lives, Kara had been the one to pull me out of my occasional funks. Besides our father's death, I couldn't remember a time when she'd been so sad she stayed in bed and ate ice cream for dinner.

I was just about to text my mom when shoes stopped in my periphery. I looked up to find Brian standing there, an impassive look on his face as he watched the field.

Brian wasn't an unattractive man. He was in good

shape and kept his dirty blond hair slicked back. It was his cunning brown eyes that made him look evil.

"Can I help you?" My eyes darted to where the pack was playing through a play.

"You're distracting them." His lips barely moved as he spoke. "When they lose, it's on you."

"Does it look like I care? It's not my fault they get distracted by my presence." I looked back at my phone. "Go coach them or something."

"They have a lot riding on these games. They just signed a major deal to have their brand be the official gear for all of United Alpha Sports. Do you really want to fuck that up for them?" He blew his whistle and walked forward a few feet to yell something about watching the middle.

Beck looked over at Brian, his hands on his hips. I couldn't tell if he was mad at Brian for stopping their play or standing near me.

I didn't know what Brian's deal was, but I didn't want to be anywhere near him, so I got up and headed for the small area that was meant for people just watching practice. No one was there, so I picked a chair next to the wall and kicked my feet up on the table.

I checked all the things I'd been neglecting for the past few days. Most of my social media was filled with pictures of omegas with their new packs. I'd had a few messages from classmates asking how I was doing with my new pack.

If I was going to answer, I would have said things

were going great. In less than twenty-four hours, I'd had an orgy of sorts by the pool and been knotted later that night by a grumpy alpha.

Things hadn't started well, and I would say they still weren't going well. I was so unsure of what I wanted and didn't want to let my hormones drive my decision to stay.

I still had time to figure things out before my heat hit. Even though it would be mild because of my suppressants, it would still lead me into wanting real knots instead of fake ones on dildos.

After scrolling through social media and noticing Kara hadn't posted anything since she made a post about her excitement for match day, I checked to see where the hell my boxes of stuff were.

I was excited to finally have more than just my suitcase, and last time I had checked, they had been on schedule to be delivered that afternoon.

"Hey, sweetheart." A deep voice made me jump and I nearly dropped my phone. "Sorry, we didn't mean to frighten you. We just saw you sitting over here all alone and wanted to see if you would like to go grab something to eat."

Three alphas that were similar in size to my pack were coming closer in the little sitting area I was in. They stopped a reasonable distance away but were close enough that, if I'd wanted, I could have smelled their scents.

"Um..." I tried to look around them, but they were

blocking my line of sight. "I'm here with a pack."

"We know, but we noticed they haven't marked you and you haven't marked them. A pretty omega like you shouldn't be sitting all alone and vulnerable." He wasn't wrong, but I didn't need to hear it from three massive alphas that could easily overpower me.

I slid my feet off the table. "I think I'll pass."

"What the fuck do you think you're doing, Miguel?" Rylan was between me and them in an instant, a fierce growl coming from him as he panted from running. "We told you five minutes ago that she's ours."

Rio joined him, erecting a wall in front of me so the three unwelcome alphas couldn't see me. "You know the rules. Don't approach an omega you have no business approaching."

"You brought an unclaimed omega into a place filled with testosterone-filled alphas. You're lucky we're the ones that came over here. Do better before you lose a sweet omega like her."

"Leave." Rylan's growl was so loud I was sure the whole facility was looking over at us.

The three alphas laughed, and Rio and Rylan turned around. The men were walking away, but one of them looked back and winked at me.

I didn't know whether to be creeped out, thankful they seemed to care, or angry that I was so fragile I had to be babysat.

"Are you okay? What did they say? Did they try to

touch you? I'll kill them." Rylan was squatting next to me and looking me over.

"Jesus. They were just trying to get me to go out with them. I had it handled. It's not like we were in a dark alley and they cornered me." I batted his hand away as he reached for my face.

The hurt in his eyes made a sick feeling well up in my stomach, and I reached for him to apologize, but he was already getting to his feet.

"It takes less than ten seconds to bite and claim an omega." Rylan crossed his arms. "You were supposed to stay on the bench."

"Yeah, well, being out in the middle of the fray was not my cup of tea." I stood, sliding my phone into my crossbody purse. "Is practice over? I'm ready to go."

I was surprised Rylan was acting so possessive. Out of the four of them, he was the most laid back, but right then, he looked ready to send heads flying.

Even if one of those alphas had bitten and claimed me, I certainly wasn't claiming them back. It would have been an infected bite for a week before healing after the claim loop wasn't complete.

"Beck!" Brian's angry yell made us all look toward the field.

Beck was marching toward us, his eyes full of fury. It made me glad he hadn't been the one to come over and send the three alphas away.

"Kane, you were supposed to keep him distracted."

Rio sighed and put himself in front of me. "Beck, calm the fuck down. You're scaring her."

I snorted. "He doesn't scare me."

"Let's go. We're leaving." Beck practically barreled through Rio and grabbed my hand, pulling me toward the locker room. "You can just shut your eyes in the locker room."

"What are you doing? Practice isn't over!" Brian was fuming as he met us halfway across the field.

"It is now. We are more than prepared for our play-off. We'll see you at the game." Beck was still pulling me, and I just went along with it because it was actually kind of funny to see him so pissed off that other alphas had given me attention.

"You still have another practice." Brian jogged in front of us and was practically running backwards with how fast Beck was walking.

Beck stopped, and I bumped into him. "We'll practice on our own. Over-practicing is a thing."

"As your coach and manager-"

"You're fired." Beck let go of my hand and stepped close enough to punch Brian in the face. "Effective immediately."

Brian *looked* like he had been punched. "You can't fire me! We have a contract!"

The last thing I wanted to cause was for them to be sued. I grabbed Beck's hand and squeezed it. "I'm ready to go."

Beck nodded and, with a huff, continued to lead me into the men's locker room. "Shut your eyes."

"I've seen dicks before." There didn't seem to be anyone in the locker room anyway. "I don't need a babysitter. I can wait outside the door."

"Over my dead body." He led me along to the far side of the locker room where there were four large locker stalls. "Rio and Rylan, go shower."

Kane laughed and sat down on a bench in front of a locker area with his name. "You are something else, man. We can't just fire Brian without just cause."

"There's plenty of cause. He fucked up Omega Match and is gaslighting us. I'm not an idiot." Beck let go of my hand and opened his locker as Rio and Rylan went to go shower. "I just wish we could use that as a reason without creating a shit storm for ourselves."

"You know I'm standing right here." I crossed my arms. Hearing him speak so negatively about what had happened with Omega Match stung. "If you're going to refer to you knotting me last night as a fuck up, then at least do it behind my back."

"What?" Kane jumped to his feet, his eyes wide as he looked between the two of us. "You fucking knotted her?"

Beck shrugged. "It's not a big deal."

That stung.

Kane spun him around by the shoulder and shoved him into the small section of wall between lockers. "It is a fucking big deal! You of all of us got to knot her first and you're brushing it off like it was meaningless. Wise up and stop acting like you don't give two shits about her when you were just now ready to kill other alphas for talking to her."

My stomach felt full of butterflies, and I couldn't decide if I wanted to run or kiss Kane for telling Beck he was being an idiot.

Beck shrugged Kane off and straightened his sweat-soaked shirt. He stared at Kane for a minute that seemed much longer and then looked at me. "I'm sorry."

What was he sorry for? Fucking me the night before or acting like an asshole?

He walked toward the showers without elaborating, and I sat down with a huff. "He's something else. Why did he even agree to do the match thing if he was going to be so horrendous?"

Kane sat down next to me and took my hand, rubbing his thumb over the top of it. The small touch had no business being so comforting. "I think he's always wanted an omega as part of our pack, he just... he's complicated."

Someone needed to tell me what the hell that meant because I was getting tired of his past being alluded to and no one saying anything about it. I knew it wasn't their place to tell me, but there were only so many chances the man was going to get.

CHAPTER FOURTEEN

Rio

Beck was losing his ever-loving mind. We couldn't just fire our manager and coach right before playoffs. As much as I wanted Brian gone, I also had to be realistic about the entire situation.

We'd fire him in two weeks after winning the championship.

After showering and changing, we went out to the parking lot. We'd come in two separate cars because Kane and Beck were going to volunteer at the food bank we were major donors to.

As much as I loved volunteering there myself, I liked the idea of spending some time with Kayla.

"What do you want to do today?"

It was just past ten in the morning, and we had nothing going on the rest of the day. We were always so busy all the time and it was nice to have a few days of rest.

"Can we go to the mall? The rest of my stuff is going to be delivered later this afternoon, but I want to get a few things and get a gift for Kara." Kayla sat in the passenger seat next to me and Rylan got in the back. "I have my own credit card."

Rylan laughed. "If you think we're letting you pay for anything, you have another thing coming."

"Yeah, but…" She sighed. "You're right, you should pay for everything. That's how it's supposed to work, right?"

"If you don't want us to, we won't." I pulled out of the parking lot and headed for a mall that was on the way back to our house. It had a variety of high-end and regular stores. It also had my favorite women's boutique that I planned on taking her to.

"Speak for yourself." Rylan made a growly huff. Since our time in the pool with Kayla, he'd become somewhat possessive. I hoped it wasn't going to start causing problems.

"It's been a long time since I've been to a mall during normal hours. Usually, once a month, there was a day we'd all go for two hours of omega-only shopping before the mall opened. It sucked because none of the food places were open." She looked out the window, her cheek on her fist. "I could really go for a soft pretzel with cheese."

"You don't strike me as the mall-going type." I turned

onto the freeway and was pleasantly surprised at how light the traffic was.

"What is the mall-going type?" She looked over at me and then gestured to her jeans and plain T-shirt. "I don't like super girly things, but I still like to shop. But mainly the reason I like the mall is the food. We're going to start with pretzels, then after we hit a few shops, we'll get frozen lemonades and corn dogs, and then for lunch, nothing beats mall Chinese food." The girl talked about food like we talked about Alphaball.

"I'll give you a corn dog." Rylan was in the middle seat and leaned forward. "Can bend you into a pretzel too."

"Oh, geez." Kayla laughed and turned in her seat to pinch his cheek. "Good thing you're cute."

"You think I'm cute?" I didn't need to look at Rylan to hear the grin in his voice. Plus, I could feel his happiness through the pack bond. While we didn't always let our emotions flow freely through it, he wanted me to know how happy he was.

"Cute as a mangy mutt." I took the off-ramp toward the mall. "We can go anywhere you want, just lead the way."

"Suck up." Rylan flicked my arm and laughed.

As I pulled into a parking spot, I became certain that Kayla was just the omega we needed.

AFTER EATING PRETZELS WITH CHEESE, Kayla led us to a map of the mall that she examined for a few minutes before she giggled and grabbed our hands.

The giggle concerned me a bit, but we'd told her we'd go anywhere she wanted to go and we meant it. Pleasing her was all I could think about, and if that meant I sat for an hour and waited for her to try on clothes or look at baubles in a shop, then that was what I'd do.

What I wasn't expecting was for her to lead us to a sex shop that had a discreet storefront and an actual bouncer at the door. He nodded to us as we entered, not even bothering to check our identification.

"I'm not sure if this is a wise idea." I was hit with way too many scents and had to breathe through my mouth. "It smells like a nest in here."

"How do you know what a nest smells like?" She led us straight back to a wall of vibrating dildos.

There wasn't anyone in the store besides two beta women behind the counter. I could tell they were betas because they didn't immediately react to us.

"I agree with Rio. You have us. You don't need dildos or fancy vibrators." Rylan picked up a pink, flower-shaped toy. "What is this supposed to do exactly?"

"You put it over your clit, and it vibrates in a way to simulate sucking. I have one. It's amazing." She grabbed a toy off the wall. "This one stimulates the clit and G-spot, plus the ass. Perfect for Kara. I think I'll get one too. I've heard good things about it."

"Um, no." I plucked the toy she was grabbing for herself out of her hand and put it back. "If anyone is stimulating any of those things it will be us. Not something someone manufactured to use solo."

She turned around and raised an eyebrow. "Who said I'd be using it solo? You poor alphas. You think toys are just for me to use on myself? Toys are friends, not foes."

"We have a display case right over here if you'd like to see what the vibrations and movement are like for the most popular of our products." The female store clerk stopped a respectful distance from us.

Rylan and I were both slightly on edge being there with our omega. All it took was one horny alpha to ruin our day.

"Oh, that won't be necessary." Kayla snatched the toy I'd put up back off the hook. "Where are your strap-ons?"

The woman's eyes darted over to me, and for some goddamn reason, my face felt hot. Why the hell was she asking about strap-ons?

"Right this way. We have quite a few choices. Do you know what size and shape you're looking for?" The woman led us a few feet to a wall of strap-on dildos.

Rylan and I were standing next to each other now, both too stunned to speak. It was sexy as hell that Kayla was so confident with her sexuality, but also... a strap-on?

"Well, judging by their facial expressions, I'd say I need the smallest possible."

"I'd recommend this one. It has a spot in the strap to put a bullet so your clit will be stimulated as you thrust. Do you have prep materials? I recommend a set of gradually increasing butt plugs."

What the what?

Rylan and I looked at each other with wide eyes, which she didn't even notice because she was examining the package hanging on the display like it was some kind of art piece in a gallery.

"Uh, Kayla, sweetheart. I think we need to discuss this in private." I wanted to give her what she wanted, but also, there needed to be some boundaries.

"I'll be at the counter if you need any more assistance. I can take these for you to free up your arms." The woman took the two vibrators from Kayla and left us staring at the wall of dicks.

"You're just kidding, right?" Rylan picked up the product the woman had recommended.

"I'm serious. You'll come so hard. I will too." She put her hand on Rylan's biceps. "Please."

Please.

The single word had a lot of power over an alpha, and I could quickly see Rylan giving in.

"I want your ass first. If I do this." He handed her the box with the strap-on in it. "Where are these butt plugs she spoke so fondly of?"

The next thing I knew, we were looking at packages of butt plugs. I didn't know there were so many kinds or that they came in different sizes and shapes.

"I think because the dildo on the strap-on isn't super girthy, these will be perfect. We just need to get you some lube and then you'll be all set." She was acting like a kid in a candy store, and I couldn't help but smile at her excitement.

She wouldn't be getting anywhere near my ass with a butt plug or dildo, but if Rylan wanted to give it a go, more power to him.

"You basically start with the smallest, leave it in doing whatever for a bit. Maybe ten minutes at first. Then you put the next in, and then the next. Hopefully, your muscles get to a point where it doesn't take as much prep." She grabbed a butt plug with a red jewel on the flared base. "This would be so sexy for you, Rio."

"What? No." I took it and put it back. "I love red, but no."

"Suit yourself, but when you see how much Ry gets off, you're going to wish you'd bought your own butt plugs." There was a teasing glimmer in her eyes, and I wrapped an arm around her, pulling her to me.

"Be careful, sweetheart. You're making the alpha in me want to punish you for being cheeky." I kissed her, capturing her gasp before pulling away. "Now, where are these bullets she mentioned?"

TWENTY MINUTES LATER, we were finished in the adult toy store and headed to the boutique I'd been aching to

KNOT SO PERFECT OMEGA

go to. Out of the four of us, I was most interested in fashion and design, which was why I made most of the decisions when it came to our clothing.

I'd studied business in college but had always had an eye for what was hot and what was out of season. My eye was drawn to clean lines, bold colors, and unique patterns.

Rylan and Beck couldn't dress to save their lives, so someone had to make up for their lack of style.

"Can I pick some things out for you to try on?" I wasn't going to take no for an answer.

"No pink and no floral." She looked around the store. "And nothing see-through. I already make you four horny enough as it is."

"Trust me, you want Rio picking out your clothes. If this Alphaball thing doesn't pan out, he could be a personal stylist for the stars. Wouldn't that be a dream, styling N'Pact?" Rylan chuckled as I shot him a glare.

We walked around the boutique, and I pointed out different things to Kayla so she could grab her size and pile them into my arms. With my arms loaded, we headed for the dressing room.

"I'm going to go find a bathroom. Here, hold this bag." He handed Kayla one of the two bags from the sex shop.

"Do you want me to take the other one?" She reached for it, and Rylan moved it behind his back. "Rylan, what... oh! Oh... you dirty boy. Go! Take a picture too so I can see." Her grin was wide and excitement was in her eyes.

"I'll show you later if you want." He winked, and then he was practically skipping from the store.

"I can't believe you've convinced him to do that." I shook my head and stopped at the entrance to the fitting room area.

"You can take those on back for her since no one else is here." The store clerk was busy looking at a magazine and didn't look up.

"Thanks." I followed Kayla back to a fitting room all the way down the aisle of doors. "Wouldn't it be better if you were in the first room so you can come out and show me?"

"You can just stand outside the door." She set the bag down by my feet and grabbed the clothes. "I'll be out in a minute."

I picked up the bag and leaned against the wall outside the door. "You know, you making me wait outside while I can hear you undressing is a cruel kind of torture."

"Is it?" She laughed, and then I heard her grunt. "I hate skinny jeans, but oh, man, they make my ass look fantastic."

"Let me see."

"Hold your horses, I need a top." She started muttering to herself,

I hit my leg with the bag and then looked inside it.

Rylan had moved stuff around and left me with the two vibrators and the bullet. I grabbed the small box with the bullet and my cock jumped at the idea that popped into my head.

I did warn her if she was cheeky with me again, she'd be punished.

She finally opened the door, and I pushed inside, locking it behind me and dropping the bag I had on the small bench beside the door. "It took you long enough."

I finally got a good look at her, and the growl that came from my throat made her eyes dilate. She liked her alpha growly, and if that was what she liked, who was I to deny her?

"I couldn't decide on the top." She adjusted the slightly sheer, royal blue blouse that gave me a direct view of her lacy black bra underneath. "I thought I said nothing see-through." She backed up as I stalked forward the two steps it took to get to her.

"It's sexy as fuck." I ran my finger along the V-neck that stopped just at the swell of her breasts. "You'll wear this out of here."

"You want other alphas to see my goodies?" She was against the mirror, and I put a hand on the wall on one side of her. The gesture only made her straighten her spine.

She had a point. "No." I captured her lips with mine and damn near busted a nut on the spot.

Her lips were pillow-soft and sweet, but the way she

kissed was all sass. She knew she had me wrapped around her finger.

I tugged her bottom lip between my teeth and then released it with a groan. My need was rising exponentially and we were in the worst possible place for that to happen.

My lips moved up her jaw to her ear, and I could feel her trembling beneath the touch of my lips. "How quiet can you be?"

"Here? In the dressing room?" She whimpered as I reached into my pocket and pulled out the small bullet vibrator. She looked down at the small pink device and her breath hitched. "Rio…"

"Take off those pants and blouse. We're buying everything. No need to try anything else on." I stood back and watched her take off the pants that fit her like a glove.

She stood before me in her lace panties and bra, and I bit on my fist to stop the possessive noises I wanted to make. This was entirely different than seeing her in her bikini.

"What if we get caught?" she whispered, resuming her position against the mirror.

"Then we get caught." I took her mouth again, turning on the vibrator as my tongue tangled with hers.

The sound was quiet, but it was also the lowest setting of five. I ran it across the swell of her breasts and then down her stomach to her panty line.

I pulled back, wanting to see her face as I punished her in both the best and worst way possible.

Her eyes closed as I slid my hand into her panties and pressed the toy against her clit. She was already soaked, her body anticipating the sweet torture I was going to do right there in the dressing room.

"Ma'am? How are you doing? Do you need any additional sizes or patterns?" the woman who had been at the counter said.

"I'm fine." Kayla's last word came out as more of a yelp as I turned up the vibrator. "I have a few more things to try on."

"All right. Just yell if you need me."

I leaned in next to her ear. "Don't yell too loud."

She grabbed onto my wrist and bit down on her lip. "I'm going to come."

"So soon?" I pulled it away from her clit and let it rest against her thigh. "We can't have that."

"Please, Nazario." Her eyes were glossy with need and, fuck, hearing my full name on her lips did something to me.

"Say it again." I clicked the vibrator to the next level, moving it just left of her clit. "Let me hear my name on those sweet lips."

"Nazario," she panted, "I need you to make me come."

I kissed her right as I placed the bullet over her clit again and clicked to the highest level. It was difficult to stifle her cry as her body came apart. Her nails dug into

MAYA NICOLE

my wrist, and I had to wrap my free arm around her to keep her from falling.

My hand was covered in her slick as she trembled through her orgasm. I turned the toy off and rubbed it against her swollen nub as her pleasure peaked and then cascaded down around us.

"Such a sweet omega, coming for your alpha." I kissed the corner of her lips, then her neck and shoulder. "Now to clean up the mess I made."

I dropped to my knees and pulled her panties down. She leaned all her body weight against the mirror as I placed one of her legs over my shoulder. I hadn't had the pleasure of tasting her sweet cunt the day before, and as I swiped my tongue through her cum, I growled, the taste everything I imagined and more.

If only we weren't in a dressing room.

I reined myself in as much as it hurt me to—and trust me, it fucking hurt—and licked her and my fingers clean.

"I think… I think we need to go." Her chest was still heaving, her face and chest flushed pink.

I stood, sliding the bullet back into my pocket, knowing I was going to smell strongly of her. That was exactly what I wanted—for every motherfucker who looked at her to know she was mine.

"We still have shopping to do, and what about all the food plans you had for us?" I pulled up her panties, which were soaked through. "Do you think you can handle it?"

She pushed a stray lock of hair behind her ear. "Of course I can. The question is, can you and Ry handle it?"

I picked up the clothes on the floor and put them back on the hangers. "You underestimate my willpower, sweetheart. A lesser alpha would have bent you over and taken you with how good you smell right now."

"And you don't want to do that?" She tugged on her jeans and grabbed her T-shirt.

"Oh, I do." I took her shirt from her and brought it to my nose, inhaling her scent before pulling it over her head. "I don't want you to share your screams for me with anyone."

She stared at me with parted lips, and I leaned in for a quick kiss before grabbing all of the clothes and walking out of the dressing room. If I didn't walk away now, I was going to say *fuck it* and give the whole mall something to talk about.

Rylan was back and had a smirk on his face as I walked past him to the counter. The woman, who appeared to be the only one working, seemed none the wiser about what had just transpired in the fitting room.

"Everything fit all right?"

"It was perfect. We'll take it all." I handed her my credit card as Kayla walked out of the fitting room area, her face still flushed from her orgasm.

"Sounds like you had really good luck today." The woman scanned the items.

"You could say that." Kayla stood next to Rylan, and

he held open the bag he'd gone off with for her to look inside. "You really did it?"

"Yup." He grinned from ear to ear. "It doesn't feel too bad."

The things we did for this omega.

Our omega.

♡ 154 ♡

CHAPTER FIFTEEN

Rylan

There's a butt plug in my ass. Words I never thought I'd say to myself.

When we'd first gone into the adult toy store, I'd been a little offended after what we had been up to the day before, but who was I to judge how she wanted her pleasure? We had made her come like it was the Fourth of July, and her wanting toys wasn't a critique of that.

Omegas were very sexual, and now I'd had a little bit of time to think about it, the more toys, the better. There might be four of us to keep her satisfied, but when her heat hit, we were going to need all the help we could get. Especially her first one after being on heat suppressants for years.

If that meant I suffered a little bit by letting her peg

me, then so be it. I was more adventurous than the other three, and so far, there hadn't been as much discomfort as expected. It was a pleasant kind of ache, and when I moved the right way, it brushed my prostate.

After paying for Kayla's new clothes, we went across the mall to Nest & Knot. Kayla had grumbled a little as soon as she saw the sign, but once we set foot inside, her demeanor changed immediately.

As hard as she tried to fight her basic instincts, the twinkle in her eyes didn't lie. Maybe she'd just never imagined herself falling into place with a pack and so she never let herself imagine all the possibilities. Life as an omega wasn't easy at first; not when teenage girls going through so many changes were moved into a school where their every move was supervised and planned out.

We grabbed a cart and followed her to the back of the store where they had every sheet option available. She gaped at the rainbow of colors and looked at us, her bottom lip between her teeth. "I already got two sets."

Rio leaned on the cart. "You came back here because you know you need more than just two."

There was some uncertainty in her eyes, which was not something I liked seeing. "You like blues and greens. Let's get some of those. We don't want to have to do laundry every day during your heat."

I went to the wall of colors and grabbed a plastic-wrapped set of pale green and threw it in the cart. She perked up a bit but then grabbed a light blue set, flipping it over to look at the price.

Rio snatched it from her and threw it in the cart. "Our money is your money, and we have plenty to spend on your nest. Go wild."

"But-"

I grabbed another sheet set and put it in the cart. "We want you to have nice things. The nest is for us too."

"You're right... I just don't want you to feel like I'm taking advantage." She headed down the aisle with bath linens. "It's just going to take some getting used to."

We loaded up on towels, washcloths, nightlights, and robes since none of us would probably want to get dressed with all the sex that would be going on. To be honest, despite taking a course in college on omegas, I didn't quite know what was in store for us when it came to Kayla.

My parents never talked about my mother's heats growing up, and whenever they hit, my sister and I were sent to my grandparents.

After Rio paid and arranged for the haul to be delivered, we headed to the food court since we'd been in Nest & Knot for over an hour and were all starving.

A few eyes landed on us as we walked into the large dining area with restaurants around the perimeter. I was usually happy to take pictures and sign autographs, but with Kayla with us, I'd probably growl and scare fans away.

"Well, crap. Now that I see all the places, I'm thinking

I want to try these Korean corn dogs I've seen all over social media." We followed her to the far side of the food court, waving back to a few people as we went.

"I feel my acid reflux already bubbling." Rio grabbed her hand as we stopped in the short line and looked up at the menu. "A corn dog with potato cubes and hot Cheetos?"

"That sounds amazing! They have a sampler box where it's their top five best sellers. We can get that and some fries." She looked from side to side at us. "Unless you guys wanted something else. I'll still get the sampler, then I'll take home the leftovers for later."

I laughed and shook my head. "This is fine. Little concerned about how this will play out with my loose asshole."

The man in front of us whipped around, his eyes going wide with recognition. I cringed and gave him a *what's up?* with my chin, my face feeling like it was covered in hot Cheetos.

I could see the headlines now *"Is star Alphaball player Rylan Abbott down and out with a loose asshole?"*

Thank fuck the man thought twice about talking to us and turned back around. Kayla put her forehead against my arm, her giggle making my embarrassment evaporate as quickly as it had come.

We went to a few more stores after eating and then headed back to the house. Luckily, the fans that did recognize us kept their distance, probably realizing we were with our omega. Being out in public with Kayla had been a concern for us since we weren't bonded, but since there weren't huge crowds on weekdays, things were going better than expected.

No one had paid us much attention before this season. It was like all hell broke loose when I broke my arm in the playoffs last season, and then it was like everyone became obsessed with us.

It was a lot of pressure and there was still a very small part of me that was nervous I'd break a bone again every time I set foot on a field. But now wasn't the time to worry about that. I'd save the worry for our playoff game in five days. Right then, I was looking forward to relaxing at home after a busy season, even if only for a few days.

"We need to figure out what we're doing in the gamer room with a nest. My sister is going to want to game later." We'd just pulled into the garage, and I walked to the front of Rio's matte red Tesla to grab our bags. "Do you game at all, Kayla?"

"Some, but I wouldn't call myself a gamer. More of a casual in the moment player. My dads have just about every gaming system." She took a few of the bags from me. "I spend a lot of my free time doodling quilt designs and sewing."

"What got you into that?" Rio plugged his car in and locked it. "It's not often you hear about women in their twenties quilting or wanting to do it for a career."

"Well, I didn't really get into it until I started at the academy and took a class, but I guess once I did, I just kept remembering how my mom took all my dad's shirts when he died and made a quilt." Sadness seemed to take hold of her, and I wrapped my arm around her waist.

"I'm sorry. That had to be tough on not only your mom but you and your sister too." Rio shut his trunk. "Is that what you're planning on doing? Sewing memorial quilts?"

"Not at first. I want to make custom or semi-custom quilts for omega nests. I think it would be hard for an omega to hand over a deceased alpha's belongings to another omega unless I have trust in the community first." She pulled away from me so she could walk into the house behind Rio. "There are a lot of specifics I haven't worked out yet."

"Like how to keep your delicious scent off the fabric?" I shut the door and we went into the lower-level living room and put the bags on the couch.

"That's an issue. Being around alphas seems to make me perfume despite taking the blockers. Maybe they're defective?" She kicked off her shoes and pulled off her socks, leaving them by the coffee table before plopping down.

"You don't really need to worry about taking them anymore unless we're going somewhere. Maybe it's time to switch brands. I overheard my mom telling my dads one time that they lose their effectiveness after prolonged use." I pushed some bags over and sat down quickly next to her, forgetting I had the plug in. I jerked straight back up, my hands flying to my butt. "Now there's an interesting feeling. Woah."

It was going to take some getting used to sitting without feeling like I was impaling myself. I carefully lowered back down, favoring one ass cheek before lowering the other.

Rio chuckled and grabbed his bag with a pair of shoes he'd bought. "I need to go take care of a few things. Don't get up to anything without me."

I frowned as he walked up the stairs. Out of the four of us, Rio was the strongest, but also the most closed off. He didn't want the role of leader of our pack and let Beck take the reins. He was a few years older than us and hadn't said why he was starting college two years late. We figured he'd tell us when he was ready, but he never had.

"Is he okay?" Kayla was a perceptive little thing. "I thought he'd want to hang out after he... you know..."

"Made you come on his hand?" I grinned and nudged her with my elbow. "You're a dirty omega, aren't you?"

She laughed and snuggled up next to me. Her scent was extra strong because of the activities she'd gotten up to with Rio. "I'm not dirty. You forget that you're the one with a butt plug in your ass right now."

"Anything for you." I kissed her and then relaxed back into the cushions. "So, when should my rump be good for the taking?"

"I want it to be the best possible because I know as soon as I'm back there, your alpha instincts aren't going to like it. In one of our sex courses, we talked about all the ways it can go wrong but also all the ways it can really empower an omega and also the alpha. So... maybe a week of you wearing the different sizes and we'll give it a go." She giggled and then started full-on laughing.

"What? Is the idea of pegging me hilarious to you? What would really be hilarious is seeing you peg Beck with no prep and no lube. He'd deserve it." The more I visualized it, the more I liked the idea. He was being ridiculous. If he'd just let himself go, he'd see how happy being around an omega could make him.

"I don't think anyone deserves that. Could you imagine the whining we'd have to hear? It's just... I was mostly joking about the whole thing because you both were so scandalized being in a toy shop and here you are wearing a butt plug for me." She looked up at me, her blue eyes full of happiness.

Fuck. This was what it was all about. Making her happy.

"If you weren't serious, I'm sure we could take the strap-on back since the box isn't open." I leaned over, reaching for the discreet black bags to find it.

"No, absolutely not!" She scrambled to stop me, and I hooked my arm around her and pulled her so she was on top of me. "Hey! That's not very nice!"

I rolled and pinned her under me. "Maybe I'm not a very nice person."

She pushed at my chest, and I grabbed her wrists,

pinning them over her head with one of my hands. With my other, I tickled her side and she squealed in delight.

Settling my weight between her legs, I stopped my tickling assault on her and brushed the hair out of her face that had fallen loose. "Stay with us."

Her squirming stopped and her eyes glossed over as if she was going to cry. "Ry..."

"Don't think of all the reasons you don't want a pack, think of all the reasons you do. How can we truly let ourselves love each other and let each other in to see the deepest parts of ourselves if there's uncertainty? I know it's scary, and I know it's not what you wanted, but let us be your alphas. Let us love you and take care of you. You don't have to sacrifice the bond of a pack to pursue your dreams. We can support you in whatever you want to do." I knew the rest of the pack felt the same, even if some of them didn't know how to say it.

"I wasn't supposed to... I'm not..." She shut her eyes and it felt like she was shrinking down into the cushions. "I only came because I had to and thought you'd all send me back... It's only been a few days. How can you already be so sure?"

"You don't feel it?" I moved my hand down to her chest, right over her heart. "Because I feel this ache right here."

A tear slid down her cheek, and I let go of her wrists to wipe it away. I knew she felt it too. It was in the way she looked at us, the way she trusted us like she'd known us for a lot longer. It was why she was crying.

"It scares me." When she opened her eyes, there was sadness in them. "To be so connected with four other people... What if... I don't think I can."

"What if what?" I could practically feel her sadness and anxiety radiating off her and started to purr to comfort her. "What if something happens to one of us?"

She nodded, her hands snaking around my waist to pull me closer. "My mom still had five mates and just one dying almost killed her. She's never been the same. I don't even want to think about if one of my other dads..." She choked on a sob, and I moved to the side of her a little so I could pull her into my chest without squashing her.

"Your dads won't let that happen. That's the beauty of a pack. We're there for each other no matter what. You can't let the tragedy in your life stop you from having that for yourself. Even a day of feeling the love in a bond will be worth any amount of pain that might happen down the road." I rubbed her back, my purr vibrating through me. I could already feel her calming down in my arms.

"What about Beck? I can't be in a pack where one of the alphas doesn't want me." She buried her face in my chest and inhaled my scent, her tears soaking through the fabric.

"He's just prickly on the outside... He gave you his knot, didn't he?" I wasn't exactly happy about that fact when he was being such a royal ass, but maybe it was what he needed to come to terms with his feelings.

"I'll always be a mistake to him. There won't be a day that goes by that he doesn't look at me and think about how I was supposed to be my sister."

A growl made both me and Kayla jump slightly.

"That's not true." Beck had snuck in, or just come in and we hadn't heard him.

We both looked over at him standing at the edge of the sectional, a vase of roses in his hand. I couldn't help but smirk a little. He was definitely on the same page as the rest of us, he just didn't want to admit it.

"Why is she crying?" He cut me an accusatory glare, his growl still coming out in little bursts of warning.

"I'm *right* here. And I was crying because I felt like it." She pulled out of my arms and propped herself up on her forearm but was trapped between me and the back of the couch. "Are those for me?"

Beck sighed, his growl dissipating as he set them on the coffee table and sat down by our heads. "Yes. I wanted to apologize for my behavior."

"I'm listening." She lay back down, but adjusted her position so she could look up at Beck.

"I've been out of line and you don't deserve how I've been treating you. I have a lot of issues I need to work through, but that's not your problem, it's mine." He slouched down so his neck was resting on the back cushion. "There's always been a lot of uncertainty in my life, and you've stirred up some of those things."

I nuzzled my face against Kayla's arm as she listened and processed what he was saying. It was the same thing

I had just told her, and I hoped she could see that of all of us, Beck needed her to decide the most.

"What kind of uncertainty?"

Beck blew out a breath. It took him a few years to even tell us about his past, so I knew it was hard for him to share. I reached over and put a hand right above his knee, hoping it gave him some comfort.

"My parents… they didn't have the best luck when I was younger, and when I was ten, they lost everything in a bad investment."

"Everything as in…" I could feel her unease start back up again. She cared, even if she was mad at him.

"We were homeless. At first, it was okay because we had a spot at a shelter, but then they both started selling drugs, which turned into using drugs. Anyway… they were both arrested when I was around sixteen, and I went to live in a group home since no one wants to foster a sixteen-year-old boy. The only thing that saved me from being homeless when I turned eighteen was emerging as an alpha and getting a scholarship."

Kayla was trembling slightly, and I started my purr up again. "That's… I'm sorry you had to go through all that, Beck."

He shrugged and scooted forward, getting ready to get up. She grabbed his hand, and he looked over at her. I felt like I was intruding on a private moment between them.

"Stay. We're going to watch a movie." She scooted so

her head was on his thigh, but that also meant her boobs were right in my face.

"You two can watch a movie. I'll just lay right like this and watch these." I put my face right on them. "Yup, this is paradise."

"You're ridiculous." Kayla's satisfied sigh and hand running through my hair let me know she enjoyed it.

I could feel her that much closer to staying, and I smiled to myself, thinking about how good life was going to be.

CHAPTER SIXTEEN

Kayla

Over the next several days, I did a lot of thinking while trying to not let myself be persuaded by how good the sex was. And that meant not letting any of them stick their dicks and definitely not their knots in me. I'd been moving way too fast in the first place and needed my head and hormones clear.

It was easier said than done.

I lay on the bed in the primary bedroom, which I'd overtaken as my own. There had been another spare bedroom upstairs, but it had been used as a closet for their athleticwear brand. That was now moved to the room on the ground floor, so Beck had his own room.

I was all for sharing rooms and beds, but I also

needed my own space. I wanted to backtrack a bit and get to know them more. Especially since I was ninety-five percent sure I was staying.

The video chat app on my phone finally connected with my sister, and I rolled over and propped the phone on a pillow. "Hey, Care Bear."

"You look comfy." She was in bed, lying the exact same way as I was. She had soft lighting on so her face was illuminated in a warm glow. "I was starting to worry you'd died from too much dick."

I laughed. It was nice to hear her joking again, but I could still see the pain and sadness in her eyes even through the video chat. "I'm abstaining."

"What? Why the hell would you do that? At least let me live vicariously through you." She sighed. "You look happy."

I curled my hands under the side of my face and wondered how much I should tell her. I didn't want our relationship to turn into secrets and I knew she wouldn't want that either.

"I am... I think I'm going to stay." I bit my lip and kept my eyes glued on Kara's for any signs of duress. "They want to bond with me."

Kara mirrored me, her hands going under her cheek. "Is that what you want? You were so adamant that a pack wasn't for you."

"I know, but I just feel... at peace around them. It's hard to explain." It felt natural, like this pack was always meant to be mine. It was a ridiculous feeling considering Kara was supposed to be the one in my place. A fact I didn't plan on telling her because it would do nothing except hurt her.

"I'm happy for you." She blinked back tears. "I think we've swapped opinions on packs."

"You don't mean that, Kara. It just wasn't the right time. I mean, think about how the whole system works. We hardly get time with any of the packs and then have to rank each other for some algorithm to match us. They might as well just auction us off instead."

"That's barbaric. I've been doing a lot of thinking about Omega Match and have decided they can't be trusted. Who's to say money doesn't trade hands? Where there's power, there's money pulling the strings." Kara almost never spoke badly about anything having to do with how omegas are treated or matched in our society. It was concerning the sharp turn she'd made.

There was still the question of how I ended up even matching when I opted out. I was sure everyone thought I was lying, and part of me still wondered if Kara really believed me.

"Are you going to start doing meetings and socials for the fall match? They told us the fall one is a lot less overwhelming."

"What if I meet a fantastic pack outside of Omega Match? Am I supposed to just ignore my feelings and make them go through the whole process?"

"How do you plan on meeting a pack outside of it? I hope you aren't thinking of sneaking-"

"No. I just... never mind." Kara sat up, and I could see her room. It was a disaster of boxes and piles of things. "I should finish packing this mess. They're moving me to the omega compound tomorrow."

"Call me whenever you need to. I love you, sis."

"Love you too." She hung up, and I was left with an uneasy feeling in my belly.

There was a soft knock on my door, and it cracked open an inch. I'd told the guys I was going to take a nap, but really had been scrolling on my phone and then talking to Kara.

"Kayla? You awake?" Kane whispered.

"Yeah. You can come in." I sat up and scooted back against the headboard. "What's up?"

Kane was dressed in jeans and had a leather jacket on over his T-shirt. Odd attire for inside the house.

"I'm going to go for a ride and then stop at a food truck event. You want to go?" He shoved his hands in the pockets of his jeans. "I thought it would be nice to get out for a bit before we leave tomorrow morning."

"A ride? Like on a motorcycle?" My heart sped up, and I scooted off the large bed when he nodded. "Hell yes, I want to go."

I looked down at my pajama shorts and tank top I'd put on to take a nap. "Let me change."

"You don't have to wear a leather jacket or anything,

but something to cover your skin would be good just in case." He sat on the bench at the end of the bed as I opened one of the boxes I still hadn't unpacked.

"I have a leather jacket I never have reason to wear." I dug to the bottom and yanked it out. "Is everyone going?"

"No, just us." He leaned back onto the end of the bed with his forearms as I started changing right in front of him. "Have you ridden on a motorcycle?"

"Yeah, my dads have them. Drives my mom nuts. I've never driven one myself though. I think they were scared I'd ride off into the sunset if they taught me how." I pulled on the jeans I had on earlier and swapped out my sleep tank for an N'Pact shirt.

"I could teach you how. I mean, not today, but once the season is over. Rio has a bike too. We could get you one." He sat up and grabbed my hips as I came to stand in front of him. "Do you have your driver's license?"

I cringed. "No. There's been no reason for me to learn to drive and it's not like omegas have freedoms where we can just go wherever we want when we want." It really sucked, and I didn't even know how I thought it was going to be possible to open my own shop with all the restrictions.

I'd have to hire at least two beta security guards to be in the shop and to accompany me to and from the shop. Might as well be a celebrity.

"What's that scrunched up expression for? There's no

♡ 172 ♡

shame in not knowing how, but I think it would be good for you to learn in case you ever need to drive." He stood and pulled me against him in a hug.

"I've driven bumper cars and on video games. How hard can it be?" The thought of driving in Los Angeles traffic gave me anxiety.

"It can be difficult. Let's go so we have enough time to enjoy the food trucks and get back before it gets dark." He entwined our fingers and led me out of the room. "Are you a fan of N'Pact?"

I looked down at my well-worn shirt. "Who isn't?"

He laughed as we walked through the house. "They live down the street. We've been over there a few times for parties and stuff. I'd introduce you but they don't have an omega, and I don't want them to get any ideas."

I zipped up my jacket as we went out into the garage. "I guess I can see why they wouldn't have an omega. Too many beta chicks to wet their dicks with... You guys must have stopped getting so many throwing themselves at you to agree to take me."

Kane stopped and I nearly ran into him. He turned and his face screamed that my comment had hurt. "Not all famous or popular alpha packs are man whores, Kayla."

I cringed. "I know... I was just joking."

But was I? My perception of alpha packs that were in the limelight was a pretty negative one. It was probably why I had such a bad reaction to Beck at first.

"I get why you would think that about us, and we definitely have had our fair share of women, but it's not like we were sleeping with new chicks every week." He backed toward the two bikes on the far side of the garage.

"How many is a fair share? Did you all sleep with the same one?" I shouldn't have asked because all it was going to do was make me jealous as fuck.

Kane grabbed a helmet and handed it to me before going to a blue Harley-Davidson street cruiser. I knew nothing about bikes, but it looked faster than a regular Harley but wasn't a crotch rocket.

"I haven't kept count. We sometimes share a woman. Sometimes we pair off. Sometimes solo." He threw his leg over the bike and looked back at me. "Don't look so pissed off about it. None of them matter."

"But that's where you're wrong. They should matter. They're human beings." I got on the bike behind Kane and wrapped my arms around him as he manually backed out of the garage. "Omegas aren't allowed to explore their sexuality with other people. It's unfair."

Kane turned and flipped down my visor. "I agree. Hold on tight."

I was already hotter than hell in the leather jacket, and the visor down just made it worse, but it was better to suffer for a short time than to end up getting road rash if we crashed.

He pulled out of the gate and headed toward the main road. About five houses down, he pointed, and

KNOT SO PERFECT OMEGA

without him even saying anything, I knew he was pointing out N'Pact's house.

It was mostly hidden behind a brick wall, trees, and hedges, but I memorized the number to look up when we got back to the house. Kara would be so jealous to know I lived so close I could simply go over and ask for a cup of sugar.

I should have asked him where we were going because, ten minutes later, we were on the freeway, dodging traffic. I'd never been scared on the back of a bike before but going between cars made me fear for my life.

Kane must have sensed my unease because his body started vibrating with a deep purr. I thought at first it was just the vibrations of the bike until we had to stop when someone was blocking the path between the lanes.

These men just knew what I needed from them, and for someone who hadn't thought they needed all the attention and comfort a pack would bring, I was soaking it up. I'd been naive to think I'd want to spend any more time alone with no alphas to take care of me.

Not just take care of me in a biological or financial sense, but take care of me emotionally. I lucked out matching with this pack because they didn't have to do the little things they'd done for me so far like taking me on bike rides, shopping with me, and helping me put together my quilt for my nest.

They didn't have to rearrange major parts of their house to accommodate what I needed and wanted. But they had. They'd exceeded my expectations, and as hard as it was to admit it to myself, I couldn't wait to see what the future brought.

Tears sprang to my eyes, and I let them fall inside the privacy of my helmet. I was going to do it; I was going to tell them I wanted to stay and bond with them.

Maybe half an hour later, Kane pulled off the freeway and drove a few more minutes before coming to a stop in a parking lot at the beach. I'd stopped crying and decided to wait to tell them until after their playoff game. They didn't need the distraction of thinking about bonding with me while kicking some Alphaball butt.

It was still sunny out, but the sun was starting to sink, and I was excited to watch the sunset so close to the water. The view from the pack's house was great and all, but no matter what they said, it wasn't really an ocean view. Seeing a speck of water occasionally when the sky wasn't smoggy was not a view.

Kane tapped my knee and I got off the bike, taking my helmet off and unzipping the jacket. I was dying a little and felt like I was burning up. It was probably in the high sixties, but with the sun and the leather, my body felt like it was at least ninety.

"You okay?" Kane asked, a concerned expression on his face as he took off his own helmet and jacket.

"Yeah, just hot." I handed him my jacket and he shoved it into a small compartment under where I had been sitting. "Safety first, right?"

"Right... I guess I'm just used to it. You're a little flushed." He put his hand to my cheek. "Jesus, you're burning up."

I didn't want to confess I was crying. "I'll just rinse my face off in a bathroom."

Looking around, I saw a public bathroom and started to walk toward it. Kane cursed and then jogged to catch up with me. "Kayla, you can't just walk off by yourself."

"The bathroom is right there." I pointed as if he couldn't see the sign in bold letters. "I'll scream if I need you."

He was holding one of the helmets still and rolled his eyes. "You're going to be the death of me. If you aren't back in one minute, I'm coming in after you."

I waved him off and walked the few hundred feet to the bathroom. It smelled horrible and was dirty as hell. I looked in the cloudy mirror and was a little surprised at how red my cheeks were.

Shaking my head, because it was ludicrous to think it was my heat—it wasn't due for several more weeks and it wouldn't turn me the color of a lobster—I turned on the water and sniffed it to make sure it wasn't gross before splashing my face.

The relief was instant, and I splashed myself a few more times before walking out with my face dripping wet. There weren't any paper towels, and I wasn't about to dry my face with toilet paper or stick it under the hand dryer.

There were two men talking with Kane, but he had his eyes locked on me the entire short distance back to him. As soon as I was within grabbing distance, he wrapped his arm around my waist and tugged me into his side.

"I didn't know your pack had taken an omega." One of the men gave me a quick once-over, his eyes looking closely at my neck. He couldn't see my shoulder, though, so there was no way he could tell if we'd bonded yet.

Kane stiffened the slightest bit. They were both alphas, I could tell from their scents wafting on the breeze. But even if I couldn't smell them, there was a way an alpha carried himself that alerted omegas to their presence.

We were outside, and there was a slight breeze, so hopefully they couldn't tell we weren't bonded yet. Something changed with an omega's scent once the bond took place. My scent wouldn't change for me or the pack, but other alphas would be able to detect a kind of warning pheromone.

"Well, it was nice to meet you. Good luck tomorrow." The second man nodded respectfully and then grabbed his friend's arm and steered him away.

Kane breathed a heavy breath out and kissed my temple. "I was a little concerned about the one when he stared at your neck. You feel cooler?"

KNOT SO PERFECT OMEGA

"A little. It doesn't help when you're pawing at me." I pulled away and grabbed his hand. "Now, where are these food trucks?"

Maybe stuffing my stomach with food would stop the ache that had started to build there.

♡ 179 ♡

CHAPTER SEVENTEEN

Kane

My whole body was tense as we walked through the crowds of people at the food truck event. I'd thought it would be fine, but my alpha instincts were going haywire, and all I wanted to do was throw Kayla over my shoulder and get her home.

I held on tightly to her hand as we stopped in the center of the large picnic and grassy area the food trucks were arranged around. "Where do you want to start?"

There were at least twenty different options and the aromas filling the air drowned out any other scents. It should have comforted me not to have to worry about Kayla's scent catching the nose of another pack, but not being able to catch her scent also made me paranoid about losing her.

Kayla looked around, her bottom lip between her teeth. "I don't know." Was that a hint of a whine in her voice?

"We'll get some food and then go sit on the beach. Lots of people make me antsy too." I led her toward a Mexican food truck since I knew she loved tacos and corn.

"Oh, they have esquites with Flamin' Hot Cheetos crumbled on top!" She was lifting to her tiptoes to see the menu that ran down the side of the truck. "They have a taco sampler. Let's get that too."

"I've never tried esquites. Seems disgusting." I made a face, and she hit me playfully on the chest. "I mean, mayonnaise in corn?"

"There's some kind of sour cream in it sometimes too. Don't knock it until you try it. You pick out a food truck too." Her mood that had seemed on edge had made an abrupt one-eighty. She was now chipper and had an excited glow in her eyes.

"Are you sure you're okay?" I put the back of my hand to her cheek, and it didn't feel any warmer than usual.

"I'm fine. I just haven't been around this many people in a long time and that motorcycle ride was hot... in more ways than one." She winked, and we moved forward in the line. "I've been worried about Kara too. Maybe once we bond, we can have her for a visit. I'm sure Omega Protective Services will allow it as long as we're taking all the precautions."

"Once we bond." I turned her toward me and grabbed the side of her neck gently, bringing her forehead to mine. "You mean it?"

"Yes." She sniffled like she was about to cry, and I kissed her gently before pulling her closer to wrap my arms around her.

"You don't understand how unbelievably happy you just made me." I nuzzled into her neck and didn't care that the gap between us and the people in front of us was widening.

"I don't want to tell the pack yet. I want you guys to focus on Alphaball." She didn't realize how hard it was going to be for me to keep it a secret, but she did have a point.

If she told the other three the night before playoffs, there was probably no way we'd get on the plane to go to Portland in the morning. A bond, especially a new one, would make us incredibly territorial and protective of her.

After ordering and getting our food from the Mexican food truck and a barbecue truck, we walked the short distance back to the parking lot and then to the beach where we found an empty bench.

We laid out the cartons between us, and she grabbed the bowl of corn and popped the lid off, lifting it to her nose. "I've loved this stuff forever and used to wish when I perfumed I'd smell like it." She took a large spoonful and ate it. "Fuck, that's good. Not better than my dad's, but it'll do."

She handed me the bowl and I sniffed it. "I'm glad you didn't smell like this." I took a bite and didn't hate it but didn't love it either.

"It's not for everyone." She lifted the plate of tacos and took a bite out of one. "You know those two guys from the parking lot have been watching us this whole time?"

"What? Where?" My focus had been on her for the past few minutes, so I hadn't noticed anything out of the ordinary.

"It's probably nothing, but they were in the food truck area and are now sitting on the tailgate of their truck in the parking lot." She handed me the taco plate. "I can save the esquites and throw it in their faces. Maybe some Hot Cheeto dust will get in their eyes."

I took a bite of the taco, turning my head to the side so I could glance in the direction of the parking lot. Sure as shit, those assholes were watching us.

They were fans of the Killer Gnomes, but I could feel at least one of their demeanors change when Kayla had come back from the bathroom. For now, they were keeping their distance, and luckily, it had seemed only the one had taken interest in my omega.

Or I was just thinking about it too much and they were just out enjoying the evening like we were.

"They aren't going to try anything with so many people around." Kayla grabbed the to-go plate of barbecue and scooted next to me. "You're growling."

"Damn right I am." I turned a bit and glared at the

two men. They weren't even looking at us now, and I wanted to kick myself for overreacting. It's not like people hadn't stared and watched me before, I just had precious cargo with me now.

"Hey. Let's enjoy ourselves." She grabbed a rib and held it out to me. "Here, open."

"You're going to feed me? I should be the one feeding you." My attention was back on her and the rib that was floating in front of my face. I took a bite as she held onto it.

"Are you ready for your game tomorrow?" She handed off the rest of the rib and grabbed one for herself.

"Yeah. We're as ready as we're going to be. Last year we were ready, but Rylan broke his arm in our second game."

"You guys should have alternate players, or does that not work when you're playing as a pack?"

"A lot of teams do have a relief player, but they're almost all a part of the pack. We never could find a fifth alpha that fit in with all of us. We agreed earlier on we were willing to deal with any negative impact of only being a quad. Last year was one of those times." I shrugged. "We have so much other stuff going on business-wise that not winning the championship isn't the end of the world, but it would push our pack to billionaire status because we'd get a lot more endorsements plus prize money."

Her eyes widened. "Billionaires? As in nine zeros?"

"Yup. Beck has been working nonstop since starting college to never be without money again. It's tiring at times, but we also have some big philanthropic projects in the works."

"Are you guys sure you don't want to trade me in for my sister? I'm not sure I'm cut out to be a billionaire pack's omega." She looked out at the ocean.

She had barbecue sauce on her cheek, and I swiped at it with my thumb. "You're perfect. Don't let how we ended up together take away from what we have."

"But you don't even know if you'd have a stronger connection with her."

Why was she talking like this? A few minutes ago, she'd been talking about bonding with us and becoming a member of the pack, and now she was offering us her sister?

"We do know, Kayla. You deserve happiness just as much as your sister does. Don't let your guilt over the situation ruin this for you." I took her chin between my forefinger and thumb and turned her face toward me. "We might not have seemed like we cared about having an omega at first... we honestly didn't until you came into our lives."

"Sorry, I'm being stupid." Her brows furrowed. "I guess I'm just worried about Kara. She's always been the solid twin and now she seems so... lost."

"You're a good sister." I gave her a quick kiss and then gestured to the food on our laps. "We should finish eating so we can take a stroll while the sun sets."

"Look at you being all romantic." Her mood did another complete one-eighty and she dove right back into her food.

My alpha instincts were screaming at me that she was going to start her heat. All the signs were there— abrupt shifts in mood, hot flashes, uncertainty—but she said she wasn't and she knew her body best.

My alarm went off at six in the morning, and I grabbed my phone to turn it off. I hadn't had the best night's sleep and the temptation to go back to bed was strong, but I could nap on our flight.

After Kayla and I had finished our food the night before and walked on the beach, we'd come home and watched a movie. She'd seemed completely normal when we'd parted ways to go to bed, but I wanted to check on her before we headed to the airport.

Apparently, everyone else had the same idea as I did because Beck, Rio, and Rylan were all coming from their bedrooms. It was eerie how we sometimes didn't even need to communicate to know what we needed to do as a pack.

I'd wanted to sleep with her, but she'd insisted we all needed our beauty sleep so we could be at our best for our playoff game later that evening. I couldn't have cared less about the playoffs at that point.

"I slept like shit," Beck muttered as we walked across

the hallway to the primary suite. "Jesus, I can smell her already."

"I told you guys she was going into heat." I reached the door first and opened it, a plume of her perfume smacking me right in the nose and the effects going straight to my dick.

The room was dark besides light coming in through the open French door. My skin prickled from the chill in the air.

Beck shoved past me, going to the side of the bed closest to the door that Kayla had made her spot. He sat down gently and pulled the covers back just enough so we could all see her.

She was beautiful when she slept and the peace on her face was confusing since I'd half expected her to be panting and sweaty from a heat spike.

"Kayla, wake up." Beck leaned down and pressed his lips to hers.

She groaned and rolled over, grabbing a pillow and tugging it under the blankets. "Go away."

"We're going to leave soon... say the word and we'll stay." I knelt on the bed and tugged the pillow away from her so she couldn't hide. "You slept with the door open all night and you're perfuming more than ever."

She rolled onto her back, her fists going to her eyes and rubbing. "Huh?" She sniffed. "I'm fine."

"Did you stop taking your pills?" Beck started stroking her arm. "If you're about to start your heat..."

"I'm still taking them." She let her hands drop to the

blankets covering her. "Even if I am about to start my heat, it'll be mild. Nothing I can't handle."

"Maybe she should come with us." Rylan went and shut the door to the balcony. "She can stay in the hotel suite, and we can post some guards outside."

"If she's about to be in heat, it's not safe for her to travel." Rio adjusted himself in his boxers. "We either need to withdraw from competition or-"

"No." Kayla sat up, the covers dropping to show her flushed, naked chest which she quickly remedied by pulling a sheet to cover herself. "You guys have been working your asses off for this. I always run hotter during my heats. I don't think that esquites agreed with me either, but I'll be fine."

Fine usually didn't mean she was actually fine.

"Beck, where's your thermometer?" I asked, heading for the bathroom.

"Left drawer."

I grabbed it and came back, ready to stick it in her ear. She batted me away with an annoyed whine. "Let me go back to sleep. I don't need my temperature taken."

"Let him take your temperature." Beck's alpha bark had the boner I'd popped quickly deflating. "You're as stubborn as a mule."

Falling back onto the pillows, she glared up at Beck as she turned her head to the side. "I'll show you a mule when I kick you in the balls."

"Do it." Beck was back to stroking her arm, and the only reason I knew he was talking to me and not telling Kayla to kick him was because he was looking at me.

Too bad. I would have liked to see her put him in his place.

I put the thermometer in her ear and pressed the button, pulling it out when it beeped. "Ninety-nine point eight. That's a little elevated."

"Kayla." Beck put his hand on her cheek. "Say the word and we'll stay."

"I don't need you guys to stay. What I need is some sleep." She pulled the covers up sharply over her head, forcing Beck's hand away and hiding herself from our concerned stares.

Beck growled and stood. "You'll call us if anything changes. Do you understand?"

"Yes. Now go before you miss your flight." She didn't uncover her head and we all shared a brief look before leaving the room. We didn't need to correct her that the plane could wait.

"What are we going to do?" I started pacing in the hall. "We can't leave her."

"She wants us to go. We'll go." Beck strode back toward his new room.

Rio had been awfully quiet, and I turned to him. "What do you think we should do?"

"Honestly? She's been going through heats for years, and if she says she's fine for us to leave..." He seemed unsure and rubbed a hand over his face. "We can come back right after the game."

"I don't know. It feels wrong to leave her when she's going into her heat. I don't care if she's been handling it before now." With one last look at her door, I followed Rio and Rylan back toward our rooms.

"It's not how we feel about it. She's fiercely independent, and as much as it goes against some of our instincts, if we don't listen to her, we could ruin things with her. Let's go, like she wants, and use this as fuel to win." Rylan might have been the youngest, but sometimes his words made so much sense.

He was right that she had her own way of dealing with her suppressed heats, and if she didn't want us around then we had to respect that.

Even if it felt wrong.

CHAPTER EIGHTEEN

Kayla

Light streamed through the windows, and I whimpered, throwing the blankets off me and letting the cool air from the ceiling fan chill my sweaty skin. I hated that I had the urge to lie naked in the middle of the bed and also pile every blanket known to man on top of me.

I blindly reached for my phone, knocking it off the nightstand and onto the floor. With a groan, I rolled over, letting my arm hang over the side of the bed but having no energy to actually grab it.

My entire body ached, and my panties were soaked through with slick. What I needed was a cold shower and an orgasm. I should have known my heat was going to start, but it made no sense when for years I'd been consistent with timing and intensity.

And this? This was much worse than any of my suppressed heats.

"Different environment, Kayla," I muttered, trying to reassure myself that this was normal and all I needed was to take care of myself and the worst of it would pass in a few hours.

But I'd been saying that since the night before and now there was an ache building in my core that I feared would turn into cramping.

I shuddered at the thought of the pain from the heat when I'd first emerged. It had been so awful I'd been ready to go find any alpha off the street to fuck me to take the pain away.

I managed to get my body to cooperate and scooped my phone off the floor before sitting up on the edge of the bed.

"Jesus, how many times did they call and text?" I pulled up the group text and replied that I had just woken up and was doing okay. It was noon and they were set to play around four.

I turned on some music and opened the nightstand where I had my collection of toys. I was in desperate need of a shower, so I grabbed the cock with a suction cup. Fucking myself in the shower seemed like a good plan.

Twenty minutes later, I was showered, and my need for cock was satiated for the time being. I pulled on a light pair of pajamas and stuck a pad in my underwear so I didn't have to change every five minutes.

An omega's heat was very similar to a beta's period, except instead of blood, we secreted a lot of pheromone-filled fluid to attract an alpha and to help us take his knot. I didn't know what a period felt like, but an omega could be hospitalized and even die from their heat if they didn't take care of themselves properly.

I pulled out the drawer with my toys and emptied it into the center of a blanket. I didn't want to have to come back upstairs again when my legs felt like jelly. I should have already been in my nest, but I hadn't wanted the guys to worry about me.

My phone pinged a few times with messages.

Beck: *Text us every hour to let us know how you're doing.*

Rio: *One of us will take our phone out to the field when we play.*

Me: *I just took a shower and had a pretty good orgasm. I'm feeling great.*

Kane: *Don't tell us that. What did you use?*

Me: *The nine-inch girthy one with suction cup for the shower. It took a while to get into a groove with it, but I was screaming out your names as I clenched around it.*

Rylan: *Don't get us hard right before our game.*

Me: *Your game is several hours away.*

Beck: *Are you in heat?*

Me: *It's fine. I want you guys to focus on winning.*

I gathered the ends of the blanket and slung it over my shoulder like Santa's bag. "Ho, ho, ho. Maybe I'm not doing fine. I'm talking to myself."

After dropping the blanket and toys off in my nest, I

went to the kitchen to find food. I was already starting to feel a need build between my legs again. I'd barely come fifteen minutes before, and a tendril of worry wrapped around my chest.

There were already waters in the former game room turned nest. Now I just needed food, so I didn't have to come back out again. Getting a reusable grocery bag from the pantry, I filled it up with snacks and then made myself a sandwich.

The first cramp hit me halfway to the nest, and I nearly dropped everything as I hunched over, a flood of wetness pooling between my legs. With a whimper, I hobbled the rest of the way, my clit throbbing and my pad feeling like it had been soaked through already.

I was grateful the pack had moved their gaming equipment and desks out. Now there was the loveseat with a small coffee table shoved in the corner, a television, and two heat mattresses piled with pillows and blankets. There was a small minifridge too, which was where I set the bag of snacks and put the sandwich inside since my appetite was gone.

Another cramp pulled at my core, urging me to seek relief.

It was going to be a long afternoon.

My shaking finger hovered over the call button, my breaths coming in pants as another cramp took hold. It felt like something was ripping me apart from inside, and no matter what I did, nothing seemed to help it.

It had been hours, and with each orgasm, the pain returned sooner and sooner. Not even the inflatable knot on a dildo was giving me any kind of relief. My vision was so blurry I couldn't even text.

I finally got the nerve to press the button, not knowing who else to call. My mom was going to freak out, I just knew it, but I needed some reassurance that I wasn't going to die.

"Hi, hun. How are you?"

Just hearing her voice set me off, and I let out a sob. "Mommy."

"Kayla, what's wrong?" The masculine voices in the background abruptly silenced.

"It hurts so bad. Why does it hurt?" I wasn't sure if she would be able to understand my blubbering so I tried to calm down. "How do I make it stop?"

"You're hurt? What's wrong?" I heard a growl and then my mom whined. "Give me that back!"

"Kay, what's going on?" The last person I wanted to talk to was one of my fathers.

"I'm in heat," I whimpered. "I need Mom. Please put her back on the phone."

"You're in heat and those fuckers left you?" he roared. There were a lot of threats and growls I couldn't decipher.

"Hun, it's me again." She slammed a door, and the

growling went away. "Aren't you still on your suppressants?"

"Yes." I sucked in a sharp breath as a cramp made my entire vagina ache. "I don't know why it's so bad. What do I do?"

"If you even missed one dose, it might be the full thing, hun. Your body knows when there are alphas around."

"I didn't miss a dose," I said through clenched teeth. "I take them like clockwork."

"Do they know? That you're in heat?"

I couldn't stop another sob from escaping. "No."

"Then what you need to do is call them this instant. They haven't played yet, but the two teams up right now are almost done."

"What do I do until they get back?" I sat up and a wave of dizziness forced me to lie back down.

"A cold shower or bath will help, although the bath will get warm quickly. Also, keeping an artificial knot inflated inside you should help a little. You didn't have any symptoms it was coming on?" She didn't sound as worried as I felt, and it was helping to relax me a little.

"I did... but I didn't think it was going to escalate into this." I grabbed my dildo with an inflatable knot. "I'm going to go. Thank you, Mom."

"Call them, Kayla. I mean it. Check in with me later, okay? I love you."

"Love you too." I hung up with her and stared at my phone. "Fuck."

I called Beck's number, and it rang and rang before going to voicemail. "Hey. I uh..." I cleared my throat, trying to hold back the whine. "Can you come home? It's um... fuck. It's hitting me hard, and I just need... please."

Jesus, I couldn't even formulate words anymore.

I hung up and pulled up the voice memo feature for the group text. This time, knowing all of them would hear it, I couldn't bite back the whine in my voice. "I thought I was going to be fine... please come home." I started crying and wanted to throw my phone. "It hurts."

They were going to lose their shit hearing the message, and I wouldn't blame them if they didn't come. I'd sent them away when they'd been willing to sacrifice the rest of their season for me.

I didn't deserve them.

My phone landed on the floor as another cramp wracked my body, and I clutched my lower abdomen. I grabbed the knotted dildo again and shoved it inside me, the relief minor. It didn't even feel good, but I pressed the button to inflate the artificial knot.

The shower seemed so far away, but I was burning up and should listen to my mom. I rolled off the mattress and crawled to the bathroom. The knot was easing the cramping, but like everything else I'd tried, it wasn't going to last long.

I didn't have the energy to keep filling up the bathtub when it got warm from my body heat, so I climbed in and turned on the shower. The cool water was an instant relief, and I shuddered as it pelted my skin.

I curled up on the floor, my relieved whimper echoing in the tub. I was going to be fine. I'd just stay under the water and wait for the pain to pass.

CHAPTER NINETEEN

Beck

By some small fucking miracle, we'd pulled off a win and were moving on to the championships. We hadn't been at our best, our minds on Kayla most of the time, but we were so good this season that didn't matter.

I'd checked my phone several times, but I hadn't heard a peep from her, even though I'd told her to text us every hour. Rio said that was a bit overreaching, and maybe it was, but I couldn't stop the worry from eating me.

She should have at least texted once to check in by now. It was nearly eight in the evening. I understood she wanted independence, but she needed to understand that our alpha instincts needed somewhat frequent assurance she was okay.

I was just about to text her and say as much when Brian came up beside me and nudged me with his fucking elbow. The urge to punch him in the goddamn face was so strong I nearly broke my phone from squeezing it so tight.

We hadn't seen him since the practice when I'd fired him. But I couldn't legally fire him until the end of the season when his contract was up. Sports teams fired coaches and managers midseason all the time, but there wasn't any reason I could share with our lawyer as to why.

It was the last time I ever trusted anyone with some important aspect of my life. So far, we'd been lucky that the people we worked with took the utmost care in doing their jobs.

Brian's mistake had at least worked out in the end.

"Will you stop checking your damn phone? We have an interview in five minutes in the media room. I need you to be focused." Brian was walking next to me as we went through the tunnel toward our private locker room.

"We? *You* don't have an interview." I went back to looking at my phone because... fuck him.

Brian let out a huff like he was trying to blow something down. "There's no reception out here anyway."

As soon as the words left his mouth and we stepped into the locker room where Rio, Kane, and Rylan already were, my phone pinged with notifications. I didn't need to listen to know they weren't good.

The growls, anxiety, and anger coming from my three packmates all at once told me all I needed to know.

"Out." I turned to Brian and put my hand in the center of his chest, pushing him back toward the door.

"What? We need to quickly debrief before you go to your interview." Brian ducked out from under my arm.

"Cancel it. Now, *get out.*" I rarely used my alpha bark during business, but Brian was long overdue to be barked at.

Brian paled, and he backed toward the door. "Beckett, what the fu-"

"Get out or I will punch you in the goddamn face!" My bark growl combo did the trick, and he ran out with his tail between his legs.

The loud bang of a fist hitting metal rang out in the locker room, and I spun around, finding Kane punching the shit out of the siding on his locker. "This is all my fucking fault!"

Rio grabbed his arm before he could do any more damage. "Stop."

"What the fuck happened?" I glanced at my phone to find a voicemail and voice message from Kayla. "Fuck. There wasn't any reception in the stadium, and I didn't even realize!"

"She's in heat. We need to go." Rylan was already out of his uniform and pulling on a pair of sweatpants. "I'll call and see if we can get on a flight in the next hour."

I toed off the cleats and brought my phone to my ear

to listen to the voicemail she'd sent hours ago. "Hey. I uh... Can you come home? It's um... fuck. It's hitting me hard, and I just need... please."

The pain in her voice fucking broke me.

I quickly changed out of my uniform, my mind on one thing and one thing only: getting to Kayla.

"She's not answering her phone." Rio had his bag already slung over his shoulder. "Our driver is waiting for us outside the athlete exit and we'll stop by the hotel to grab our stuff and check out before going to the airport."

"There's no time for that." Kane still didn't have a shirt or shoes on but was heading for the door.

Rylan put himself between Kane and the door, his ear plastered to his phone. "Well, when can you fucking get us a plane or a helicopter? Approval? Do you know who we fucking are?"

We were losing our minds and I needed to take charge before one of us did something really stupid.

I tugged on my shirt and then grabbed the phone from Rylan. "This is Beckett Thomas. We need something approved for an emergency. What can you do for us? Are there commercial flights available? We are going to Burbank or LAX."

Buying our own damn private plane was now moving to the top of my priority list.

"They are booked solid. The best I can do is three hours from now. That's when we'll have a plane available and can get it here." The man on the phone sounded

KNOT SO PERFECT OMEGA

like he would rather be talking to anyone else other than pissed off alphas. "Will that be good for you?"

"It'll have to be." I pinched the bridge of my nose, trying to think of any other way we could get to Kayla faster.

"I recommend getting here as soon as possible in case we're able to accommodate you. There's just four of you?"

"Yes. We'll be there soon. Thank you." I hung up and shoved the phone into Rylan's chest. "Calm down. We all just need to calm down. Put on your clothes and shoes. We'll swing by the hotel on the way, and then hopefully something will be available sooner."

I didn't bark, but my voice was sure and firm, which was what this pack needed if we wanted to make it to Kayla in one piece. The last thing we needed was for one of us to lose it and end up on a no-fly list or worse, arrested.

We finished changing as fast as possible and headed out the athlete's entrance. Since we were supposed to be in a press conference about our win, no one was waiting to snap pictures or ask us questions, so we made it into the SUV with no fanfare.

Our stop at the hotel was quick, just long enough to throw our shit in our bags and check out before we were back in the car and on the way to the airport.

We all kept calling Kayla, but she didn't answer. I didn't think I could wait, at best, two or three hours to make sure she was okay.

"We need to get cameras installed in the house as soon as her heat is over. Let's call Michelle and see if she'll go over and check on her." Rio was scrolling through his phone as if the answers to all our problems were inside it.

Michelle was our publicist, but even so, I didn't trust anyone to go into our house when our omega was in heat. "No. What good will that do?"

"What if she's hurt?" Kane had been dead silent since the locker room.

"Then what? They cart her off to the hospital where we can't protect her? She's probably sleeping or left her phone somewhere." I was sure of one thing, no one was touching our girl but us. "Her heat just started today, or maybe last night. She isn't going to die."

I didn't think.

I blocked out all the emotions coming through the pack bond we shared, unable to handle them any longer along with my own.

The SUV pulled into the parking lot of the private jet terminal of the airport and we piled out, grabbed our bags from the back, and rushed inside. Once we got on a plane, it would take about two hours to get to L.A. and then another twenty or thirty minutes to get to our house if we landed in Burbank.

It was nine o'clock, so the terminal was empty besides us. I marched right up to the counter and waited patiently for the man to look up from his computer, but

I only had so much patience. And that patience was two seconds.

"Excuse me. I'm Beckett Thomas."

The guy finally looked up and glanced over at the rest of my pack, who had moved into the waiting area. "That was fast. I have some good news and some bad news."

I couldn't stop the growl from coming out. "What's the bad news?"

He didn't seem put off at all by my growl. "The good news is there's a plane landing in an hour. The bad news is it needs fuel and some minor maintenance before it can take off again, so the best we can do on such short notice is a departure time of eleven-thirty."

"What about this plane that's right outside? It looks like they are getting ready to leave. We can pay whatever is necessary." Rio came to stand next to me at the counter and I was grateful because I was about to bite the guy's head off.

"I'm afraid that's a private plane that isn't part of our fleet. We have coffee, water, and snacks while you wait."

Rio tugged me away as my fist curled around the handle of my suitcase. "We can have Omega Protective Services check in on her. It's going to be fine."

I sat down heavily next to Kane and put my head in my hands, feeling defeated. My job was to protect my pack, and right then, I was doing a shit job of it. Maybe we should call OPS to check on Kayla. But then what?

They take her away because we couldn't take care of her?

Honking came from the parking lot and a party bus pulled up outside the door. Four women came down the steps dressed to the nines in minidresses and high heels that would break a neck.

They stood off to the side giggling and squealing, and then I saw why. Payne, Alvaro, Cal, and Tate of N'Pact came down the steps.

I personally didn't see their appeal, but women and a lot of men went nuts over them and they ate it up like it was a feast laid before them. We'd met them a few times when they'd invited us to parties at their house, but none of us were into dealing with the type of betas that followed them around.

"I am not in the mood to deal with a bunch of knot-tyboppers right now." Rylan slumped further in his seat. "Maybe they won't notice us."

"Oh my God! It's the Killer Gnomes!" one of the women shrieked as soon as they walked in the door.

"My ears are bleeding," Kane muttered. "Shoot me now."

"Do you think they just picked those chicks up from the stadium?" Rio crossed his arms and watched them all gather around the check-in desk with the band.

"Probably." I stood to pace, unable to sit still, and tried calling Kayla again. It went straight to voicemail. What did that mean? Had she turned it off? Did the battery die?

"All right, ladies, take a seat in the beta area. We'll board in ten minutes." Alvaro, the leader of their pack, gestured to the other side of the waiting room.

There wasn't a beta area in this small terminal.

I shook my head as they came and sat in the seats across from where we were sitting, eyeing us with curiosity. We should have been over the moon at our win, but we looked like a bunch of depressed assholes ready to snap at any moment.

My phone rang and Brian's name flashed on the screen. I wanted to decline his call but also wanted him to leave us alone for the foreseeable future. "What?"

"You're canceling all of your media for tomorrow?" He was pissed and not a single ounce of me cared. "You have contractual obligations to uphold. What about the photoshoot for *Alpha Heat Magazine*? It's for the cover!"

"If they can't understand that we need to get home to our omega, they can fuck off. We're also canceling our practices."

"You barely won your games today. We need to be on the practice field every day until the championship game."

"That's the stupidest thing I've ever heard come out of your mouth. Do you want us to lose? We need rest, and we also need to be with our omega."

"Oh, so now you want her. Is that why you've run off? What did she do? Spread her legs and now all of a sudden you love her?"

I growled, the chatter from the band and the girls

they brought going silent. "You don't get to talk about her like that."

"Why? She's affecting something we've worked hard for all season! Is she in heat? Is that what this is?"

"That's none of your fucking business. The championship doesn't matter if she needs us!" I was clutching the phone so tight I swear I heard a crack. "We'll forfeit if we need to."

"No, no! This is great news! Her starting her heat is perfect to give us the extra boost we need to seal the win. The championships are in Los Angeles, so you wouldn't have to be gone from her for long. What would be even better is if you bonded with her."

Was he actually fucking serious?

"I'm hanging up now." I hung up and threw my phone in my seat. "Motherfucker is going to get punched in the face."

"I'll hold him for you," Rio agreed.

"You guys having a rough time with your new omega?" Tate seemed unsure if he should ask, but the kindness in his blue eyes didn't go unnoticed by me. I couldn't be mad that he was asking.

"Just trying to get to her. She um... unexpectedly went into heat. We can't get ahold of her and there's no plane available until almost midnight." I stopped at the window, looking out at the tarmac. "There isn't a chance you're flying back to L.A., is there? Maybe we can catch a ride."

"There are only eight seats," Payne, the one member

of N'Pact that didn't quite fit with his black hair in his eyes, black eyeliner and nails, and tattoos covering most of his visible skin said. "But I'm down to kick the chicks off the flight. They're hot, but too damn loud and lacking some brain cells from too much hairspray."

"Should the celibate one really be making these kinds of decisions for the pack?" Cal, who had a crazy glint in his eye, turned to Alvaro. "Let's vote."

Alvaro rolled his eyes and stood, walking toward the girls. "Ladies, I'm afraid we have bad news. There's just not room for you on the flight anymore."

"Aww, but Alvie." One of the women whined like pretending to be an omega would help her cause.

"What did you just call me?" he growled, stepping closer to her. She shrank back in her seat. "My name is Alvaro to the likes of you. Now get out of here before I call our security."

I didn't know what the hell that was about, but I wasn't about to ask.

"Fucking groupies," Payne grumbled.

"You don't know how much this means to us. Thank you." I extended my hand to Alvaro as he walked back toward us. "We owe you."

Alvaro shook my hand and then reached for my bag. "Come on. Let's get you home to your omega."

CHAPTER TWENTY

Rio

The two-hour flight back to Los Angeles felt ten times as long as it was. I'd really been trying to not think about my past since Kayla had arrived, but now that she was in heat, old wounds were coming to the surface.

None of my packmates knew about my past before them, and they never asked. It had never felt like the right time to talk about it, but now with my stomach knotting and my throat threatening to cut off my air supply, I needed the reassurance it wasn't about to happen again.

I'd barely survived the pain at nineteen. I didn't think I could survive it again.

After the plane had landed, N'Pact let us use their limo while they called for another ride. Our pack had been stuck in our own heads the whole flight, so we hadn't talked to them much besides to express our gratitude multiple times.

We were about ten minutes from the house when I finally grew the balls to talk to them about the anxiety and fear I knew they could feel through our bond. They probably thought I was concerned about Kayla, and while I was, I knew she was going to be fine.

I rolled up the privacy window between the back and front of the limo and three sets of eyes turned to stare at me in question. "I need to tell you guys something that I've been keeping from you."

Beck crossed his arms over his chest and nodded his head. I could feel a tendril of disappointment from him, even though he had no clue what I was about to tell them.

"Go on, man. What is it?" Kane leaned forward, his arms across his legs.

I stared out the window, trying to figure out where to start. "You all know I come from a very traditional, wealthy family. Part of that tradition is to build packs before their children even emerge."

"Shit." Rylan was next to me and put his hand on my shoulder in support.

"I was part of a pack before I met you guys. None of us liked each other, but we did the bond and tried to make things work because that was what our families expected of us." The memories of the first few months of our bond were painful to recall.

There was so much fighting for the leader position, which was one of the reasons I forced myself not to give in to my instincts to fight Beck.

"Then the omega promised to our pack came of age after her two years at a boarding school. She'd already been forced to go off her suppressants, so by the time she moved in with us she was already starting her heat." A tear slipped out and I let it fall onto my shirt. "We got her through it, but then when it was time to bond with her…"

"You don't have to finish if it's too painful," Beck said softly, surprising the shit out of me.

"No, I need to, because as much as I've tried to pretend it's no longer stuck with me, it is." I wiped another tear from my face. "She decided she didn't want us. It fucking hurt, but then the next day she was gone and so was one of my packmates. They ran off together."

"Fuck." Kane leaned back in his seat. "That's rough."

"It took me a good year to heal enough from it to want to move on. I enrolled in school and then met you guys and it just felt right. I thought I'd have more time to reassure myself that history wasn't going to repeat itself, but here we are." I looked at each of them and hated the pity I saw on their faces.

"That's not going to happen. We're all in this together." Beck reached over and grabbed my hand. "We're brothers."

"But what if she decides she only wants one of us? There's nothing saying she can't do that." We were all seeing Kayla through rose-tinted glasses because she had quickly become everything to us, but what if the same wasn't true for her?

Kane grabbed Beck's hand and then Rylan's. We were all connected, and I felt our bond strengthen. "She is going to want all of us. She told me she wants to bond with us... she was just waiting until after our championship."

"And you didn't tell us?" Beck's frown deepened.

"She didn't want me to. She let it slip the other day." Kane shrugged, not giving a shit. "She's ours and we're hers. There's no question about that."

His reassurance meant the world to me, and my shoulders relaxed for what felt like the first time in days. "I'm sorry I didn't tell you guys."

"You had your reasons, but know that you don't need to go through things alone. I know we aren't the mushy feelings type of pack, but we're here for you." Rylan moved his hand from my shoulder and took my other hand. "I have a confession since we're having a moment here as a pack."

My eyes narrowed slightly. "You are the most open of all of us. What could you possibly be hiding?"

Rylan gave me a withering glare, but through our bond, I could only feel happiness seeping through the layer of worry that had settled there over Kayla.

The limo turned down our street and we all waited for Rylan to share. Right as the car pulled to a stop in front of our gates, he decided to speak with a heavy sigh.

"I wore a butt plug during our game, and it gave me an extra pep in my step. You should all consider getting your own sets so Kayla can-"

"Absolutely fucking not." Beck let go of everyone's hands and he suppressed a smile. "Let's go take care of our omega."

I WAS HARDER than a rock when we made it up the front steps to the front door with our bags. The others had no clue what was about to be unleashed as soon as we opened the door, but I did.

As soon as Kane unlocked the door and it opened a crack, I could smell her perfume. It was like a punch to the gut with its slightly bitter note, signaling duress.

"Fuck me, that's potent." Kane opened the door all the way and practically stumbled inside, his cock no doubt immediately harder than stone. "Kayla?"

I dropped my bags by the door and went straight for the nest, one thing on my mind and one thing only. Beck had the same thought and was two steps behind me as I started kicking off my shoes and ripped my shirt over my head.

She'd been waiting for hours for us and I couldn't even imagine the pain she was in from needing a knot to fill her. A possessive growl came from me as I pushed open the door and found it empty.

"The bathroom." Beck shoved past me, his shoes and shirt discarded and his jeans undone.

The only light coming from the bathroom was the soft glow of a nightlight. Fear pooled in my gut as I stepped in behind Beck to find her asleep, curled in the bottom of the tub.

"Little omega, we're here." Beck stepped over the ledge of the tub and scooped her up. "She's fucking freezing."

She whimpered and tried to get closer to Beck as he stepped out and carried her into the room. "It... hurts."

I reached out and stroked her damp hair before Beck knelt on the mattress and set her down gently. "We're going to take care of you."

Her eyes were cracked open, and she looked at both of us before her eyes slid to the door and then closed again. "So cold... and hot." She shivered violently and her breaths came in soft little pants.

Fuck.

"Get undressed. She's going to need all of us tonight." I practically ripped off my slacks and boxers and yanked off my socks. "She needs the strongest alpha first."

I let that hang in the air for a minute before dropping into the bed. "Beck, get behind her. She needs all the skin-to-skin contact we can give her."

He didn't even attempt to argue, which was a rare treat. His pants were off in an instant, and I helped her sit up so he could move behind her. She relaxed back into him, sighing and spreading her legs wide.

She had a damn dildo in there, the end of it taunting me that it wasn't my cock. I grabbed it and started to ease it out of her, and she gasped. "Knot."

Batting my hands out of the way, she pressed something on the end of it and then slowly pulled it out of her.

I damn near nutted at the sight of her slick on it and at her swollen cunt waiting for my cock. "Kane and Ry, help her keep her legs bent and open."

I grabbed the dildo from her and brought it to my mouth. She sucked in a sharp breath as she watched me with heavily hooded eyes while my tongue licked the length of the fake cock.

The need to take her was so strong, I couldn't wait anymore. Beck was behind her, purring and stroking her breasts, and Rylan and Kane were getting situated on the mattress to hold her open for me.

I tossed the dildo to the side, a needy growl rumbling in my chest as I licked my lips.

"Alpha..." She panted, her hands trembling from where they rested just above her pussy. "Please."

I moved into position, and in one smooth roll of my hips, I was buried inside her. She cried out, her hands moving to the top of Beck's as he kneaded her breasts and played with her nipples.

"We're so sorry we weren't here." Beck purred in her ear. "But we're here now and we're going to take the best care of you."

My balls tingled as I began pumping in and out of

her, trying to hold myself back from being too rough. Now was not the time for me to get carried away when she was so fragile.

"Did you at least win?" she mumbled, arching a bit as I hit just the right spot inside her. "Harder. I need it harder."

"We won." Kane took the leg he had ahold of and straightened it in the air, kissing down the length of it while Rylan did the same.

I grabbed Kayla's hips and gave her what she wanted. With hard, fast snaps of my hips, I had her whimpering and crying out for us to make her come in no time at all.

Her pussy clenched around me as her orgasm took hold of her, her increased slick helping me work my inflating knot into her. I came with a roar, my eyes rolling and muscles straining as I rutted into her, trying to get in as far as possible.

We were locked together, my dick throbbing with every pulse of cum that shot into her. Her body was flushed, warmed from the touching and purrs we lavished her with.

"I'm going to put her on top of me. It'll be more comfortable." I didn't know if that was one hundred percent true, but I was ready to cuddle with her without the others being practically right on top of me.

Kane and Rylan let go, crawling away. And that was when I saw it. The butt plug.

"Rylan." I barked a laugh as I wrapped Kayla's legs

around me and leaned down to let her loop her arms around my neck.

She wrapped herself around me with weak limbs, and I lay down with her on top of me, her body going limp as soon as I was situated on the pillows.

"What?" He stood and stretched, his hard cock bouncing and the barbells running down the length glinting in the light from the hallway.

"Some things I don't need to see." Beck reached over and grabbed a washcloth from the stack on the night-stand. We'd at least been smart about preparing some things for this.

"What?" Kayla tried to lift her head, but I stroked her hair, urging her to stay still.

"Rylan is wearing a butt plug." I started purring and she melted into me. "He thinks it made him play better today."

Beck wiped Kayla's back, and I gave him a questioning look. "Her ass was rubbing against me." He finished and threw the rag in the laundry basket in the corner.

"What took you so long?" Kayla muttered against my chest before yawning. "You didn't answer. I thought you didn't care."

"There was shitty reception at the stadium. We didn't even realize... we were careless and we're sorry." I moved my hands to her back, rubbing in reassuring circles.

Kane and Rylan moved about the room taking the used dildos and vibrators into the bathroom to clean.

Beck lay next to us stroking Kayla's back, his eyes never leaving her. "Rest, little omega. Because when you wake up, we're going to make up for all the pain we put you through."

"Don't call me that…" her voice trailed off as she fell asleep on top of me.

Why we'd all denied our pack this feeling for so long weighed heavily on me, but maybe there was a reason.

Her.

CHAPTER TWENTY-ONE

Kayla

It felt like I was floating on a cloud, my mind not completely awake yet, but my body sensing the warmth and comfort around me.

I still wasn't completely sure I wasn't just hallucinating. The pain had been so bad for so long I wouldn't have been surprised if I'd forgotten to turn the cold water off and been swept away into hypothermia land.

I hated how fragile heats made me feel. With this one being full-blown and then some, I'd never felt weaker, curled up in the bathtub, waiting for my pack to come.

I was angrier at myself more than anything; I'd sent them away when, in the back of my mind, I knew something wasn't right.

The smell of something delicious broke through Rio's scent, and I lifted my head from his warm chest to sniff the air like a dog. Rio was awake, his dark brown eyes watching me as he pushed a clump of hair out of my face.

I didn't need to touch my hair to know it was a tangled mess. It had been in a sloppy bun, but with the rolling around in pain and writhing on the bathtub floor, it felt tangled as fuck.

"How are you feeling?" A line formed between Rio's eyes, and I reached up to smooth it with my thumb.

"Horny and hungry." I wiggled on top of him, seeking the friction of his cock against my clit. At some point, he must have slid out of me after his knot went down.

He groaned and rolled me over so I was under him. "Kayla, I can't begin to tell you-"

I silenced him with a kiss, not needing any more apologies. They would probably spend the rest of their lives making up for the fact that they weren't there when my heat hit.

Our tongues tangled together and the ache between my legs and in my lower belly quickly became painful. I needed another knot and I needed it now.

I heard the door open as Rio ground his dick against my clit. The bed dipped, Kane's warm smoky scent making my blood boil. There was the faint scent of bacon too, which made my stomach grumble with hunger. I hadn't eaten since our date.

Rio's lips left mine, and I whimpered from the loss of contact. But they were quickly replaced by Kane's and

Rio rolled off me so Kane could take over. I didn't know how long it had been since they'd gotten home and Rio had knotted me, but none of that mattered; I was going to need them all before I was satisfied.

Kane kissed me like he hadn't in months, and I wrapped my legs around him, pulling him closer to me. He kissed down my neck, sucking on a spot that he seemed to like the most.

"That's where you'll bite me." It wasn't a question so much as a proclamation that the spot was his to take when it was time.

"Yes." He pulled back to look into my eyes. "I'm sorry we weren't here. I should have listened to my instincts."

"No. You listened to me. That's more important sometimes." I smiled, and he chuckled, moving his lips to my nipple and sucking it between his lips. "Fuck me, that feels good."

I wanted to take things slowly but also wanted him to flip me already and pound into me. My hips moved against him, my slick coating his dick as he plucked my other nipple between his fingers.

"How do you want it, sweets?" Sweets. I liked that.

"From behind. Fucking rail me into the mattress." My voice had turned needy, and I didn't care for a single second because it seemed to light a fire in Kane's eyes to match his scent.

He bit one nipple while pinching the other, and I cried out, my cunt feeling like it was going to cramp up on me. With a pop of his lips as he released me, he moved off me and flipped me like I weighed nothing.

"Show me that ass, Kayla girl. I want to admire what I'm about to fuck." He smacked one cheek, making me squeal with delight.

Jesus, I was lost to these alphas.

I got to my knees and rested my forearms on the bed, my ass in the air, preening like a fucking peacock, and I loved every second of it. "Do you like what you see, Alpha?"

He growled deep in his throat in approval, and I wiggled my ass, presenting it to him for the taking.

"It's a tough decision whether to fuck your ass or this sexy pussy." He ran his hand over my cheek and then between my legs, cupping my sex possessively.

"I need your knot," I whimpered, pressing into his hand as he slid a finger in. I sighed and rested my forehead on a pillow. "No teasing."

"Your wish is my command." He removed his finger, and I heard the distinct sound of him sucking his finger before he lined up with my entrance.

His cock filled me in one sharp thrust, my body lurching forward with the force. I cried out, my back and neck arching like I was a cat stretching.

"Tight and wet as fuck." His hand cracked against my ass again, and I clenched around him. "You like that, Kayla girl?"

"Yes!" My whole body was alive with feeling and my

core ached for an orgasm and for his knot to fill me. "Again, harder."

His fingers dug into my hip, and he pounded into me, our skin slapping against each other in an erotic symphony of sexual bliss. He smacked my ass again, harder this time, making me yelp. It was the good kind of pain that quickly crossed into even more pleasure as my pussy clenched and flooded with slick, ready to take whatever he had to give me.

He reached around me, his fingers going straight to my swollen clit. I cried out as he rolled it between his fingers, my orgasm slamming into me. He worked his hips until his knot was firmly inside me, the noises coming from him strengthening the tidal wave of pleasure pulsing through me.

My body practically convulsed as the first rope of his cum shot into me, his roar telling me just how much pleasure my body was bringing him. I started to collapse onto the mattress, but his arm hooked around me, keeping my hips up as he finished spilling into me in short little thrusts that had me seeing stars.

Every centimeter of my body was tingling, and my chest heaved as my orgasm waned and I went limp underneath him. He shuddered with one last thrust and lowered me to the bed, his body weight pressing into me briefly before he rolled us onto our sides.

"Are you okay?" He peppered kisses along the back of my neck and shoulder, his arm hanging loosely over me and resting by my belly button.

I was too tired to answer and instead put my hand over his, entwining our fingers. I was more than okay.

A DIFFERENT KIND of pain woke me what couldn't have been more than a few hours later. I had no concept of time, my body and brain only really focused on the constant need that simmered between my legs. But what I needed now was food, or I was going to keel over from starvation.

Kane was gone, but in his place, wrapped around me like a protective shield, was Beck. My pussy immediately clenched at the realization he was cuddling with me, and I scrambled from the bed before my hormones got any ideas about needing him right that instant.

He groaned and rolled over onto his stomach, clutching the pillow I had just been sleeping on, but he didn't wake up. They all had to be exhausted just as much as I was. They'd won a game and then come back here for a different type of game.

I tiptoed to the bathroom and caught a glimpse of myself in the mirror. My hair was a disaster, and I attempted to take the ponytail holder out, only to find it stuck in the tangled mess. I was too weak to care and quickly used the bathroom and washed my hands and face. My body was sticky and gross, but a shower could wait until after I ate because I was damn near about to pass out.

Grabbing the soft terrycloth robe I'd hung on the back of the door as part of my nest preparations, I went back into the bedroom and let out a little squeal when I ran straight into a chest.

"Jesus, Rylan, don't sneak up on a girl like that." I pulled on the robe and secured it so he wouldn't get any ideas just yet. "I need food, and you'd better not tell me you have some right between your legs."

I looked around for my phone and found it charging on the entertainment center. My parents were probably so worried about me. Taking it off the charger, I swiped it open and found no messages.

"I hope you don't mind, but as soon as we plugged it in, the notifications were going crazy from your parents, so we sent your mom a text that we were here, and you were fine." Rylan came behind me and wrapped me in his arms.

"Thank you." I went back through the texts with a sigh. "I should put a password on this so you guys don't see all the dick pics guys send me."

"Haha," Rylan said dryly and then glanced over at Beck sleeping. "He hasn't slept, so let's give him some peace."

He grabbed my free hand and led me from the nest room, shutting the door quietly behind us.

"Why hasn't he slept?" I stopped him and turned him to face me. "He's not having regrets, is he?" If I was an insecure omega before, them sending me away after getting me through my heat would make me even worse.

"Not at all." He pulled me to him, his purr soothing my worries, which seemed to be exacerbated by my heat. "He was taking care of business stuff, then he walked the perimeter of the property about ten times, making sure it was secure, and then he made some phone calls to get beta security guards out front."

"What? Why?" I had felt safe in their house, but maybe I shouldn't have.

"N'Pact knows you're in heat... that's how we got here; they let us take their plane with them." Even he seemed a little worried about that.

"You really think they'd try to break in here because they know I'm in heat? They haven't even met me." I didn't want to believe that alphas could be so driven by their instincts that they'd take an omega in heat by force.

"It's better to be safe than sorry. Then he's paranoid about Brian. I can't wait until we can officially fire his ass."

Brian. Just his name made me want to vomit. "What did Brian do?"

"He had the balls to ask if you purposely stopped your pills to start your heat. Like, why would that matter anyway? It's your body." My mouth fell open at the accusation, and Rylan put his hands on my arms in reassurance. "We do *not* think you did it on purpose. But maybe you missed a pill or two by accident?"

"No. I have an alarm on my phone that goes off every day. Fuck Brian."

"He was enraged we're all for forfeiting the championship too if we need to. I don't see why he cares so much. He gets paid regardless of if we win or lose."

"He's an idiot." My brain was still latched onto the pill issue. Even if I had stopped them, it wasn't like I knew it was going to start when it did. "I do need to call my doctor and ask about why I'm going through a full heat when I take my pills every day at the same time."

"Maybe we're just so sexy, we caused it." Rylan kissed my forehead and then led me away from the nest.

It was almost six in the morning and the house was darker than usual. As soon as we were in the main living room, I could see why.

I hadn't even known the floor-to-ceiling windows had giant roll-down blackout shades. It made the house that much more appealing. All it needed now was some new décor and it would feel like home.

Kane was asleep on the couch and didn't stir as we walked past him into the dining room where Rio was at the table using my sewing machine.

"What are you doing?" I let go of Rylan's hand as he continued to the kitchen, and I went to stand behind Rio, wrapping my arms around him and putting my chin on the top of his head. He was working on my quilt, and it filled me with warmth.

"Well, you had the one sample block made and all of the fabric pieces cut. I hope you don't mind." He had just

KNOT SO PERFECT OMEGA

finished a block and cut the thread. "It took a few YouTube videos, but I think I've got the hang of it. Only pricked my fingers a few times."

I bent over his shoulder and kissed his cheek. "Thank you. Maybe you can be my first employee."

He turned and captured my lips, but I quickly pulled away. "None of that. I need food and a shower before any more sextivities can take place."

Rio laughed. "It's just a kiss."

"A kiss turns into tangling tongues, which turns into me thinking about tongues in other places, which then-" He silenced me with another kiss, laughing against my lips. "Thank you. I was headed down a dark path there. Food. I need food."

My core was already starting to ache with need again. I was at least grateful for the small reprieve their knots seemed to give me. The thing was, in the back of my mind, I knew the worst was yet to come.

CHAPTER TWENTY-TWO

Rylan

My tongue flicked at Kayla's clit, her body trying to squirm from Beck's hold on her. The woman was insatiable, and we were teaming up now to keep her satisfied. I'd lost count of how many times I'd given her my knot, and I was fucking exhausted. We all were.

Well, except for Kayla, who seemed to become more and more energetic with each orgasm. Her body craved us and wanted as much of our seed as possible to increase the likelihood of her becoming pregnant. Good thing she had a birth control implant because we were definitely not ready for any babies.

"Yes! Right there!" Kayla lifted her hips off the bed, grinding against my face as her orgasm hit her. Her body trembled and her pussy flooded with even more slick, preparing for our cocks.

I'd been going at her cunt with four fingers, making sure she was ready to take Beck and me, but first I wanted something else.

"Hand me the strap-on." I turned my head to look over my shoulder at Rio, who was sitting on the loveseat next to Kane.

"Wh… what?" Kayla's voice shook as she sucked in air, recovering from her high. "Are you serious?"

"Yup." I sat up and took the strap-on Rio handed me. "The vibrator in here already?"

"Yes, and it's on and has a fresh battery." Rio went back to the loveseat and kicked Kane's foot to get his attention. He was zoned out, probably in a sex haze. "Let's move this so we can get a better view."

"We don't need an audience for this. If you two want to go cook us some food or something, that would be great." I grabbed Kayla's arms and pulled her up to her knees. "You need to stand, babe. You wear it like underwear. I mean, I could undo the straps, but that would take forever."

"Nope. I think we're fine right here." Kane grunted as he and Rio moved the couch.

Kayla stood on shaky legs, and I held the harness for her as she used my shoulders for support. I was face to face with the dildo that was going to be in my ass in a matter of minutes. My cock jerked in anticipation, and I grabbed the base of the dildo and could feel the light buzz of the vibrator.

"Are you going to suck my cock, baby? I want you to choke on it." She thrust her hips forward, hitting my cheek with the fake penis, a giggle escaping that sweet mouth of hers.

We all laughed, and I pulled her arm so she'd drop back down to the mattress. She held her hand out to Beck, who had grabbed a bottle of lube. We were operating like a fine-tuned fucking machine.

Kayla squirted some lube on her hand. "On your hands and knees, hot stuff. Show me that ass."

The alpha in me growled at her command, but I fought off my instincts and did as she said. I'd already taken out my butt plug, so I was as ready as I was going to be.

"I think I might be into this," Rio said with a laugh. "Next, we need to talk Beck into it. I'd love to see him in a submissive position."

"This is not a submissive position," I growled. "I'm more alpha than any of you fuckers for letting my omega explore something like this."

Beck smacked my ass with a loud crack. "That's right, listen to the man and be quiet as his omega explores his ass."

I winced because the fucker smacked hard. "You fuckers better sleep with your eyes open or you might find yourself choked by a giant dildo shoved down your throats."

More laughing ensued as Kayla dripped lube down my crack. "Boys, let's be nice or I'll kick you out."

"Maybe you should anyway..." Nervousness suddenly coursed through my body, and I wasn't so sure this was a good idea.

"You ready?" Kayla said to me and only me. She seemed to block out the other three, staring into my eyes as I looked over my shoulder. "Maybe you'd be more comfortable on your back."

Why didn't I fucking think of that?

I quickly rolled over and grabbed my knees, feeling a lot more exposed wide open like I was. With the way I was lying, only Beck and Kayla could see, though. "I'm ready. No need to stretch it."

She moved in close and lined up the tip at my hole. I shut my eyes and tried to relax and pretend I was just putting in a butt plug. The dildo was a little thinner than the biggest of the butt plugs, so I had no reason to be nervous.

It vibrated a little from the vibrator that was at the base and that made things ten times better as she slowly pushed in past the first ring of muscle.

She hummed in satisfaction. "Breathe, Ry. Relax."

I released the breath I was holding, and she pushed in the rest of the way, farther than I'd ever gotten with a plug. I groaned, feeling the stretch and a satisfying fullness I never could have imagined.

"How is it? Are you okay?" Kayla stroked my calf,

and I finally opened my eyes, letting my feet fall to the bed.

"Fuck me, omega," I growled, grabbing onto my dick and giving it a few hard pumps.

"This is hotter than expected," Beck mumbled as Kayla pulled out and then slowly pushed back in.

"I'm not going to break, Kayla. Fuck me like you like to be fucked." I lifted my hips, pushing her deeper.

It took her a few thrusts to figure out a rhythm, and each time she pulled out, the dick pressed against my prostate and made a lightning bolt of pleasure run down my spine to my groin.

Beck moved in behind her, and to my dismay, she stopped for a few seconds before she surged forward as he thrust into her.

"Oh, fuck." She braced her hands on my stomach and leaned forward a bit as Beck set a rhythm along with her that had my cock leaking all over my hand as I pumped it furiously.

Skin slapping and groans filled the room as I was fucked into the mattress. My orgasm was right on the precipice, and I squeezed my knot as I fell over the edge. My vision lit up with sparks and my balls felt like they were seizing up as I came harder than I ever had before.

"Holy fucking shit!" Kayla cried out as she barreled toward her own orgasm, her body flushed with the exertion of fucking me.

I was barely over my orgasm, my hand and lower

abdomen a mess, but I was already getting hard again. My refractory period was shorter than usual thanks to her hormones making our bodies react.

I quickly unhooked the straps on her toy, glad there were two ways to take it off, and threw it to the side. "Have her sit on you, Beck."

"What are you…" Her eyes widened as Beck wrapped an arm around her and pulled her backward, so he was in a seated position and she was reverse cowgirl.

Even though she was wet enough, I grabbed the bottle of lube, and with a few pumps of my hand on my dick to get it nice and slick, I was hard as stone again.

"But, Beck… he's already in there." Her eyes widened as I got into position, lining the tip up on top of Beck's dick. "I can't fit two dicks!"

"Yes, you can. My whole hand was practically in you just a while ago." I slowly slid in, and we all groaned in unison as things got very tight.

"I think I'm going to come just watching this," Kane said from next to Rio. I'd hardly been paying them any attention.

After a few breaths to adjust, I started moving, my dick sliding along Beck's. He moaned, his fingers digging into Kayla's hips as he held her still. "Fuck, those piercings feel amazing."

It surprised me that Beck had even agreed to try this with me in the first place.

I picked up my speed, warmth and pressure making

my skin prickle and my knot ache. "I'm going to come." I leaned forward, kissing Kayla as I slid my dick out of her. There was no way we were going to fit two knots in her.

Breaking our kiss, we adjusted so she was back on her hands and knees with Beck behind her. I moved to my knees, and she wrapped her slightly swollen lips around me.

She whimpered as she took me all the way to the back of her throat, tears filling her eyes as she fought the urge to gag. She slowly pulled off, running her tongue along the underside of my length, teasing my Jacob's ladder piercings.

Beck came with a growl, and I knew his knot was inside her when she sucked hard and her body trembled. This was single-handedly the hottest sex I'd ever had, and with that thought, my balls drew up and I exploded in her mouth.

She took every last drop of me down her throat, her moan strangled as she swallowed. She released me, and I collapsed back on the bed with a smile on my face.

There was no greater feeling than pleasing my omega

A FEW HOURS LATER, I climbed into the passenger seat of Beck's SUV, holding onto the handle and carefully lowering myself onto the seat. There was a slight soreness, but the way it had made me feel in the moment was worth it.

Kayla's two pill bottles shifted in my pockets, the pills clacking together as I reached to shut the door. After a marathon heat spike, things had finally calmed down enough for her to call her doctor back at the academy, and now Beck and I were on a mission to get her new ones and drop the old ones off.

Her doctor didn't understand why her heat was so crazy. Even if she had accidentally missed a dose, she said it wouldn't have been as painful as it was or spiked like it had.

The pharmacy was only a few miles away, which was the only reason Beck and I had agreed to go. It wasn't at the top of our priority list to get new pills, but Kayla wanted them in case she decided to still take them. Plus, she wanted to know if something was wrong with the ones she had.

"Man, I never thought I'd say this, but I don't think I have any more cum in me." I buckled my seatbelt as Beck backed out of the garage and gate.

He waited until the gate closed all the way before taking off. "How does your ass feel? She... um... really let you have it."

"It's just a little sensitive, but nothing I can't handle." I looked over at him staring straight ahead at the road. "You all right with, you know... our dicks rubbing?"

He glanced over at me as he came to a stop at a stop sign. "I nearly blacked out when I came."

"Sex is definitely fun with her. I've never felt so comfortable laughing my ass off in bed with a woman." I stared out the window as we turned onto the main road toward the pharmacy.

"She's ours, that's why. No one before has even come close." Beck sounded wistful, which was interesting to hear. He wasn't one to get all sappy. "I want to bond with her. It's been killing me not biting her neck these last few days."

"Same, but she wants to wait until after the championship. I say screw the championship." I unhooked my seatbelt as the car pulled into the parking lot. "We don't need the money or the fame."

"You know she won't let us do that." Beck got out and I trailed behind him into the pharmacy. "We don't want to disappoint our fans either."

He was right, but that didn't mean I had to like it. Now that Kayla was in the picture, I didn't want to spend weeks traveling for games next season. If she was going to start her own business, she wouldn't want to come along with us. But that was a worry for another day.

We needed a few supplies, so I grabbed a handbasket by the door before we headed to the back of the store where the pharmacy was. No one was in line, so we stepped right up to the counter and rang the bell.

"Can I help you?" A man came from around the corner of a shelving unit full of medicines.

"We're here to pick up two prescriptions for Kayla

Sterling and to have these tested." I put the two bottles on the counter. "Her doctor should have called."

"Ah, yes." He stepped up to the counter and grabbed the bottles, examining them. "Let me take a look at them."

He opened the heat suppressants and tapped a few out into a little cup. He prodded them and narrowed his eyes before grabbing a pair of tweezers and bringing one out to examine it closer.

"What is it?" Beck leaned forward, trying to see what the pharmacist was looking at.

"These don't have the brand symbol. See?" He dropped it in his hand and turned it over. "It's blank. It should have an omega symbol on both sides."

"Maybe the manufacturer didn't put one on by accident?" I asked hopefully. "What does it mean if there isn't an omega symbol?"

"The pharmacist that filled this bottle would have noticed when they were counting the pills. They signed the side of the bottle that it was checked." He pointed to initials across the label. "Your omega didn't notice they were blank? One of the first things they're taught is to examine their pills before taking." He grabbed a larger plastic tray and dumped the whole bottle in it. "I'll have to send these to the lab to be tested to know for sure what they are, but they aren't heat suppressants."

"Then what the fuck are they?" Beck was starting to grow agitated, and I put a hand on his back. "What about these?" He pushed the perfume blockers toward him.

The pharmacist grabbed another tray and emptied them. "These are correct, but if she was taking a placebo pill, then it wouldn't have worked that well." His eyes went to our necks. "And if you aren't bonded with her yet, she would naturally release more perfume anyway to grab your attention."

"Placebo pills? What are those?" I could feel Beck's anger through our bond and hoped he didn't jump through the opening and strangle the pharmacist.

"Sugar pills, basically. No ingredients that would affect anything. Sometimes an omega will take them if they want a break from the heat suppressants. If they want to continue them in the future, it's easier to get back to the routine of them if they are taking a daily pill. Very similar to beta birth control pills. I'll send them off, so we know if they're something else." He put the perfume blockers in the pill bottle and handed them back. "Let me get the new bottle of suppressants."

He moved to a wall of bins, and Beck growled low in his throat. "She knew. She's supposed to check them every day."

"Don't be ridiculous. Do you even hear what you're saying? Why the hell would she take placebo pills and not just stop taking them if she wanted to get her heat? Hell, she wanted us to bring them here to get looked at. Someone fucked with her meds." I pulled him away from the counter and pushed the basket at his chest. "Go get the shit we need. We don't need you to snap on this poor guy. It's not his fault."

He ripped the basket from my hands and stalked away to get the supplies we needed. I knew he was just upset that our omega had been taking an unknown substance for who knew how long, but I just hoped the progress we'd made wasn't just wiped away.

CHAPTER TWENTY-THREE

Kayla

I stood under the warm spray of the shower, finally able to enjoy getting clean without the water moving over my sensitive skin making me horny. Just as I had expected after the first full day of my heat, things had gotten worse, but with four alphas to satisfy me, it hadn't been bad at all. Had they not come back when they did, I would have been in even more pain as the peak of my heat hit.

There was always the possibility this was just a lull and soon I'd be craving knots all over again. For now, I was enjoying not feeling like a sex-crazed lunatic. I was sure the guys were too.

Turning off the shower, I grabbed a clean towel and dried off. My body ached from all the different positions it had been in, and after I ate dinner, I was hoping to sleep through the night. Beck and Rylan were supposed to be grabbing pizzas on their way back from the pharmacy.

Braving clothes, I pulled on a clean pair of panties and a soft, sleeveless nightgown that fell to my mid-thigh. There was no point bothering with anything constricting. The best part of it was that it had pockets.

I quickly brushed my hair out and threw it up in a bun, not caring that it was still dripping a little.

"Kayla, the guys are back!" Kane yelled from the other side of the bathroom door. "You good?"

I grabbed my phone and turned off N'Pact's last album, putting my phone in one of my pockets. It made the nightie a little heavy, but I was waiting for Kara to text me back.

"I'm great." I opened the bathroom door and grinned as his eyes traveled down my body. "Should I put on real clothes?"

"Not at all. Just surprised to see you in a dress is all." He wrapped an arm around my waist and pulled me closer. "I like."

"It's a nightgown, not a dress." I shoved at his chest. "Don't start. I finally feel somewhat normal again. Probably just a lull, but I'm going to enjoy it."

"Party pooper." He kissed my cheek and backed up. "Want to eat in your nest or the kitchen?"

I scrunched my nose because the room smelled like sex and was a bit stuffy. "I think we need to air this room out a little. That might help me not be a nympho.

The smell does something to me. So do all the naked chests."

He walked out of the bathroom and grabbed a stray shirt from the floor. I immediately snatched it from him and threw it across the room. He laughed and took my hand, leading me to the kitchen where the aroma of pizza made my mouth water and my stomach flip with hunger.

"You guys better have gotten a whole pizza just for me." My feet came to a screeching halt when Rio, Rylan, and Beck all turned to look at me.

I don't know how I knew, but something was wrong. They weren't smiling, and they all had this glint in their eyes like they were about to murder someone.

Grabbing the hem of my nightie, I resisted the urge to hide behind Kane. It was so fucking embarrassing that my immediate reaction to them looking pissed was to cower.

"We got you what you asked for." Beck grabbed a paper plate and opened several of the boxes. "Let's eat."

"What's wrong?" I wasn't moving until I figured out what had crawled up their asses and died. "Did something happen?"

Rio held out a plate to me. "Come get your food, sweetheart. We'll talk after we eat."

Kane put his arm around my waist and led me to the island. He was as tense as I was, and I didn't think he had any idea what was going on either.

We took our plates out to the patio, the sun only a

line on the horizon. I couldn't enjoy the view, though, when I was trying to think back to all the things I had said and done during my heat spike. Could they be having regrets about me now?

I thought things were final between us, but maybe the pegging had taken it too far. It was a pretty domineering position to put an alpha in, even if he had agreed. Was I not omega enough for them?

My phone rang just as I was about to sit down, and it startled me so much I nearly dropped my plate. Rio grabbed it from me and set it on the table while I fished my phone out of my pocket.

"Oh, it's my doctor already." I accepted the call and lifted it to my ear, walking out into the small yard next to the pool. "Hello?"

"Hi, Kayla. This is Dr. Wilkins. Do you have a minute to talk?" I heard some screaming children in the background and wondered if she was calling me from home. It was past the time she was normally at the academy's health clinic.

"Yes. Did you already find out if something was wrong with the pills?" I headed toward the railing that was on the edge of the cliff. It had scared me a bit at first, but unless there was a massive earthquake and I just stood there, I wasn't going anywhere.

"Did your mates not talk to you yet?" A door shut and the screaming children were muffled. "Are you with them?"

"Yeah. They're eating. Why?" I looked back over my

shoulder, and they were discussing something. Probably me.

"That's interesting." She sighed. "The pharmacist is sending your tablets to be tested but called me right away to tell me he thinks they were swapped out with placebos... sugar pills."

My heart nearly stopped beating, and I backed away from the railing a step so, if I dropped my phone, it wouldn't be lost forever. "What?"

"Have you been checking your pills every day before you take them?"

Crap. "It was a new bottle I just opened the night before I left. They had the symbols. I always check."

Tears welled in my eyes. I was a sporadic checker when it came to the pills, and I couldn't recall checking the entire time I'd been here.

"But you didn't do a daily check? Kayla, you know how important that is." She let out a frustrated sigh, and I sniffled back the tears. "It's okay, mistakes happen. I was concerned that the whole lot of those blockers were incorrect, but if you're sure they had the symbol..."

"Someone switched them," I whispered, looking over my shoulder to find four sets of eyes on me before hastily turning my eyes back toward the darkening skyline. "What do I do?"

Tampering with an omega's pills was a serious crime, and if one of the guys had swapped them out... My stomach cramped, but not from my heat.

Why would they do it? Why make me go through a heat when we were just getting to know one another?

"They got your new pills. If the seal is broken, don't take them and call me back. I want you to take three with a meal tonight, tomorrow morning, and tomorrow evening to stop your heat. Then go back to your normal schedule of taking them."

I whimpered and heard the chairs scoot out from the patio table. "They're coming."

"Don't confront them. Until we get this sorted out, we don't know what they're capable of. I'll call you tomorrow with a plan after I speak to Omega Protective Services. With the pack being so high profile, I'm not sure how they're going to want to proceed to get you somewhere safe so the proper investigation can be done."

"But if I just ask them, then-"

"Kayla, I know you want to trust them after going through your heat with them, but I'd rather act with an abundance of precaution and make sure you're safe. Your safety is priority number one. When and if they do share what the pharmacist said, you can be upset, but don't point fingers."

Arms wrapped around me, and the scent of cinnamon and cloves washed over me. Only now, instead of enjoying the scent, it made me want to gag.

A memory hit me like a tidal wave and my knees felt like they were going to buckle, so I pulled away from Beck and grabbed onto the railing with my free hand.

The meet and greet conversation. Beck and Brian were talking about what would happen if an omega went into heat during her pack's season. The pack would be more aggressive, which would be a good thing for them.

"Kayla? Do you understand?" Dr. Wilkins snapped me back to the present, although it felt like I was floating above, looking down at myself.

"Yes. I understand. Thank you for checking in on me." I hung up and stood there for a moment, collecting my thoughts.

"Kayla, is everything okay? What did your doctor say?" Rylan stepped up to the railing beside me, leaning on it with one arm.

"She was just checking in and wanted to make sure I got my new pills and dropped the old ones off." I plastered on a fake smile and turned to mimic his stance. "Did you get my new ones?"

"Yes." He put his hand on my forearm. "We wanted to wait until after we ate to talk to you about what the pharmacist said."

Beck growled, and I looked over at him standing a few feet away, his fists clenched at his sides. "Might as well tell her now."

I didn't take my eyes off Beck as Rylan started to talk. "Well, he said your suppressants are possibly sugar pills and he's going to send them to be tested."

My head snapped toward Rylan, part of my act that I didn't know that already. "What?"

"They weren't real. That's why you got your heat. Someone fucked with your pills." Beck was closer now, and my skin prickled with uncertainty. "How did you not realize-"

"Beck," Rylan warned. "Who would have fucked with your pills though?"

You. Beck. I don't know.

I bit my lip and tears sprang to my eyes, but not for the reason they were thinking. "This is all my fault for not checking them every day."

Rio, who had been standing by the edge of the pool watching, walked over to join us. "You shouldn't have to check them. No one has been in the house since you've been here. Could someone at the academy have swapped them?"

"Possibly." I looked back out at the city in the distance. When the sky was clear, the Hollywood Hills really did have a million-dollar view.

"The cleaners haven't come, have they?" Rylan asked.

"No. I told them not to. We were going to have them over to meet Kayla, but with everything going on and her heat starting, that hasn't happened yet." Rio put his hand on the small of my back and I resisted the urge to stiffen.

I just wanted to go lock myself somewhere and think about everything. The only plausible explanation at the moment was that one of them had done it to give them an edge. My hormones were a natural performance-enhancing drug to them.

"The pizza is getting cold. Let's eat." Kane was still at the patio table. It was weird that he hadn't come to see what the problem was.

The fact was, I didn't really know any of them. There I was, just thrown into their lives when they hadn't wanted an omega in the first place. I should have dug my feet in more about coming here.

And to think I'd almost bonded with them.

IT WAS KILLING me not talking to the pack about the pills, but even I knew how serious of a situation this was. Either someone at the academy pharmacy had seriously fucked up, or I was being used.

But the question was, why?

Why had I matched with them instead of no one at all? Was someone in the Omega Match offices working with the pack to manipulate the system? Had everything they told me been a lie?

I should have called Omega Protective Services right away when I'd matched after opting out. No one wanted to get them involved, but maybe they could have put pressure on the Omega Match administration to take another look at what had happened.

Or they were in on it too.

As an omega, I knew quite well how delicate my designation was. There were only so many of us, and the impact we had on the most powerful people made us both highly regarded and vulnerable.

If there weren't strict protections and protocols for us in place, I was sure we'd be sold, passed around, and treated like nothing more than breeders. Despite all the safeguards in place, I was starting to realize that maybe I didn't pay enough attention to what went on with other omegas.

The nest door unlocked, and I stiffened. After eating, I'd told the guys I wanted to be alone and locked myself in the room. I'd had a little more heat pain, but after popping the three suppressants, it seemed to evaporate into thin air.

I pretended to be asleep as Beck came into the room. If I hadn't been awake, I wouldn't have heard him, but I was on edge and could hear the smallest of noises.

The mattress dipped, and he lowered onto it behind me and wrapped an arm around my waist, trapping me against him. "I know you're awake."

Despite my mind screaming at me to run, my body melted against him like we were two spoons nestled next to each other. "That's not creepy at all."

He chuckled, his nose running along my neck to a spot I had noticed he licked and sucked the most. "This is where I'm going to bite you." He kissed the spot and my nipples hardened against my will.

"Beck… I'm tired." My traitor of a pussy clenched as he kissed the spot. "Don't you need to sleep? Aren't you guys going to have any practices before your championship game in a few days?"

"No, we don't really need to practice anymore. We're confident we'll win now that we know the other three teams in the championship. Our biggest threat is the Raging Skeletons, and we've never lost against them."

"You'll be riding on the hormones still in your system from my heat too." I bit my lip; saying that was a risky move.

"We will." He nuzzled my neck and sighed. "Don't think I didn't notice how weird you got after your doctor called."

"I got weird after you guys told me my heat suppressants were tampered with. Who would do that to an omega unless they wanted to take advantage of them?" I couldn't stop myself. I knew the doctor had told me to keep my mouth shut, but I just couldn't. Not when he was cuddling up to me and pretending everything was fine.

He stiffened, and I thought he was moving off the mattress, but instead only moved so he could roll me on my back to see my face. I looked away and he grabbed my chin, making me look at him.

"You think we messed with your pills?" The hurt in his voice was thick, but that didn't mean it wasn't an act.

"What other explanation is there? You benefit from the heat." I cringed as his jaw ticked in anger. "Put yourself in my shoes. What would you think?"

"That you wanted your heat so we'd grow attached

and would bond with you." He lacked any power behind his words, but they still stung.

"That's not fair. I never asked for this, but I gave it a chance because I felt an inkling of something in my gut telling me to. Maybe it was just gas."

He let my chin go and put his forehead against my shoulder. "Just... trust us, okay? We want you and wouldn't do something to jeopardize that."

All I could really trust was myself, but every fiber of my being was telling me to trust them too.

CHAPTER TWENTY-FOUR

Kayla

I t was the day of the championship game and had been two days since I found out about my pills and started questioning everything and everyone. I'd gone from being on cloud nine to being ten feet under, and I was running out of oxygen fast.

I hadn't heard a peep from Dr. Wilkins about what to do. She'd called to check on me and I'd told her that I didn't believe the pack had anything to do with my pills. She was just an impartial third-party and was being as objective as possible, which meant they were at the top of her suspect list.

We'd decided since my heat had just finished, it wasn't a good idea for me to go to the game. Even if I had felt comfortable going, it didn't change the fact that

I was an unbonded omega, and even if I had ten beta security guards, I would worry.

So now I was stuck at home, watching pre-game highlights on the large projection screen. At least I'd get to see an up-close view of my men when it was game time.

My phone buzzed, and I smiled seeing my sister had finally texted me back after I'd texted her the night before. It was unlike her not to immediately check her phone when she woke up or before she went to bed.

Kara: *Sorry, I just got up.*

Me: *It's almost noon.*

Kara: *So? You used to sleep until noon on the weekends. I'm making up for all the lost time.*

Me: *Point taken. I was up at seven seeing my pack off to their game day festivities.*

Kara: *You didn't want to go?*

Me: *Yes and no. It would just distract them with me being fresh off my heat...*

Kara: *Why do I get the feeling that... means something? I appreciate you not saying much about all the nesting and sexing you've been doing, but I think I can handle hearing about it.*

Me: *It's not that... okay, maybe a little. We discovered my heat suppressants were tampered with. They were all blanks.*

My phone immediately rang, and I sighed, answering it. "Well, hello, stranger."

"What do you mean they were all blanks?" The

concern in her voice was not something I had wanted. She didn't need any more stress in her life.

"They're testing them, but they were placebo pills or something. I just opened and checked them before leaving, so..." I left that piece of information hanging between us and Kara was silent for at least a minute. "Care Bear? You there?"

"So, I'm guessing if you're still there at their house that you don't think it was them... that doesn't leave too many people."

"Dr. Wilkins was supposed to be handling it on her end and contacting OPS, but she didn't say much about it when she called to check on me yesterday. I want to believe it wasn't my pack, but who else could it have been? Literally no one has been in the house."

"But where were you keeping the pills? In your purse?"

"No. They were in my suitcase. Shit, there's a ton of people who touched that thing. The driver to the airport, the front desk person at the terminal, the baggage handler-"

My heart plummeted into the pit of my stomach.

"Kayla? What is it?"

"Brian. He was alone with my bag for at least ten minutes... he... he told me to go explore the house and I didn't even think... oh my God, why would he do that?" I started shaking so bad I had to put my sister on speakerphone and put the phone down.

"Breathe, Kayla. What do you need me to do? I can

probably steal a car and be there in a few days." Kara sounded dead-ass serious, and it immediately snapped me out of the panicked feeling in my chest.

"What? You can't even drive! No... I need to call them and tell them... none of this makes any sense."

If Brian did swap out my pills, what exactly was he up to? He could have done that just as easily with Kara instead of 'accidentally' mixing us up. Which led to bigger and crazier questions... was someone working for Omega Match making under the table deals to fuck with the matches?

"I can drive if I need to. How hard can it be?" She was starting to sound like me.

"I'll call you back later, all right? I need to figure this all out before OPS decides to have the pack arrested or something." That would be a worst-case scenario. They wouldn't arrest them without a thorough investigation... I didn't think.

"Just be careful, sis. Love you." Kara hung up after I returned the sentiment.

The game started in just a few hours, so my pack was probably resting or in interviews. They had said they would all keep their phones on them and on. They'd even made sure the reception at the stadium was good.

I was just about to call Beck when my phone rang with a call from Dr. Wilkins, scaring the crap out of me.

"Dr. Wilkins! I think I know who switched out my pills." I fell back onto the soft cushions of the couch, my heart thudding in my chest. "The team's manager,

Brian. He had my bag for a bit and I just didn't think of it."

"Are you sure? Why would he swap out your pills? In any case, two OPS agents are at your front gate. They're going to take you to an omega compound while they run their investigation."

"What? No way." I jumped up and nearly tripped over the rug as I ran to one of the display panels that controlled the security system and lights.

An unmarked SUV was parked across the street from the gate, and I could see two people inside it, although not clearly.

"This is going to be a high-profile case. Now is the best time to get you to a safe place so they can do their jobs. There will be a media circus as soon as the pack is taken in for questioning." She was speaking but I could hardly hear what she was saying over the ringing in my ears.

I had to warn them.

"Kayla? Are you there?" I didn't know how long Dr. Wilkins had been talking, but I finally snapped out of the daze I was in staring at the SUV out front.

"I'm here. I don't want this. Let's just forget this even happened, okay?"

"Sweetheart, I know you want to protect them, but even if they didn't switch your pills, someone close to them did. We don't know if they put him up to it or what his motivation is. You aren't safe there right now."

"I'm not going. I can stay here while OPS does their

investigation." The last place I wanted to go was an omega compound, which was ironic considering just a few weeks ago it was the only place I could think of.

This was my home. This was my pack. This was my life and future.

I'd never cared much about any of those things until matching with the pack, and now I had them, I didn't want to let them go.

"They have a court order. If you don't go willingly, they will come in and get you." She sighed. "I know this is tough, but if they didn't do it, then you'll return to them when the investigation is closed."

"And how long will that be? A few days?" My mind was starting to whirl, and I ran to my nest where I had been sleeping and grabbed jeans since I was in pajama bottoms.

"A few weeks... a few months. Depends on how much they cooperate."

"A few months!" I shrieked, shoving my feet into slip-ons. "Just tell them what I told you about Brian and they can investigate him first."

"Open the door for them. They aren't the enemy, Kayla."

The doorbell rang and I ran back to the living room, seeing the view of the front door on the display signaling someone was at the front door. How the hell did they open the front gate?

I hung up on Dr. Wilkins and quickly dialed Beck's number. "Come on... come on."

"Hello?" Fucking Brian. What the hell was he doing answering Beck's phone?

"Uh… can I speak to Beck?" I watched in horror as one of the OPS agents got a crowbar from a bag they were carrying. "It's urgent."

"They are in an interview at the moment. Can I take a message?" Fuck. Fuck, fuck, fuck.

"OPS agents are here, and I need to speak to him immediately." *You fucking two-faced asshole.*

"I'll give him the message." He hung up, and I resisted the urge to chuck my phone in anger.

The agent lifted the crowbar to the door, and I did the only thing I could think of… run to the backyard. I disarmed the alarm so they wouldn't know I was trying to run. I should have paid more attention when Rio was explaining how to just turn off the alarm to certain areas of the house.

I ran along the back and to the side of the house, dialing Kane's number next. He picked up right away. "Kane-"

"Kane's in an interview. Are you trying to be a pain in the ass?" Did Brian have all of their phones? Why the hell would they leave their phones with him?

"Who is it?" I heard Kane ask from a distance.

"Someone trying to reach you about your car's extended warranty."

"Wait!" *Click.*

Motherfucker. They had no clue he couldn't even be trusted with watching cell phones. There was no use in my trying the other two, plus I needed to get away so I had time to come up with a plan.

I ran down the stairs on the side of the house next to the garage and peeked around the edge. The agents had pulled into the driveway and left the gate open. If I could just make it out, I could hide nearby until they left or until the guys realized I had been the one who had called.

Maybe I should let OPS take me, otherwise, I was going to murder a beta and end up in prison.

I took a deep breath and sprinted across the driveway to the gate, not looking back as I rounded the edge of the gate onto the sidewalk. Now what?

I continued running, hoping by the time they realized I wasn't in the house, I'd be somewhere safe.

The street and sidewalk sloped downward out of the neighborhood, and I picked up speed. I was flying across the pavement, my breaths ragged and my feet burning from the flatness of my shoes.

Until I wasn't.

My foot caught on a crack from a piece of cement that was slightly lifted, and I went flying forward, my phone smashing to smithereens as I collided with the ground.

I cried out, my hands and knees taking the brunt of the fall. My wrist twinged and blood oozed from the scrapes on my palms and forearms.

It took everything in me not to just lie there and wallow, but I had to keep moving because the agents would see me when they left. A woman sprawled out on the sidewalk would be hard to miss.

My phone was busted, the screen in a million cracks, and I slid it into my back pocket, hoping the contents on it were salvageable.

I started walking, looking for anywhere that might be a good place to hide when the gate right in front of me slid open and an SUV pulled through.

N'Pact.

The SUV stopped right in my path across the sidewalk as the driver scanned the street. If I could just dash in through their gate, I could hide there until the championship was over.

The back window rolled down and one of the members of N'Pact, Cal, stuck his head out. "Hey, you all right?"

I looked over my shoulder, worried the agents were right behind me. "I'm fine. I just…"

Cal opened the door and got out. "You're hurt. Is there someone we can call for you?"

"Cal, leave the girl be. We were supposed to be at the stadium half an hour ago." I knew that voice. Alvaro Estrada, alpha of the pack that made up the band.

"The stadium? Can you give me a ride?" They wouldn't try anything, would they? I was out of options.

Cal's eyes darkened as he stepped closer to me. "Who do you belong to, omega?"

My jaw opened at the protective tone in his voice.

"Thomas pack. They... I... my phone is broken. I need to get to them."

"Cal! Come on, man!"

Cal turned his head. "Shut up! This is the Gnomes' girl." He turned back to me. "What is going on here?"

"OPS. Please. I need to get to them." I didn't like to purposely whine, but I did, and all the heads in the SUV turned to look out at me.

"OPS? Are they mistreating you?" Cal lifted his hand like he was going to reach for me, but then thought better of it.

"No, it's complicated. I'll tell you on the way?" I knew it was risky being scared and getting into a vehicle of alphas, but I had no other choice. "They would do the same if your omega was in trouble."

Cal narrowed his eyes, his nostrils flaring slightly. I didn't know what button I'd pushed, but apparently them and omegas were a sensitive subject.

"Get in the front. We're respectable alphas, but you also smell amazing and are injured." Cal walked around the back of the SUV to the passenger side. "Out."

The security guard or whoever it was jumped out and moved to the back without question as Cal held open the door for me.

"Thank you." I breathed a sigh of relief as he slammed the door and got back in the back. "Kara is going to lose her shit when I tell her I got a ride from N'Pact."

I<small>T TURNED</small> out that N'Pact was singing the National Anthem and were late for the pregame rehearsal. I'd never been more grateful that they were well known for showing up late for events.

They unfortunately did not have any of the guys' numbers and had only talked to them on social media, which I knew they wouldn't be checking on a game day or really at all.

I'd just show up unannounced. That was probably for the best because if Brian knew I was coming, he'd try to stop me.

Forty-five minutes before game time, we pulled up to the entertainer and player entrance, and the driver, a nice beta named Jonathan, rolled down his window at the security hut.

The security officer came to the window with his tablet and peered into the car. "You're late. I have N'Pact plus two. No mention of them bringing anyone else."

"Last minute change of plans. She's our VIP guest," Jonathan explained smoothly. "Is that going to be an issue? If so, we're going to have to take her all the way back to the Hollywood Hills, and well…"

The security guard glanced at me and sighed before returning to the security hut and grabbing some badges. "She'll need to stay with you at all times and wear her badge."

"Got it. Thank you." Jonathan grabbed the badges

that were on lanyards and passed them back to Alvaro, who distributed them as we pulled through the gates and into a parking lot at the back of the stadium.

"You'll stay by us until we find your pack," Alvaro directed as he handed me a VIP badge. "If we find out you've been lying to us..."

"I'm not." I put the lanyard around my neck and checked my hands before getting out of the vehicle. They were scraped up, but luckily there had been a first aid kit in the SUV and I'd been able to clean them up. Too bad there wasn't a spare cell phone.

Payne gave me a withering stare as he shut the back passenger door. "They are going to kick our asses."

Cal came up beside him, slinging an arm around him. "Why would they do that, Payney boy?"

"She smells like us now." He grunted and shoved off Cal's arm.

I lifted the hem of my shirt and sniffed. It was an odd mixture of my scent, theirs, and my own pack's. It didn't smell bad in the slightest, but I could see why Payne was a bit concerned.

Glances were exchanged among the members of the band and Alvaro pinched the bridge of his nose, reminding me of Beck. "Let's go find your pack."

CHAPTER TWENTY-FIVE

Kane

I was in this surreal sort of headspace as we sat in the locker room, waiting for our time to go warm up in the training facility.

Kayla wasn't answering our calls and texts, and we were on edge. She might have been taking a nap, but that didn't explain why her phone went straight to voicemail—unless she'd turned it off.

We'd started our day with a delicious spread for breakfast with Kayla then headed to the stadium for a practice and debrief on the schedule for the day. After that, we'd showered and done several interviews, including a segment for one of the sports broadcasts on how Alphaball is played. One would think doing anything before a game would leave us tired, but it only amped us up more for our games.

Brian had been surprisingly quiet since arriving shortly after us. Maybe he'd finally realized his time with us was over. We didn't make the decision lightly since we'd have to find a new manager and coach.

"I'm going to check the cameras," Beck muttered from across from me.

We had several cameras around our property, but none in the house. That might need to change if Kayla was going to be staying there by herself often. If she'd let us. The reason we didn't have any inside in the first place was because we weren't confident that they wouldn't be hacked.

"We're up on the practice field and then will be going straight out into the stadium for the National Anthem." Brian didn't look up from his phone he'd been texting away on for the last several minutes.

The four of us stood from where we were lounging around in our small locker room. We had on special edition all royal blue uniforms with our signature pack of gnomes with butcher knives in hands screen printed on the front and last names on the back. The blood-red cleats had our gnome printed on the side with a printed signature. The look would be launching on our Alpha Fit website at the start of the first game.

It had been Rio's idea to do an exclusive limited run of our championship uniform, and our website tech team was already anticipating a sell-out within minutes of going live.

I grabbed my cell phone and followed my pack out of

the locker room, texting Kayla that I couldn't wait to see her later.

"Did we leave the gate open?" Beck fell into step beside me. "I could have sworn I waited for it to be shut. Am I losing my mind?"

"No, I'm pretty sure you shut it because in my head I was thinking about what a lunatic you were for blocking the car that pulled up behind us while it shut." I grabbed his phone as we walked down the corridor. "Let me back it up. We left at what? Nine?"

We made it to the practice area and Brian nearly clotheslined me as we filed in through the door. "Put the phone away."

"Dude. What the actual fuck? I am a grown-ass man." I rarely lost my temper, but I was about to. I shoved past him and backed the camera footage up to nine when we left.

"We are less than thirty minutes away from game time now. I need you four to focus. Surely your omega is fine."

"Weren't you the one who pushed for us to have an omega?" Rylan snapped, setting his phone down on a bench and taking off down the half-field doing high knees.

"The gate was definitely shut." I put the feed on a slow fast forward.

"Here, I'll watch the damn thing and you go get warmed up." Brian held out his hand for Beck's phone.

"It's on three times the speed." I handed him the

phone and put mine on the bench next to Rio's and Rylan's.

I took off across the field, running through the quick agility drills we did before every game and then grabbed a weighted ball to toss back and forth with Beck to warm up our arms.

"How the hell are we going to focus if we're worried about Kayla? We should have just brought her with us and kept her next to us the whole time," Rio said from next to me where he was tossing a ball with Rylan.

"Like we'd be able to focus with her here. We'd be looking for her every second. She's probably just taking a nap or something." If we thought things were bad now with us worrying, when we bonded it was going to be crazy.

"She said she was going to watch us so she should be texting or calling us back soon." Rio caught the ball and didn't throw it again. "I think I'm good with my warm-up since our first game will be like playing for fun."

"You can say that again." Beck jogged in with our ball and we walked as a pack over to the benches where Brian was to grab our phones. "Anything on the camera?"

"No. It seems to have opened by itself. Probably needs to be checked by a technician." Brian handed Beck his phone back. "All ready to win this thing?"

"Do you even have to ask?" Rylan walked to the door leading back to the main corridor of the stadium. "Let's roll some heads!"

We all shouted in agreement and my excitement started to grow. I was stronger, faster, and had more energy than I had in months. There was no way we were giving up the win.

Outside of the practice room, the rest of our team was waiting for us, including our team doctor in case one of us was injured, our publicist, and a photographer. Waiting on the field for us were a few teenagers we'd met at the foodbank when volunteering, who would be giving us water and our towels when we needed them.

We liked to keep our game day entourage small so we weren't distracted by them, so the rest of the people that made our team tick but didn't need to be on the field were in a private box to watch the game.

There was a commotion back down the hallway where our locker room was, and we all turned at the exact moment Kayla came barreling through two security guards that were in the hall outside the door.

One of them snagged her around the waist and practically threw her into the wall, pinning her there with his massive body.

The growls that ripped out of the four of us were unlike anything I'd ever experienced. I'd growled plenty in my life, but never from somewhere buried so deep inside it almost felt like it was from another person.

The security guards and Kayla all looked our way as N'Pact rounded the corner at the end of the hall at a sprint.

We moved toward the security guards and Kayla as a

wall of raging alpha. Beck was slightly in front of us, his body taut and ready to fight. *"Let her go."* His bark was fierce enough to immediately cause the security guard to back off Kayla.

"Damn, I think my nuts just retreated a little." Cal cackled from where they were approaching from the opposite side of the corridor. "See, we told you that running ahead was a bad idea, Kayla."

"Back up," Beck barked at the two men, who were also alphas but had claim bites on their necks. "She's ours."

The guy who had shoved her against the wall held up his hands and backed up several steps, heeding Beck's warning. "Our apologies, but when we tried to stop her for her credentials to be in this area, she didn't have them, and then when we asked who she belonged to, she said no one and ran. We were just doing our jobs."

Pride swelled in my chest, not just because she'd gotten around two massive security guards, but because she hadn't changed even after her heat left her dependent on us.

I was the first to her and put my hand on her arms. "What are you doing here, sweetheart? We've been trying to call you."

Knocking my hands away, she bent over with her hands on her knees, her breaths coming in pants from running. "Broke my phone. Had to escape OPS. Brian."

"OPS? Escape them? What does Brian have to do

with that?" She held up a finger to tell me to give her a minute while she caught her breath.

She straightened suddenly, her eyes going straight past us to the empty hallway behind us. "Where is he?"

At the same time, Beck stepped past the security guards to N'Pact, his fists clenched at his sides. "What the hell are you guys doing here and why do you smell like our omega?" Beck stepped toward N'Pact, his fists clenched at his sides.

If they laid even a finger on Kayla, we were going to beat their asses so they were singing the National Anthem out of their assholes. Rio, Rylan, and I moved to stand shoulder to shoulder with Beck, blocking our omega from their view. The security guards had moved back from us, and they weren't threats with them being claimed by an omega.

"Woah, man. We just gave her a ride here. She took a fall right outside our gate as we were leaving." Alvaro lifted his chin in Kayla's direction. "She's taking off again. Feisty little minx, isn't she?"

She was sprinting down the corridor and nearly ran into a wall turning a corner. We took off after her, not really knowing what the fuck was going on with her but not willing to let her run through a stadium full of who knew how many alphas who were just looking for an omega to claim.

"Kayla!" Beck barked as we rounded the same corner just as she leapt onto Brian who had quickly been walking away.

"You son of a bitch! What bet? Was that about your extended warranty? I'm going to kill you!" She was yelling loud enough that a few doors along the corridor opened, and staff poked their heads out.

Brian fell to his knees and then rolled, but Kayla had attached herself to him and reached around to hit his face.

"Get off me, you psycho!" Brian was about to roll over on top of her when we reached them and pulled Kayla off of him. "Jesus! Keep your fucking omega on a damn leash!"

"What the fuck did you just say?" Rio shoved him into the wall, and I grabbed his arm to pull him back.

"I heard him! Just now! He said something about betting!" Kayla twisted away from Beck and Rylan, and I tried to grab her around the waist but was too late.

Her knee collided with Brian's crotch, and he fell to his knees, his phone dropping to the floor and his hands going to cover his junk. "Fuuuuucccck!"

"Kayla, that's enough." I rarely used my own alpha bark but did this time because we didn't need her getting an assault charge.

I grabbed Brian's phone, which was still connected to whoever he was talking to. The name was unfamiliar. "Hello, who is this?" The call ended and I threw the phone down next to Brian, sending a crack across the screen.

"He messed with my pills." Kayla was vibrating with

rage but hadn't moved since I told her that was enough. "It makes so much sense now!"

"Gnomes! You have five minutes to get yourselves into your position on the sideline!" our publicist yelled down the corridor. "Do I need to send security?"

"Yes!" Beck yelled back to her.

"Thank God. It's about damn time you realized she's playing you." Brian used the wall for support as he got to his feet.

Was he fucking serious? I let Rio go, and it was my turn to shove him into the wall. "What game are you playing? You fucked with our omega's pills?"

"What? What are you talking about?" he spluttered as I pressed my forearm against his chest. He didn't try to fight me because he wouldn't have been able to get past four alphas and a rabid omega.

"Her pills. They were swapped with blanks." His eyes widened at this revelation, but I couldn't tell if it was from shock that her pills were swapped or because he'd done it and been busted. "So, when did you do it? Hm? We changed our security code as soon as we got home. Does that mean you broke into our house?"

"Why would I mess with her pills? Her heat doesn't benefit me." He sneered and narrowed his eyes on who I could only guess was Kayla standing behind me. "That little cunt never wanted to be here."

"Where do you want us to take her until the police get here?" The two security guards plus a third came down the corridor we were in.

KNOT SO PERFECT OMEGA

"Not her. Him." Beck pulled Kayla against him protectively.

"On what grounds?" Brian was practically foaming at the mouth now and started trying to get out from under my arm. I put on more pressure.

"Tampering with an omega's heat suppressants." Beck kissed Kayla's temple. "We have a new coach now."

"You can't be serious." The security guards went on either side of Brian and I let him go. "You have no proof!"

"I'm sure as soon as we check the security footage in the corridor and get the video and sound evidence of what you said to whoever you were talking to, we'll have all the proof we need." Rio picked up Brian's phone. "I'll be holding on to this."

Security led him away from us, and I tuned out the bullshit he was spewing about putting us on the map and Kayla being manipulative.

Kayla pulled away from Beck and stood in front of us. "You are all fools! You gave him your phones? Did you really think someone was calling about your car warranty?"

My cheeks heated, and I honestly didn't have an answer to that. I was always getting spam calls, so it didn't surprise me in the least when he'd said it.

"You really think he's the one that swapped your pills?" Beck asked, stepping forward, but she stepped back. "Kayla, don't shut us out."

"I'm not shutting you out." She crossed her arms.

♡ 275 ♡

"You have a game to play, and if you touch me then you aren't going to be able to focus. And I don't know he did it for sure... but he got my bag while I was exploring the house when I first got there. I didn't think anything of it until earlier."

"And what about OPS?" I checked the time on my phone. "Shit, we need to get out there before they start the National Anthem."

Things with Brian were far from over, but for now, we had our omega safe with us and we had a game to play.

CHAPTER TWENTY-SIX

Kayla

When Beck said they had a new coach and kissed my temple, I'd only been partially paying attention because I was focused on Brian and suppressing my urge to kill him.

I'd followed Brian down the hall and around the corner when I heard him say to whoever he was on the phone with to double the bet. I didn't know much about the sports world, but what I did know was that anyone in United Alpha Sports whether it be players, coaches, or other support staff wasn't supposed to be betting on games.

Things were starting to come together now that I'd heard that little tidbit of information right from his sleazy mouth. He'd switched my pills so I'd go into heat and make the pack more aggressive. That was some hopefulness on his part that it would happen by the championship.

But then again, I'm sure there was more to it than that. I wondered if they would let me torture the information out of him. I could see him now; venomous scorpions latched onto his nipples, knife precariously close to cutting off his dick.

I probably need to cut back on reading dark mafia romances.

My heart was in my throat as I stood on the sidelines of the Alphaball field. It was much more intense being up close to a game and hearing the noises and facial expressions the teams made. Whoever had decided that throwing weighted balls at opponents as a form of defense was sick.

N'Pact was at my back, acting as my bodyguards in a way. After they rocked the house singing the National Anthem, they had a brief conversation I wasn't able to hear, but they'd come over to surround me.

They felt more like brothers if anything, and just like when I'd gotten a ride from them, I felt comfortable being around them despite none of us being claimed.

The Killer Gnomes were on the third round of their game against the Raging Skeletons, and it had been close the whole time. Both teams had easily beaten their opponents in their first games, the wins only seeming to make them even more aggressive.

The crowd roared as Rylan ran toward the Gnomes' goal, the thirty-pound ball tucked under one arm but situated slightly in front of him. The other team still had their ten and twenty in play and while one of their players headed for their own goal, the other was running after Rylan with the ten-pound ball.

With an overhead, two-arm throw, the Skeletons' player threw the ball at Rylan. The game was quite barbaric with throwing balls at each other, but it wasn't much different than being tackled.

Beck had been running along with the two and as the ball released, he dove in front of it, taking a hit right to the chest just as Rylan made it within scoring distance.

"And with a brutal save to the chest, Thomas is down, saving Abbott from what might have been a repeat from last year's playoffs. Abbott is nearing the goal! Will he... he scores! Gnomes just need ten to win!" The announcer's excitement was amping up the crowd to near deafening loudness. I was glad I had a headset that muffled the roar. "And Thomas is up! He has the ten! But Dominguez is right behind him! Thomas throws! Oh, ouch! Dominguez takes him to the turf! The Gnomes win!"

The headset crackled on, which I got to wear as their coach—not that I did anything besides relay anything important to the team. "We need a doctor for Thomas. He hit his head going down."

My heart jumped into my throat as those on the sidelines swarmed the field in celebration and Beck left my line of sight.

I started to move forward onto the field and Payne

grabbed my arm. "Let me go! Beck's hurt!" I didn't know if he could hear me, but he must have, because he said something to the rest of the pack, and they tucked me between them before moving out onto the field.

Payne put his arm around my shoulders as we shoved through people. For being the quiet broody one of the group, he had been surprisingly sweet.

We got to the goal area, and I shoved my way through the throng of people to find Beck just sitting up, a grin on his face.

The whine that left me drew every alpha's attention as I bolted forward the final few feet and threw myself onto him. He rocked back a bit but stayed upright, wrapping his arms around me.

His purr started and he nuzzled his face into my neck. "I'm okay, little omega."

I was pretty aware of all eyes on us and felt my cheeks flame. "What did I say about calling me that?"

"Guess you'll have to punish me later." He chuckled and then moved me off his lap so we could stand.

"Are you sure you're okay?" He looked fine, but concussions couldn't always be seen. "We should get you to the hospital."

He kissed my forehead. "The doctor will check me out when we're back in the locker room."

"Sorry, man." The player who had tackled him to the ground stuck out his hand to Beck. "Good game. Looking forward to kicking your asses next year."

Rylan came up behind me and gave me a bear hug,

lifting me off the ground. I squealed and spun as soon as my feet were touching down. He had a huge grin on his face and dove in for a kiss.

Warmth and comfort enveloped me on all four sides as my pack surrounded me. They'd won, and as excited as I was, I knew there were more serious matters we needed to deal with.

I KNEW AS SOON as we set foot in the tunnel from the field that something was wrong. My omega senses were tingling, and I squeezed Rio's and Beck's hands as we walked toward the locker room. They must have sensed it too because their relaxed demeanors were quickly replaced with tension.

We turned the corner, and there was a group of OPS agents and police officers outside the locker room. Their heads immediately turned our way and my stomach plummeted.

"This should be fun," Rylan muttered. "Didn't the security guards take Brian to the security office?"

"They're here for me. I ran from them at the house." I pulled free of Beck and Rio and walked farther in front of them.

The police were the ones that reacted though. They walked right past me. "Beckett Thomas?"

"That's me." He sighed, seeming to already know what was about to happen. Why else would they be asking him to identify himself?

All the happiness I'd felt over the win vanished as one of the officers stepped forward. "You're under arrest for possession and use of heat stimulant pills." The officer took out his cuffs. "Turn around."

"What the fuck?" Beck took a step back. "I don't know what the hell you're talking about."

"You have the wrong guy. Brian Stokes was taken by stadium security for tampering with her pills." Rio didn't move from where he was standing but put his hand on Beck's back, stopping him from retreating."

"We've found heat stimulant pills in his bag matching the same pills that were given to Ms. Sterling." One of the OPS officers held up a clear evidence bag with two containers of pills. "We also found the heat suppressants that we believe belong to Ms. Sterling."

This couldn't be happening.

"That's insane! She's my mate, I wouldn't do something like this to her!" Beck's face turned red, and his hands were shaking at his sides. "I haven't seen those pills before."

"Are you going to make a scene or are you going to come willingly?" The officer never took his eyes off Beck. "Given the circumstances, I would suggest your full cooperation."

"Just go, Beck. I'll call the lawyers." Rio had his phone out and to his ear.

"Wait! Don't I have a say in this? I think it's a little soon to be making arrests when you haven't dusted for fingerprints or done anything else. They could have been planted there!" I put myself between Beck and the officer, ready to protect him from being taken from me.

"Ms. Sterling, you're going to have to come with us until we get this sorted. We might have found the pills in Beck's possession, but the entire pack is implicated in this." One of the women who worked for OPS stepped forward, a saddened expression on her face. "I know this is tough, but let us run our investigation."

"You can run your investigation while I stay at the house with my pack." I was almost twenty-three freaking years old; they couldn't force me to go to an omega compound.

Could they?

"The other alternative is to go with your family. We'll have to send two beta OPS agents with you, but it should be fine since you are no longer in your heat. I'll need to confirm with your mother when her last heat was. Either way, you aren't going to be able to stay with your pack while we ensure your safety."

My shoulders slumped, and I felt like I'd been kicked in the gut. "She only gets them once a year now and she just had it about a month ago." If there was no way they were going to let me stay with the pack, then going to my parents was at least something. "What about Brian? He was betting on the game."

Everyone seemed to be forgetting about that slime bucket, and I wasn't about to let him get away with something so heinous. It was one thing to switch out my heat suppressants, but to replace them with heat accelerants…?

Only omega doctors could prescribe those, and only under certain conditions. Omegas that took them usually had a medical condition of some kind or their heats didn't trigger their mate's rutting, meaning they couldn't get pregnant.

But for an omega in good health to take them? No wonder it had been like World War III in my womb.

"Let's go grab a bag from the house and then we'll do a formal interview at OPS's headquarters before we take you to your parents.'" The other OPS agent came forward and gently put her hand on my arm.

"Go, Kayla. It's better that you aren't in the middle of everything." Beck stepped around me and looked over his shoulder. "It'll be okay. Let us get all of this situated so you can come home to us."

"But… I…" The OPS agent gently pushed at my shoulder to get me moving. "Wait. Let me say goodbye."

I moved back toward Beck and threw my arms around him. He sighed into my neck, kissing me there before pulling away, his jaw set with tension and anger. "He won't get away with this."

"No. He won't." I kissed him before he went to the officers who didn't handcuff him, but placed him in front of them as they headed toward the exit at the end of the corridor.

"Kayla girl, it's going to be okay." Kane turned me to face him, and I buried my face in his chest as he started purring. "Think of this as a little vacation to see your family."

It wasn't going to be much of a vacation knowing OPS were going to be breathing down my back the whole time I was there. It's not like omegas that were born into a pack could just return home whenever they wanted. There were too many variables when it came to omega safety.

"We should be celebrating and bonding, not... this." My eyes filled with tears, but I refused to let them fall. "It's not fair."

"When this is all over, we'll go on a nice long vacation somewhere secluded where it's just us, okay?" Kane stroked my back and pulled back to tilt my chin up. "We aren't going anywhere."

Kane moved out of the way and Rio took his place, kissing me gently. "We'll make sure Beck's taken care of. Don't worry, this will all be figured out."

Rylan took my hand, and I moved into his arms. "There's nothing you can't handle, curly. You'll be back in our arms in no time at all."

A tear escaped and he wiped it with his thumb. I'd just given in to the idea of them as my pack, and now they were being taken away from me.

With shaky legs, I joined the two OPS agents, one a beta and one an omega, and they flanked me on both sides as we headed down the hall away from my pack.

CHAPTER TWENTY-SEVEN

Rio

Watching Kayla walk away from us made my heart feel like someone had put it through the meat grinder, reshaped it, and shoved it back into my chest cavity. I couldn't stomach the thought of losing another omega. I wouldn't survive this if she was taken from us.

The hallway cleared, leaving me, Rylan, and Kane alone, the only sound the distant noise from the stadium. We walked in silence into the locker room, which was trashed, all of our bags and gear strewn about.

"Fuck." Rylan dragged his hand down his face. "What are we going to do?"

We came together in the middle of the mess, our arms wrapping around each other's shoulders, our foreheads coming together. Our bond was a mess with anxiety, anger, and fear. We needed to stick together now more than ever.

"We're going to get our brother and omega back." I leaned my weight on them and they did the same. Together we were strong and we'd make it through this.

"But what if-" Rylan started, pain in his voice.

"The lawyers are on getting Beck a quick hearing and release. I'll request video footage from the hall to see if anyone came in when we weren't in here." I squeezed their shoulders, then released them. "Brian's not going to admit to anything, so we're going to have to come up with a plan in case there's nothing on video and there are no fingerprints."

I pushed my turned-out duffle bag off the bench and sat down. I didn't understand why they had to make such a complete mess of our shit. I wondered if they'd been to the house or if they had the proper documents to even do a search. It was a Sunday, so it wasn't like a ton of judges were working to grant permission.

"We torture his ass." Rylan started to pick up his things off the floor. "Make some cuts and rub some lemon and salt on the wounds. He'll tell us what we want to know."

Kane sighed and took off his jersey before throwing it across the room in a ball. "Fuck this. Kayla was right. We're fucking idiots. As soon as that whole thing went down with Omega Match, we should have been more cautious and done some digging into it."

"No one expects someone they trust to be so decep-
tive." I kicked off my cleats and pulled off my socks.
"Let's shower, then go see if Brian is still in the security
office. I have his phone. We need to crack his passcode."

"Let me see it." Kane held out his hand and I held it
out for him. "He uses a swipe password and I've seen
him do it enough."

The screen had a crack across it, but it had already
buzzed several times since Alvaro had handed me it
along with my phone after the game. If we could poke
around in it before giving it back to him, maybe we
could find something.

Kane swiped his finger in a pattern, cursed, then
tried again. "See. Easy. Just had to try it a few different
ways." He handed it back to me and I felt hopeful we'd
find something. "I'm going to go shower really quick."

I opened up Brian's text messages. There was a
group text with us, a few others that looked to be busi-
ness-related, and then one from someone named
Brandie, who had sent quite a few over the last few
hours. I read them out loud for Rylan and Kane to
hear.

Brandie: *Done.*

Brandie: *What happened? Are you okay?*

Brandie: *Do we need to worry? I told you to not be an
asshole.*

The conversation didn't make sense out of context
and with such vague messages. I pulled up his call log
and saw she had been who he'd been talking to when

Kayla had heard him talking about betting and she'd attacked.

Why did that name sound so familiar?

I went back to the message and took a second to think of what to say without drawing suspicion from her that it wasn't Brian.

Me: *Beck's been arrested. OPS took Kayla.*

Brandie: *They don't suspect anything?*

Me: *No. They're fools. When can we expect the money?*

Brandie: *Tonight. I've arranged everything.*

Me: *What's arranged exactly?*

Brandie didn't answer me back, and I cursed. Not even a second later, the phone rang with Brandie's name appearing on the caller screen. I was going to take a risk.

"I'm going to answer and talk to her." I cleared my throat and accepted the call. "What?" I whispered, making my voice a little less deep since Brian's voice was higher.

"I didn't want to put that in text. You're deleting all the messages after you read them?" The voice sounded so familiar, but I just couldn't figure out where I'd heard it before.

I quickly put her on speakerphone and unlocked my phone to pull up my video so I could record the call. "Yes."

"My transport to the airport will be there to pick me up in a few hours. They think I'm going to go visit my family but will be landing in L.A. around nine. The money is being sent to the offshore account."

What the fuck?

"Huh?"

"Jesus, Brian. Don't you fucking listen? Are you still meeting me at the airport or do I need to get to your house?"

I made a grunt of confirmation as Kane's eyes went wide and his mouth fell open. Rylan looked ready to punch something. I was feeling the same way.

Kane cleared his throat. "Brian, the press is waiting. Get off your damn phone."

"I bet you're glad you'll be free of those ungrateful assholes. I can't wait to finally be together, boo bear," Brandie whined.

I cringed and made a kissing noise before ending the call and stopped my recording, a million emotions running through me at once.

"Who the fuck was that?" Kane asked, moving to his locker area and picking up some clothes to put on.

"Some chick named Brandie. Why is that name so familiar? Do we know a Brandie?"

Rylan shoved his gear into his bag. "Wasn't that the name of the chick that answered at Omega Match when we called?"

"It was." Kane growled. "That was a number Brian had given us."

How long had those two been planning all of this? There were so many questions. "I'll call our lawyers and have them get on to notifying OPS and the police about this. Kayla probably hasn't even left the parking lot yet."

I texted her quickly that we were working on getting her back. "Let's go see what Brian has to say for himself."

THIRTY MINUTES LATER, we were leaving the stadium, and I still couldn't believe the two alpha security guards had let Brian go. I thought of all people, they'd understand how serious tampering with an omega's pills was.

They said they had no jurisdiction to detain him, and their protocol was to release people they detained if the police weren't going to arrest someone. The police briefly questioned Brian, then said to let him go.

We had no idea what Brian was capable of, and who knew what he was going to get up to now. All I knew was I was on edge from not having Kayla with us. It was our job to protect her, and we'd failed miserably.

Did we even deserve her?

My phone rang as we pulled out of the back lot of the stadium, avoiding all the traffic. We could have used our regular driver to bring us to the game, but we wanted to have a vehicle to leave in as soon as we were done.

I fished my phone out of my pocket and glanced at the screen, seeing it was our publicist who had been handling canceling the press conference and rescheduling interviews. It was a shit show for her, but that was why we paid her good money.

"Here, I can't concentrate with this traffic." I swiped

to answer and handed the phone to Rylan in the passenger seat, who put it on speaker.

"Hello? We have you on speakerphone. We just left the stadium and are going to hopefully pick up Beck if the lawyers can get the whole thing situated." Rylan propped his elbow on the center console and turned the volume up so we could all hear.

"About that... I take it you guys haven't heard. It's all over the internet already." Michelle sighed. "They took Beck to Ocean View Medical Center. He passed out in the back of the police car."

We'd been so caught up in winning and then dealing with the police and OPS, we hadn't thought to have the doctor check him over before they took him.

"Do you know anything else?" I asked, pulling into the left-hand turn lane so I could turn around to go the other way toward the hospital.

"They won't release any information to me, but they should to you guys. Are you headed there now? Do you want me to meet you there?" I could hear Michelle's high heels clicking wherever she was walking.

"No. Get some press releases prepared and in contact with the lawyers to see what they want to say about Beck being arrested as well as Brian's termination and, hopefully, his arrest."

"You guys are really making me work." She laughed nervously. "I hope this all works out for your pack. I only spoke to Kayla for a few minutes, but she really is a good fit."

"Thanks, Michelle." Rylan hung up and put my phone in one of the cupholders. "Fuck!"

"It's going to be okay. It's just a concussion." I didn't feel so reassured by my own words but had to keep a level head. "We need to call Kayla and tell her."

Kane was already on his phone. "Hey, Kayla girl. Beck's been taken to Ocean View Medical. We're on our way there now. We'll call you when we have more information." He hung up and tossed his phone on the seat. "It went to voicemail."

"Her phone broke, remember?" I ran a hand down my face.

This day couldn't possibly get any worse.

CHAPTER TWENTY-EIGHT

Rylan

There was a lot I could handle emotionally, but I was reaching my limit. Why did the universe decide that it wanted to shit all over us?

I truly felt like an absolute idiot and a lame excuse for an alpha for not protecting Kayla. There had been so many red flags, yet we'd ignored every single one of them from the second Kayla walked through our door.

Brian pressuring us to finally find an omega and insisting it be Kara.

Kayla telling us she'd opted-out of matching.

Brian putting her down and claiming he got Kayla and Kara mixed up.

Kayla's heat coming fast and hardcore.

If it had been any other pack telling me the woeful tale, I would have told them that there was no way they

KNOT SO PERFECT OMEGA

could have known someone in their inner circle would deceive them. Brian made good money, but apparently not enough if he was betting on us.

"You're thinking too hard," Kane said, opening the passenger door for me.

I hadn't even realized they'd gotten out of the car, my thoughts spinning and trying to distract me from the lead ball sitting solidly in my stomach. "Sorry."

"Don't apologize." He pulled me into a hug as I got out.

"Gnomes! Do you have any comment about Beckett being carted away by police and then passing out in the backseat of their cruiser?" A reporter with a cameraman came right up to us by the car, shoving the camera and microphone in our faces.

"There have been reports that Beckett tried to run off with the omega who was seen with N'Pact, is that true?" Another reporter with just a phone came from out of nowhere.

How did these people find us so quickly, and where the hell did they get their news from? Did people seriously believe everything just because it was written on the internet?

"We're coming to you live from Ocean View Medical Center, where Beckett Thomas has been rushed after LAPD took him into custody following the Killer Gnomes' championship win. Nazario, does this mean the Killer Gnomes days are over? Will you be kicking Beckett from the pack?"

Rio growled at the reporter, and she jumped, backing up a step. *"Get out of our way,"* he barked.

I would have given him a high-five if it wasn't such a precarious situation. I fucking hated paparazzi and news reporters that didn't respect that this was our lives they were intruding on. And for what? To have the breaking news story?

We walked in a solid line of alpha to the emergency room entrance. There were several security guards out front keeping reporters back. If one of them really wanted to get in the hospital, though, it wasn't like security could stop them if they lied and said they were sick.

One of the guards lifted his chin at us as we passed by. The emergency room was busy, and the clerks and nurses behind the reception desk look frazzled.

We got in the line to wait our turn but one of the nurses behind the desk recognized us immediately and gestured for us to follow her. She led us to the elevator and scanned her card. "They just took him up to a private room on the fourth floor. As soon as you step off the elevator, make a right and the nurses' station will be right there. I'm not sure what room."

"Thank you," we said in unison as we got on the elevator and pressed the button.

I leaned heavily against the wall, my adrenaline crashing and my body feeling like it weighed two times as much. "No messages from the lawyers yet?"

Rio glanced at his phone. "No. They said they'd

deliver the video recording to the appropriate people, but it might be a few hours."

The elevator dinged to announce our arrival on the fourth floor, and we followed Kane off and to the right. The smell of food wafted from somewhere, and my stomach growled. It was just after five in the evening, but after playing as hard as we did, I was starving.

A male nurse swiveled around in his chair and saw us approaching the nursing station, his jaw dropping open at the sight of us. He seemed to have forgotten how to speak as we stopped in front of him.

"We're here to see Beckett Thomas. The nurse in the ER said he was just brought up." Rio knocked on the counter with his knuckles, which immediately snapped the man out of his trance.

"Oh, shit. I mean… crap. Oh, man. Damn it." He took a deep breath and stood. "I'm sorry. You're just… wow. You're all so much more attractive in person."

I couldn't help but smile at how flustered he was. "Thanks. Did they bring Beckett up here?"

"Yes! He's in room four-twenty-one. Right down that way on the left." He pointed. "Great game, by the way. Hopefully, everything will be okay with Beck."

"Thank you." Kane nodded at him, and we walked quickly toward Beck's room.

Now that we were closer to him, I could feel how stressed he was through the pack bond. He wasn't even bothering to put up a wall to stop us from feeling it.

The door was cracked open, and I knocked before

pushing it open to find him lying in bed, hooked up to an IV and heart rate monitor. He had what looked like a folded washcloth over his eyes and the room was dark besides a dim light next to his bed.

"Hey," I whispered. I knew he was awake since I could feel his emotions. As soon as he heard my voice, relief replaced his anxiety. "We're here now."

"Took you guys long enough," he croaked.

Was he joking right now? It was so unlike him, especially considering the situation.

I sat down on the end of the bed and put my hand on his leg. "How long are you in for?"

"Overnight and then I guess they'll take me to jail. Surprised they didn't cuff me to the bed, but the officers didn't come up here with me." Beck moved the washcloth to his forehead and cracked his eyes open. "It's so bright in here."

Rio pulled a chair up next to his bed and took his hand. "You idiot. Shut your eyes."

Kane sat on the other side of the bed. "If the cops didn't come up here with you, that probably means they are dropping the charges. We found out some shit, but right now, you need to sleep."

The door to the room crashed open and we all jumped, Beck groaning from the noise and the intrusion of light from the hallway.

"Fuck, pushed it a little too hard." Kayla came in like a tornado and rushed toward the bed, her face red and tear-stained. "Beck…"

She burst into tears, and I jumped up since I was closest to her and guided her toward the bed. I wanted to hug her and comfort her but knew she needed to make sure Beck was okay. He winced as she crawled onto the bed with him but then sighed like a weight had been lifted off of him as she snuggled into him.

I quickly shut the door to give us privacy and to reduce the light in the room before grabbing another chair and pulling it next to Rio.

We were together once again, and I didn't know about the others, but I planned on never letting Kayla go.

BECK HAD FINALLY FALLEN ASLEEP, and we'd gotten comfortable in our chairs we'd pulled around his bed. The OPS agents had filled us in a bit about what was happening with the investigation, and for now, we were breathing a little easier.

They weren't taking Kayla, and Beck wouldn't be taken to jail unless new evidence came to light about him being involved. We all knew he wasn't, and the OPS agents didn't seem to think he was either.

They'd also already had Brandie detained since she lived in an omega compound. Kayla and Kara knew her from when they were classmates together at the academy. Brandie was a few years ahead of them, and now she worked for Omega Match. From what Kayla told us, Brandie hadn't matched before leaving the academy.

As for Brian? No one knew where he'd run off to, but the police were looking for him.

"I'm going to go get some food. The cafeteria is open until eight," I whispered. "I'll bring you guys back something?"

"Yeah, whatever is fine. I'm starving, though, so please don't bring back bird food." Kane slouched down in his chair, his neck resting on the back of it.

We were all going to be sore in the morning. Not just from the way we were sleeping, but from not doing any recovery or stretching after our brutal game. Maybe they could move us to a pack room if one was available. The nurse was supposed to check on it for us, but this hospital only had two available and he wasn't sure if they were occupied.

"Can I come with you? I need some air." Kayla carefully scooted off the bed and stretched.

We all watched her as her shirt rode up a little. She noticed and rolled her eyes before grabbing my hand. "Not the time, boys."

"There's always time for appreciating our omega." I kissed her cheek and entwined our fingers before leading her out of the room.

The lights were a little dimmer now and the floor was mostly quiet besides the sounds hospitals couldn't get rid of. I didn't know how anyone could sleep with the beeping and whooshing sounds of oxygen and blood pressure monitors.

The hospital cafeteria was in the basement, and we took the staff elevator to help avoid any run-ins with the public. Our pack was plastered all over the internet with speculation about what had happened both with Beck being in the hospital and our omega.

We hadn't publicly announced we'd done Omega Match—we wanted to wait until we were bonded—but now the world knew we had an omega and that something had happened to cause OPS to take her.

The stories were ridiculous and mostly focused on Beck doing something to her since he'd been arrested. While they hadn't cuffed him, a few people saw him put in a police car and that was all it took.

We entered the cafeteria which had mostly doctors and nurses sitting at tables. They didn't pay us any mind, focusing on eating their food in the little time they had.

Kayla yawned and led me over to the cafeteria-style food line. "Chicken nuggets and fries sound good."

A woman came from the cash register and pulled on gloves. "They just brought these out too so they're nice and fresh. The last of the night."

I wouldn't consider previously frozen food fresh, but it was at least not going to be soggy. "Can we get five orders to go?"

She whistled. "You're going to clean me out for the night. They come with a fountain drink too."

"I'll get those." Kayla kissed my cheek and went to

the beverage machine by the cash register right behind me.

"She's a very beautiful woman. You're a lucky pack." The woman smiled, grabbing five to-go boxes and putting them on the counter.

"We really are. She's the missing puzzle piece that makes us complete." Maybe the hunger was making me corny.

"Well, I wish you all the best. Lord knows marriage to just one man is hard enough. I get home from work, and he expects me to cook and clean, even though I work more hours than him and take care of the kids. I can't imagine having four husbands, although maybe at least one would help around the house and know their way around the bedroom." She put chicken nuggets in each of the boxes and then started with the fries.

It sounded like she needed to reassess her marriage, but it wasn't my place to say that. "We aren't so bad."

Being an omega in a pack of alphas wasn't quite the same as a beta female having a group of beta men. I'm sure that could work too if they really wanted it to, but they didn't have the instincts and drive like we did to make the omega the center of our world.

"Oh, good. I'm glad one of the others came down to help carry the drinks. I can put these in bags for you too so it's easy for you to carry them all." She started closing the lids.

"Excuse me?"

"Your omega and one of your pack members just left.

Crap, why didn't they take the drinks? I don't have any drink carriers." She was stacking the boxes to carry.

I wheeled around, not seeing Kayla at the drinks fountain anymore, and the drinks were sitting there on the counter. She wouldn't just leave, would she? If Rio or Kane came down to help her, I would have felt them or at the very least smelled them.

Although, come to think of it, there was very little scent in the hospital because they pumped specialized de-scenting spray through the vents. They should do it in all public buildings, but the shit is expensive as fuck and still couldn't mask a perfuming omega.

"Kayla?" I walked into the seating area and looked around, wondering if she'd gone looking for straws or a drinks carrier on the endcap with the napkins and condiments.

A doctor who was eating alone looked up from the book he was reading. "She left with your coach."

It was a good thing I was in a hospital because my heart stopped.

CHAPTER TWENTY-NINE

Kayla

I filled five cups with ice and was excited to see it was the good crunchy pebble kind. The ice could really make or break a soft drink.

The day was turning around after a cluster fuck of problems. I hadn't expected to feel so broken when OPS took me and had been trying to think of a way out of the whole situation when Kara messaged me asking about Beck.

The OPS agents weren't going to bring me to the hospital at first, but when I threatened to jump out of the vehicle, they turned the car around. I'd like to think it was my threat and not the omega agent advocating for me. It probably didn't hurt that shortly after that the main OPS office called with new information.

I knew that man was the scum of the Earth from the second I met him.

Something hard pressed into my back and a mouth brushed my ear, causing me to shudder. "You whine, and I'll shoot you and your alpha before hunting down the rest."

Brian.

I bit my lip hard enough to draw blood to stop my whine. He pushed me around the end of the soda machine and out through a door that someone at the serving station wouldn't be able to see. The few people that were eating in the dining room area were too busy looking at their phones or chatting to notice anything amiss.

To an outsider, it would look like one of my mates leading me away, their hand on the small of my back. But there was definitely a weapon pressed against me.

"What do you want?" I had to figure out a way to get away from him without getting shot or getting someone else shot in the process.

"Well, seeing as I no longer have an omega, I'm in need of one." He took me to the stairwell, reached around me to scan a card he had, and urged me forward.

I didn't even want to know how he'd gotten the keycard. Had he killed someone for it?

No, Kayla. This isn't like some action movie.

I put my hands up, stopping him from pushing me into the secluded area. "Shoot me then. I'd rather die than go with you."

"So dramatic." He laughed in a way that chilled me to my bones and then kicked me in the back of my knee, sending me to the ground on my hands and knees with a yelp of pain. Leaning over me, the gun pressing into my skull, I whined, hoping someone would hear it.

That pissed him off and he grabbed my ponytail, yanking me to my feet. "Shut up. Just shut up!" He shoved me forward into the stairwell. "Move."

My scalp burned as he maneuvered me by my hair, and I nearly fell down as we went up the steps. I was going to make a break for it as soon as we were out of the stairwell. I had to. There was no way I could let him take me.

The first floor had the emergency department, which had plenty of security. Brian surely wouldn't open fire in a room full of people, would he?

We stepped onto the landing in front of the first-floor door when the intercom chimed. "Code purple stat. Code purple stat."

"What the fuck is code purple? Open the door." He let go of my hair but kept close to me. "Not a peep or facial expression, do you understand?"

"Yes." I opened the door, which was right next to the elevators.

One of the elevator doors opened as soon as we started walking into the corridor, and Rylan, a doctor, and a security guard appeared.

"Ry-"

Brian grabbed my ponytail again and yanked me

back into the stairwell. "Go. Up! Now! I swear I'll open the door back up and shoot him in the fucking face."

Tears streamed down my face as I climbed the next set of stairs. "Just let me go. This isn't going to end well."

There was a small window in this one, and he cursed as he saw security rushing toward it at the far end of a hall. "Go! Up all the way to the top!"

"No!" I elbowed him and he grunted before slamming my head into the door.

Things went a bit fuzzy, and then I was floating. He heaved me over his shoulder like a sack of potatoes and started up the stairs. I groaned and squirmed, but he had his arm around me tight and was stronger than I expected him to be.

"Help!" I croaked, hearing the door below slam open. "Help!"

Brian picked up his pace, carrying me as if he was in firefighter training and racing to beat a time. If he dropped me, I'd plummet down the steps, so I stayed still, trying to think of what to do when we were on flat ground again.

We burst onto the roof not more than a minute later, and I rolled my body, causing him to drop me. I fell onto my side and scrambled away from him as he loomed over me, my eyes going to his hand that had a fucking stapler in it.

"You don't even have a gun!" I kicked my feet at him, but he managed to grab one of them and pulled me across the helipad that was lit up. "What are you doing?"

"If I can't have my omega, then they can't have their omega." He gave my leg a hard yank, and I screamed, hoping someone would come to my aid.

Where is security? They should be up here by now.

As soon as I had the thought, the roof door opened, but Brian was already yanking me to my feet by my hair. I was going to cut it off as soon as this was over.

He wrapped a forearm around my neck and one around my waist, tugging me backward toward the edge of the roof.

"Please, Brian. Stop!" I tried to kick backward, but the way he was holding me made it impossible, and his feet were moving at just the right distance from mine that I couldn't stomp with enough force.

I dug my fingers into his arm and threw my elbows back, but he ignored whatever pain they were causing him.

"Freeze!" Two security guards were on the roof, their weapons drawn and pointed at us.

There was no way they could shoot him without also hitting me, and we were at the edge of the roof where there was a two-foot-high barrier between us and falling to our deaths. The roof was meant for heli-copters, not for people to be in a standoff on it.

The elevator doors dinged, and Rylan, several secu-rity people, and two police officers poured onto the roof. I could hear Rylan growling from clear across the space, a few other growls mixed in from the others.

KNOT SO PERFECT OMEGA

"Let her go!" Rylan barked, starting to move forward, but was stopped by an officer.

Brian grunted but readjusted his arms around me, lifting me farther off the ground and stepping backward onto the roof ledge. "It didn't have to be like this, but oh no, your little cunt ass had to go and ruin everything."

"Please," I begged, the fight leaving me for a moment to try to figure out how I could get away without falling off the roof. "You don't have to do this. We can all sit down and talk, and maybe you and Brandie can-"

"Don't you say her name!" One of his arms went back to my neck, pressing hard into it and cutting off my air for a moment.

"Why?" I croaked. "Why me? Why?"

The cops were on their walkie-talkies, and Rylan was pacing, his eyes never leaving mine. He would have stormed over to me and ripped me from Brian's arms, but even I could see the fear in his eyes at seeing us standing on the ledge which was about two and a half feet wide.

"Sick and tired of alphas always getting everything. The fame. The fortune. The fucking omegas." His arm loosened a bit around my neck. "They have everything!"

It was my opening. He was raging on, rambling about alphas and my pack, and I let my body go limp. His loosened hold gave way and I fell to the ledge, my body tangling with his feet.

He stumbled backward, his arms flailing to get his

body to move forward, but it wasn't enough to keep his feet on the ledge.

I screamed.

Brian screamed.

Rylan screamed.

I scrambled around, my adrenaline pumping through my body so fast I felt like I was outside of myself, watching a robot take over my body.

Brian's stomach hit the ledge, his arms reaching, trying to find something to grab on to. I reached out to him—I don't even fucking know why—and let him grab onto my forearms. I did the same, our arms locked together as the weight of his body pulled both of us.

Someone landed on my back, stopping my slide. Every muscle in my body hurt like it was being twisted and yanked through a small hole. My vision tunneled, the edges of it going dim, but all I could see were Brian's fearful eyes staring back at me.

I could have just flung myself onto the roof and to safety, but I couldn't let someone die. Brian might have been threatening to jump off the building with me, but from the look in his eyes now, I didn't think he had wanted to go that route.

His plans had failed, whatever they entailed, and now he was just a small, desperate man whose life was now hanging on by a thread.

"Grab his other arm," one of the other men said, lying next to me and reaching forward to pull Brian. "Pull her."

There was a lot of grunting, and my shirt rode up, my stomach scraping along the cement ledge as we were pulled to the safety of the roof. Arms wrapped around me, and then I was sitting in Rylan's lap, his fresh-cut wood scent surrounding me.

"What the actual fuck." He buried his face in my neck, his purr vibrating both of us. "Why'd you do that, crazy woman?"

I trembled violently, despite the purring. "Did they save him?" I managed to get out between chattering teeth.

"Yes." He rubbed a hand over my back. "You're safe now."

"Let's get her to an exam room," someone said. "Kayla, can you stand?"

I attempted to stand, but I was shaking so bad Rylan had to hand me off to a doctor while he got to his feet. He took me back in his arms and I put my head against his shoulder.

"Did you hit your head?" The doctor reached for my chin, looking me over. "She has a bump on her forehead."

"He smashed my head against the door." All at once, the pain started.

My forehead, scalp, knee, and arms hurt. Plus, my stomach was in knots and felt like it was on fire from being dragged across the cement. I groaned and tried not to cry.

The elevator dinged and we got on it, Rylan turning

to face the roof. Brian was laying in the center of the helipad, his hands cuffed, his head turned to the side watching us.

I'd saved him but also hadn't.

As the doors slid shut, I knew he'd have to live with what he did. Hopefully for the rest of his life behind bars.

CHAPTER THIRTY

Kayla

There was no tired quite like the tired after being held at stapler-point and almost being yeeted off a roof by a deranged beta. I'd ended up with a mild concussion, an adrenaline crash that felt like I'd been hit by a bus, and some bruises and scrapes.

Considering the alternative was death, I think I fared well.

Brian was in jail, held without bail until his trial, and Brandie had spilled all of their secrets. Their love affair that started online had turned into a toxic spiral of hating alphas and omegas. She hated Omega Match because the only way for her to get out of living in the omega compound was to match with an alpha, and she'd wanted Brian, who was just a beta.

They were planning on running off together to a

country that didn't have such strict regulations for omegas and alphas, and to do that they needed more money than Brian had. They wanted to be set for life, and Brian knew sports betting was a good way to double his money.

At first, Brian had planned on Kara and the pack being matched so the pack would benefit from her heat. But then Brandie had the idea to swap us to try to bring Omega Match down.

She had hoped me or the pack would raise a big stink about it but didn't anticipate that we wouldn't.

Brian had gone along with Brandie's swap plan because he hated Omega Match just as much as Brandie and he didn't need Kara specifically. It was just easier for him to convince Beck to agree to an omega if she was perfect in every way.

Part of me really hated that I'd been right all along about Omega Match messing up. If Kara would have put them, she would have matched with them. Even though Kara reminded me "would have" was exactly what it was.

It had been almost a week since everything had happened, and each passing day I was becoming more and more like myself. There had been a lot of movie watching, video games, sleeping, and snuggling.

But no sex and definitely no bonding.

I didn't know if they were giving me time to heal completely or if they had changed their minds with everything that had come to light. I might not have wanted a pack at first, but now I couldn't see myself without them. The thought of being without them was eating me inside.

I needed to just rip the Band-Aid off, but sitting at the kitchen table eating dinner with the four of them just made me nervous about what might be my impending doom.

It might have also been the unbonded omega in me starting to wear down. Damn hormones.

"You didn't eat very much," Kane remarked as he got up from the kitchen table and started to clear it.

"Not very hungry tonight." I'd only eaten a few bites of my lasagna and salad.

"Are you feeling all right?" Rio reached over and put the back of his hand against my forehead. "Your forehead is a little warm."

I rolled my eyes. "I'm fine. Your hand is hot."

Rylan stretched and then stood. "Well, I'm going to go game since I'm not on dish duty. Who wants to join me?"

Both Kane and Rio put their dishes on the counter by the sink and followed Rylan out of the kitchen, leaving me and Beck to clean up the dishes. We hadn't had to do them all week and I guess our vacation was over.

"Bring me the rest of the stuff off the table and I'll throw all of these in the dishwasher." Beck headed to the sink and began rinsing and stacking dishes. "You know you can talk to us, right?"

"Hm?" I wrapped the leftover lasagna with foil and put it in the refrigerator. "I do talk to you."

"I mean about what happened... about the pack... about everything." He glanced over at me as he put two plates in the dishwasher.

"Oh." I brought him the rest of the dishes from the table and started taking rinsed dishes from him to load. "I'm handling it."

"Are you? You won't set foot in your nest, you aren't sleeping well even with two of us surrounding you, you-"

"Are you going to send me back?" I blurted, nearly dropping a plate.

"Kayla..." He turned off the water and dried his hands. "Why would you think that?"

I shrugged and shut the dishwasher, avoiding his stare that did things to my insides. "Just a feeling."

He trapped me against the counter, his arms on either side of me. I looked him straight in the eyes, even though I wanted to look at the floor and whine like a rejected little omega. I could fight against my true nature with every ounce of effort, but at the end of the day, I was still an omega and still could only fight myself so much.

"We've been giving you space. You usually tell us what you want and need... is that not right?"

"On a normal day, yes." I bit my lip and grabbed onto the front hem of his shirt. "But nothing's been normal, and I guess... I just needed some reassurance."

"You're ours," Beck growled, his fingers grasping my chin to stop me from looking away from him. "Tell me what you want. Anything, and it's yours."

"I want you to bite me. All of you." God, it felt good finally saying it.

His green eyes darkened as his pupils dilated and his body vibrated with pure alpha energy, his chest puffing up a little in a show. This was it. It was going to happen.

"We'll do it my way." His voice sent a thrill down my spine and straight to my core.

"Yes, Alpha." I whimpered, my perfume blossoming around us and causing him to shut his eyes and inhale deeply.

He picked me up, my legs and arms wrapping around him. He carried me so effortlessly, and I fit snug against him as he walked out of the kitchen, and through the dining room and living room. "We have a surprise for you."

"A surprise?" I didn't know if I was up for any crazy surprises their four brains might have concocted.

"I think you'll like it." He was carrying me down the hall toward the nest, and I frowned. "Trust me."

I loved my nest, I did, but after everything, seeing it left a bitter taste in my mouth. I was sure eventually I'd use it again, but for now, I had no reason to and was perfectly content finding a quiet room in the massive house to hide under a pile of blankets when I needed.

"What did you do?" I tried to turn my head as he got to the slightly cracked open door.

"Shut your eyes." He was back in alpha mode, his bark causing my eyes to quickly close in compliance. I could have fought him on it, but there was no need to fight anymore. I was surrendering.

Their scents enveloped me as he walked into the room, the click of the door closing us in. My skin tingled with awareness that they hadn't gone off to play video games but had come here instead.

"We want this to be a sanctuary for you. A place that gives you comfort, and we know you've been avoiding it."

What didn't they know? I hadn't told them my feeling about the nest, but they were observant and me burrowing in the beds upstairs instead of in my nest was probably a dead giveaway.

"Open your eyes, Kayla girl."

I slowly opened them, gasping not at the three naked alphas lying in wait, but at the room. Everything was different. The walls had been painted a light blue and the ceiling was now almost black with strands of twinkling lights spread across it. The ceiling fan was replaced with a chandelier that emitted a warm glow of light.

But the best part was the actual nest. They'd replaced the thin nesting mattresses I'd previously bought with a platform low to the ground. The nesting mattresses were thicker and covered in light blue sheets to match the walls. Hanging from the ceiling were panels of thick dark blue fabric which was tied back for now but would enclose the nest from everything.

I wiggled out of Beck's hold and went to a chair and ottoman that had been set up to replace the loveseat. Folded over the ottoman was the quilt I had been working on for myself. I brought it to my nose and inhaled, all of their scents pouring into me. They'd finished it, and it was more perfect than I could have imagined.

Beck moved behind me, his hands going to my arms and rubbing soothingly. "Do you like it?"

I inhaled shakily and didn't trust myself to speak, so I nodded. I set the blanket down and turned, throwing my arms around him.

"We can't undo what happened, but we can move forward together... as a pack. We love you, Kayla, and anything you could ever need or want physically or emotionally is yours. We give ourselves to you." Beck sounded more certain than I'd ever heard him.

I pulled back, tears threatening to spill over, so seeing him was a bit more difficult. "I love you all too."

His lips found mine, his arms banding around me like they were never going to let me go. I could sense the others watching us, and that mixed with my emotions made my entire body come alive and my panties dampen with slick.

Beck moved to my neck, sucking on the spot where he was going to claim me with his bite. There were a lot of different ways a pack could claim an omega, but the strongest bond was made when the leader knotted the omega and the entire pack bit her one after the other and vice versa.

His hands went to my shirt and lifted it off, his eyes glued to mine. He undressed me slowly, almost painfully so, and my body trembled with need.

"Get on the bed. They'll get you ready." My nipples hardened to sensitive points as he steered me toward the three alphas waiting for me.

The bed was huge and could easily have fit all five of us comfortably. Kane, Rio, and Rylan were lounged around it naked, their cocks already hard. I crawled on, briefly appreciating that it was the perfect combination of soft and firm. I was unsure of where to situate myself with the three of them.

"Come here, sweetheart." Rio patted the empty spot next to him in the center of the bed.

As soon as I was where he wanted me, he pounced, flipping me and pinning me under him as he took my mouth. His cock pressed against my center, and I couldn't stop myself from grinding against him.

His lips moved down to my neck and then to my nipple, while one of his hands cupped my other breast, his thumb brushing over my sensitive flesh over and over at the same pace as his tongue.

Rylan scooted on one side of me and Rio moved off me to give him better access. He kissed me, his hand moving between my legs. When his fingers made contact with my wet center, he groaned against my lips.

A hand circled my ankle and was replaced by lips that began kissing up my leg. I was experiencing sensory overload from the three of them lavishing me with affection.

"Spread her open for me." Kane's voice wrapped around me like a thick blanket.

I spread my legs for him, and Rio hooked his arm around one and pulled it open wider for Kane. Rylan ran his fingers through my folds and then used them to part my lips for Kane.

"Look at our beautiful omega, ready and waiting for us," Beck said from the foot of the bed. He hadn't moved from his spot but had taken off all of his clothes. "Perfect in every way and just for us."

"The perfect treat." Kane kissed my inner thigh and then buried his face between my legs, his purr vibrating through me as he sucked my clit between his lips.

"Yes!" I broke away from Rylan's lips, needing to come up for air. I was at their mercy, and I didn't want it any other way.

My orgasm built fast and someone's fingers thrust into me, crooking in just the right way to hit that spot inside me that sent me toppling over the edge.

Rio and Rylan were taking turns kissing me, and Kane continued his assault on my pussy as I rode out my orgasm.

And then the bed dipped slightly, and Kane moved to the side, Beck finding his home between my legs. Kane moved around to the top of the bed to lie by my head, giving him access to my neck. It was a tight squeeze with all of them, but they didn't seem to mind being so close.

"You're ours, Kayla Sterling." Beck thrust into me, and I cried out, my orgasm still making every nerve-ending sensitive.

"I'm yours." I was ready for them to mark me and make me theirs. I'd been ready.

Beck slid in and out of me, going deeper and deeper with each thrust. My body tensed slightly as his knot pushed into me, swelling, and locking us together.

"*Bite her, Rio,*" Beck barked.

"*Mine,*" Rio growled before the brief sting of his bite where my shoulder met my neck made me clench around Beck, who was circling his hips in the most delicious way.

"*Kane, bite her.*"

Rio licked the bite he'd made and moved a bit so Kane could get to the spot he'd been itching to bite.

"*Mine.*" His growl was filled with emotion, and he bit me just above where Rio had, their bites slightly overlapping.

"*Rylan, bite her.*" Beck sounded as if he could barely contain himself. His neck muscles were straining, and his pupils were completely blown.

"*Mine.*" Rylan bit the opposite side of my neck, the thrill of having three bites causing another orgasm to overtake me.

As soon as Rylan lifted his face from my neck, Beck

roared as if his heart was being filled so full it had burst, and he exploded inside me, his mouth descending on my neck. *"Mine."* His bite overlapped with Rylan's and nearly made me black out from the emotional punch it brought.

It was the bite that tied all their bites together as one in a bond that I could swear I felt wrapping around every part of my body and taking root in my heart.

Beck licked his mark and tilted his head to the side, offering me his neck. I'd read about this plenty, but doing it was a completely different thing. My body took over and I struck him like a snake, my teeth easily breaking his skin. The smallest amount of blood hit my tongue and my body shuddered in pleasure, another strand of the bond slipping into place.

Licking the small wound so it would heal quicker, I bit the others, each one adding to the bond, their warmth and happiness pouring into me in waves. It was as if an emptiness that had been inside me all this time that I never realized was there was being filled.

As the tendrils of our bond connected us, Beck moved me so I was lying on top of him, his knot firmly in place. The others would knot me later, but for now, we lay with our bodies touching, our bond flowing through us and letting us feel each other in a different way.

They were finally mine and were the perfect pack for this knot so perfect omega who was perfect to them.

The End